NERO'S
FIDDLE

A. W. EXLEY

Be the first to hear about new releases, occasional specials and giveaways. My newsletter comes out approximately 4 times a year. Follow the link to sign up:
eepurl.com/N5z5z

Author's Note:
This book uses British English

THE ARTIFACT HUNTERS:

DEDICATION

To Mike, who got out but didn't forget his little sister.

Thank you for everything. I'm also blaming you for the speeding tickets…

CHAPTER 1

London, Tuesday 10th December, 1861

SNOW lay thick on the ground, chestnuts roasted by the fire, and Inspector Hamish Fraser stared at the remains of one poor sod who would never drink his eggnog. Any unusual death in the London area required the presence of an Enforcer and Fraser long ago became accustomed to taking the Christmas shifts. He let other men have precious hours at home with their families as the holiday approached.

"Name?" he asked over his shoulder as his eyes scanned the scene, trying to discern natural from artificial in the death before him. Soot stained the ceiling, a near black patch hung over the bed and then radiated out in a star pattern to fade to a pale grey before it touched the walls. A grimy tide line encircled the patterned wallpaper as though thick, viscous smoke had filled the room to neck level before draining away into the winter night.

"Nigel Fenmore, aged seventy-two, lives alone," Sergeant Connor read off the notebook dwarfed by his meaty hand. "Neighbour downstairs complained about the smell, popped her head through the door to check on the old fella and then she started screaming at the street boys."

Fraser drew a careful breath into his lungs. Before entering the room they all smeared a menthol cream under their noses. The bedroom was permeated with a sharp, yet sweet aroma no one wanted to become overly familiar with——that of slow-roasted human flesh.

"Any family?" His gaze took in the mantel piece, bare except for a cleaned skull residing on one end. The cream bone now sported black spots and stains, empty eye sockets the only witness to events that unfolded in the room. The nightstand lacked any personal objects and held only a candle and a stack of books. On top sat an open medical text book, a pencil held in between the pages. Scratchings in the margins showed Nigel added his own commentary to the text of the book. A sole gas lamp hung against one wall and struggled to throw sufficient light.

Since the house was bereft of the new electric lights, the Enforcers brought in hand-held lanterns. The handles were cranked to generate a charge that lit the bulb. Several were dotted around the room and under different circumstances they would have been a pretty sight. The yellow light chased away the shadows hiding against the soot-ridden walls.

Connor's notebook held his attention, so he didn't have to look at anything else. Unstoppable in the heat of battle, he had no stomach for violent ends served up cold, or crispy like the current case. "No family. Apparently he dedicated himself to his job and never married. No by-blow children or distant relatives that the neighbours know about. They say he mainly kept to himself these days. Rheumatism kept him inside a lot, so they didn't worry when they hadn't seen him for a couple of days."

The bedroom contained scant furniture; a double bed with a blackened steel frame stood opposite the door and dominated the small space, made even smaller by the Inspector and three Enforcers crammed inside. Next to the bed sat a foot; the flesh of the ankle was charred and an edge of white bone protruded from burned flesh. The more unnerving sight, the one making the room hum with adrenaline, was what their eyes couldn't see.

The thing their brains shouted was absent.

The coverlet laid flat over the mattress, no lumps or bumps to show a body slumbered underneath.

Connor peered at the limb on the floor and used the tiny notebook as a shield in case the foot leapt at him. "Is that all?"

Fraser gestured to the other side of the bed. "There's a hand on the other side, fallen to the floor. It is also charred through at the bone and detached from the body."

"Not much to go on, then," Connor said.

A barely suppressed snort came from one of the other Enforcers at the unintended pun.

Fraser heaved a sigh. He didn't have it in him to reprimand the men; humour was their way of dealing with gruesome deaths and besides, Christmas was nearly upon them. He settled with glaring at the men in the dark blue uniforms. They presented an unusual sight in the bedroom, with black leather harnesses around their upper bodies and waists supporting a multitude of gadgets; from glow sticks and magnifying goggles to handcuffs and electric truncheons. The street pounders were used to chasing down criminals and using their size to pin targets to the cobbles. They were useless standing around impersonating occasional tables in a room with roasted body parts.

"Do you think someone cut him up and torched the body?" Connor asked. He shifted from foot to foot, but held his position at his inspector's back.

Fraser shook his head. "The room is not burned, only singed with smoke damage. It takes quite a conflagration to cremate a body. And I am no expert, but the foot does not look severed. Nor does the head."

"I'm trying not to look too closely at that," the sergeant said, raising the notebook so it blotted out the object in question.

Fraser moved closer. The head rested on the pillow, eyes closed in slumber and a red and white striped nightcap with a decorative pom-pom slumped to one side. The horizontal white lines were now soiled and stained grey. The neck ended in charred flesh and protruding bone, like the foot and hand.

"Let's fold back the bedding and confirm our suspicion. You two, move out of the way." Fraser gestured for the other Enforcers to stand back, to give them a modicum more room for the grim task. The men edged closer to the walls, but held themselves away from the wallpaper coated in human soot.

Connor heaved a sigh and tucked his notebook into his tunic pocket. He stepped to the other side of the bed. Each man took hold of the top corner of the soiled quilt. Gaily coloured squares sewn together by hand were now soaked in the fumes, fats, and liquids that leaked from the body underneath. Connor stuck his pinkies out like he held a porcelain teacup but probably just didn't want to touch the quilt.

"Ready?" Fraser asked, and with a nod they lifted the coverlet, peeled it down the mattress and then let it fall in folds over the end of the bed. With the cover disturbed, the sharp odour escaped and magnified, spiralling up to fill the room and cutting through the menthol cream adorning moustaches and upper lips.

Oaths filled the room, followed by the sound of gagging. One of the Enforcers rushed to the window and purged the contents of his stomach onto the skeletal roses below.

Underneath the bedding lay a mess of black ooze, ash, and tiny fragments in the rough outline of a body. Phantom limbs stretched to where the foot and hand once resided. A dark mark the only evidence of the neck that once supported the detached head.

"What a way to go," Connor muttered, holding a hand over his mouth and breathing through his fingers.

Fraser contemplated the pile of detritus; all that remained of a once vibrant human life. He had scraped something similar from his hearth before resetting the fire. The only remaining parts were those left uncovered by the blanket. It appeared as though the fire burned under the quilt and never escaped its confines. "Fetch Doc. If we attempt to move the mattress we will disturb what is left and I believe he will want to see this in situ. And grab the photographer too, so we can document the position of the remains."

One of the Enforcers nodded and rushed for the door, glad of the excuse to escape the ghastly scene and the smell forcing its fingers down his throat.

"It's not right," Connor said under his breath, trying in vain to only breathe out and not in. As a tactic it didn't work for him, and eventually his lungs forced him to draw several deep breaths to make up for the previous oxygen deficit.

"It is a highly unusual death." Fraser's attention remained on the deceased. The serene expression on the dead man's face unnerved him most, as though he never felt his body melting to ash and fat under the blankets. He blew out a long sigh, his mind trying to make sense of the evidence and determine if this was a case of foul play, or perhaps the result of a stray spark from the unguarded fire or a cigarette.

His visual survey of the room failed to find any evidence that Mr Fenmore was a smoker, no pipes or tobacco sitting on a table or in a drawer. A richly enamelled guard depicting game birds encased the hearth and ensured the fire stayed contained. Although a candle sat by the bed, the item was new and the pale wick appeared to never have been lit.

No obvious means of accidental fire.

"We have encountered murderers who have attempted to destroy the evidence of their crimes in flames, but this is the first death I have seen in a bedchamber where nothing else appears damaged." He removed his bowler hat and ran his fingers through his sandy curls. Christmas time and so many people died alone, many by their own hand. The influx of deaths kept the Enforcers busy. The men would rather spend time with their families, whereas Fraser's Christmas would be celebrated by moments of stolen oblivion with a bottle and a bobtail.

"Our other cases were easier. Most people don't stuff themselves in a drum, pour oil over their bodies and then toss in a match. But this?" Connor gestured around the room. "How did the body burn to nothing and not torch the entire building? And what's with that horrid sludgy grim coating everything. I wouldn't want to be the next tenant in these rooms; you can scrub the walls, but you'll never get the stench out of the timber."

A brief smile flickered over Fraser's face. Only Connor would concentrate on the clean-up. He was a rarity among men; the large sergeant delighted in tidying his home and often relieved his wife of housekeeping duties. "Perhaps this death is natural in origin, and our services will not be required beyond today."

The sergeant shot him a look and a shudder ran through his bulk. "There's nothing natural about this."

Fraser's memory banks sparked and he recalled stories seen in medical and crime journals. "Have you heard of spontaneous human combustion?"

Connor frowned. "Nope."

"I have read of such rare cases, but never seen one." Over and over his mind traced the body outlined on the mattress. "Some would call it the fiery vengeance of God."

The sergeant shifted on his feet, eager to leave the room, but forced to stay by Fraser's presence. "Please tell me we don't have to bring Him in for questioning?"

Fraser smiled. "No, apparently this is a natural phenomenon. We can only speculate, along with the neighbours, as to what sin this poor soul committed to warrant such a fate."

Voices on the stairwell announced the arrival of the Enforcers' doctor and the technician hauling his photographic equipment. Through the open doorway to the parlour, Fraser watched as Doc stomped his feet to shift lingering snow and shrugged off his heavy overcoat. He thrust the coat at the Enforcer loitering in the adjoining room. "Make yourself useful and hang on to that, lad."

Pausing in the doorway, the physician rubbed his hands together with glee. His eyes widened on seeing the charred outline burned into the sodden mattress. He looked like a child with an early Christmas present and Fraser had removed the wrapping. "Oh I say, what have you got for me? Could it really be spontaneous human combustion?"

"Nigel Fenmore, neighbour found him this morning," Fraser said.

Doc paused and frowned. "Fenmore?" His gaze roamed the room and took in the book on the bedside. "I had a tutor at medical school called Fenmore." He shook his head and walked toward the bed and then stopped. He turned to Fraser. "Let's get this done. Was he a drunkard?"

There was a common held belief that only drunkards suffered from spontaneous human combustion. Whereas the reality was drunkards were most likely to kill themselves by falling into the fireplace. In their stupor they would be unable to rise and so burn to death.

"Only drank in moderation," Connor answered from the all-knowing notebook.

"Well, then, let us see. There hasn't been a genuine case in England since the seventeenth century. The ones I've seen are all alcohol-ridden sots who fell asleep next to an open flame or dropped a cigarette onto their bedding." Doc moved to the side of the bed and stared at the charred outline.

Fraser helped the technician set up the tripod and camera and they took a series of exposures from either side of the bed and one of the strange tide mark around the walls. Before long he gave Doc a wave to indicate he had finished and the doctor moved forward.

He dropped his metal case and pulled on the top two handles. A tray popped up. He picked up magnifying goggles and settled them on his head. He turned a lever on the side and various lenses rotated over his eyes before he determined the correct magnification. Then he selected a metal lunch box and a pair of tweezers.

"Hold this for me, Hamish." He held out the open tin to Fraser.

The uniforms settled in for a long night as the doctor sifted through the sludge, lifted fragments with the delicate prongs, and placed them in the small box. He exclaimed over each bone fragment and gave his assessment of where in the body it originated. After two hours the Enforcers' medic declared his search finished. He used a trowel to collect the remaining human sludge and deposited it in another box.

Fraser gave a sigh, his night not over yet. He would need to complete the paperwork to record the movement of the small tins to their new residence under the city. The morgue.

Lowestoft, Sunday 15th December, 1861

CHRISTMAS approached and found Cara and Nate living in the Lyons country estate to the north of Lowestoft. The brooding house straddled two different landscapes. On one side, steep cliffs towered nearly a hundred feet above a churning ocean. On the other side the estate levelled out to hundreds of acres of flat fields, grazed by sheep, cattle, and horses.

Nate's family built the house in a dark gothic fashion decades before anyone else considered gothic fashionable. Not that anyone fashionable would build in such an eerie manner with towers and turrets, a widow's walk, and downpipes crawling with strange creatures. Under their feet ran a network of tunnels, leading to a system of caves that wound their way to the private cove at the base of the cliff. The secluded beach and access were ideal for smuggling.

When Nate arrived out of the blue one morning and introduced Cara as his wife, the housekeeper fainted dead away. The house had lain bereft of feminine input for many long years. On her first night in the decrepit building Cara suggested torching the place as a belated Guy Fawkes bonfire.

On exploring the rambling house, she found the structure was sound, it just needed its ghosts laid to rest. Nate's ancestor chose to build the monolith in a dark, near black stone, making the house look like a haunted mausoleum that superstitious locals burned centuries ago. All it needed was lilies growing around the circular driveway to complete the picture of mourning.

Cara declared that a dark-panelled parlour with wide French doors overlooking the rear garden would serve as their breakfast room. She refused to be shoved in the formal dining room, with no windows and numerous severed animal heads as decoration. Today she attacked her breakfast while Nate scanned the morning business papers.

"Was Helene happy here?" she asked mid-bite of toast, her ever curious mind wondering about the history of the sad, and mad, countess.

The corner of the newspaper twitched. "I believe so. She spent twenty years here and I remember her laughter from when I was a child. Although it faded to silence as I grew older."

Cara glanced around the room. Despite the maid's best efforts, spiders clung to the corners. Fed a constant diet of insects, they grew to a size that almost enabled them to duel with feather dusters. "Did she stay here? The house feels like her."

The newspaper dropped to reveal the quirk of a lip. "No. There is a cottage by the lake. I can show you if you want." He reached out a hand for the coffee cup.

"Yes, please." Cara picked up the porcelain creamer. "By the way, I've asked her to come spend Christmas with us."

Nate snorted hot coffee over the morning newspaper and began coughing. He tossed the newspaper to the tablecloth.

Cara poured cream and cast a glance at her spluttering husband. "Maybe we should have divorced. I seem to have a knack for breaking through your poker face."

The footman detached himself from the wallpaper and rushed forward to dab at the coffee splatters on the linen cloth, but Nate waved the servant away. "There's nothing wrong with my poker face, woman, it's the live mortars you lob at me over toast that cause problems for my composure."

Cara added sugar to her coffee and stirred. "Well, she declined anyway."

Nate leaned back in his chair; the steel blue gaze penetrated to the concern eating away at his wife, the one she tried to conceal from their bond. "Jackson will visit her over Christmas and make sure she's not alone."

A sigh ran through her body, knowing that if anything happened, Helene would not meet her oncoming fate solo. "Good. I eventually figured out he is her little canary. Honestly, that man is like a crème brûlée."

Having regained his equanimity, Nate raised an eyebrow. "Care to elaborate on your analogy?"

She picked up a silver spoon, and tapped her boiled egg until the shell cracked. "Smack that hard exterior and underneath he's all warm and gooey."

"I am not." A gruff voice sounded from the doorway. The large and scarred bodyguard blocked the view beyond. "Ready when you are, gov." He nodded at Nate.

"Are so," Cara said. Turning in her chair, she threw her arms wide and gave him an equally wide smile. "I have a spare hug, want one?"

Jackson uttered an oath and threw up his hands. "I don't know what you see in that woman. I'll be outside." He cast a wary glance at Cara, in case she rose and pursued him, and then hurried out into the hallway.

Nate waited until Jackson disappeared and then gave a deep laugh. "Stop tormenting him. If you keep poking him with a stick don't be surprised if he bites one day." Rising, he gave his wayward wife a trail of kisses on the exposed nape of her neck.

"He's all bark." She tilted her head to give his lips better access and laid down the gossip sheet, no longer holding her attention. The main headline speculated about the sudden and unexpected emergence of haemophilia in the royal line, threatening the life of the young prince. Cara's focus drifted to Nate's discarded paper, where the headline proclaimed *Duke of Albany, Prince Leopold's life in the balance. Again.* She tapped a fingernail on the line of text under her hand, new threads forming in her mind.

"Nolton said he had proof that the Duke of Kent was not Victoria's father. Do you think it's true, that she is illegitimate and that's why the prince is sickly?"

Nate straightened and placed his hands on the back of her chair. "Rumours have always circulated that John Conroy was the duchess' lover. She wouldn't be the first woman to keep the identity of a child's father to herself."

Cara chewed her bottom lip. Had they saved Victoria from Hatshepsut's Collar only to lose their queen to the infidelity of her mother? Was Nolton right, and Victoria was never the rightful heir to the throne? "But to do that with a royal child?"

Nate's lips brushed the back of her neck, distracting her train of thought. Cara raised her arms to pull his head closer as she spoke. "I am expecting Amy this morning. I have brought in reinforcements to help redecorate. Plus she needs to escape London after the dissolution of her engagement to John Burke. Apparently he is being unpleasant about it and spreading rumours, she is quite ruined in the eyes of the *ton*."

"Hmm." He made the noise deep in his throat, tickling her ear. "I'll see to it that he stops."

A shiver ran down her spine, wondering what fate would await Sir John if he continued telling his tales about Amy. Perhaps he would be lodged in one of the soundproof cells far beneath the Lyons airship hangar. She made a mental note to extract the entire sordid story from Amy.

Jackson stuck his head back around the door. "The Hellcat is coming in."

"Excellent." Cara picked up the linen napkin off her knee, and dropped it on to the table. "Amy was bringing up crates of fabric and wallpaper samples with her."

Nate narrowed his eyes. "No chintz."

A smile broke over her face. "But I hear it's all the rage in London."

"No *chintz*." He growled out the syllables.

❧◈❧

Cara tugged the fur-trimmed hood of her jacket tight around her face, to keep out the freezing wind blowing from the ocean. She dashed across the weed-strewn lawn toward the Hellcat, avoiding the sheep sheltering by the unkempt hedge. The sleek airship landed with the feline maiden bow figure pointed to the sea, her wooden locks strewn back across the prow as though she too fought the arctic gusts.

Loki's men tied the lines to the mooring bollards sunk in the lawn with heavy cast iron rings in the tops. The gangplank swung down and a figure wrapped in purple wool descended and rushed toward Cara with outstretched arms.

"Oh, Cara," Amy said as the two women met and embraced. "London is just horrid, but Captain Hawke rescued me and left their curtains twitching."

Cara smiled. "Come inside to the warmth and tell me all about it."

Amy stopped and stared. Her mouth hung open as her gaze roamed the dark house where nightmare creatures wrapped clawed hands around the downpipes and window ledges. The blackened windows made the turret appear like a skull with sunken eye sockets hovering above the main building. "Oh good grief, it's hideous."

Cara laughed. "If you think this is bad, wait until you see the inside."

Amy turned wide eyes to her. "So you need my help to set fire to it?"

"That was my first reaction, too." The two friends burst into laughter and headed up the wide stairs to the warmth.

Outer clothes were shed and handed to bemused staff before Cara ushered Amy into a small drawing room. The spiders here were smaller in size and the flock wallpaper had seen better days; but the overstuffed sofas, abundance of cushions, and roaring fire made it passably comfortable.

Cara threw another log on the fire before taking a seat. "So you didn't mind me sending Loki to fetch you?"

Amy let out a sigh as she plonked down. "Oh, Cara, Captain Hawke was ever so daring. He landed his airship right outside our house, in the middle of the street. He stopped all the traffic. I'm sure poor old Mrs Higgins from next door clutched at her curtains so tightly she pulled them from the rail."

"Made a bit of an entrance, did he?"

A maid brought the tea tray and set it on the low table between the women.

"Oh yes. He swung over the side on a rope, just like a pirate on the high seas."

Cara poured tea while Amy told her tale of the dashing captain.

"He waltzed up the front path followed by two crewmen and demanded I accompany him."

A whisper of concern flew through Cara's mind. *I hope Loki didn't take advantage of Amy.* The pirate often held court at Su-Terre as the Trickster, a man who gambled favours and usually won.

"He was ever so gallant and gentleman-like. He let me hold on to the wheel and fly the ship." Amy's deep brown eyes shone with excitement, her troubles forgotten for the moment.

As though summoned by her thoughts, the door opened and the captain appeared. "Everything all right with my two favourite ladies?"

Amy blushed and held a hand to her chest. "Oh yes thank you, Captain Hawke."

Cara gave a fixed look to Loki. *Thank you*, she mouthed, over the top of Amy's head.

He gave a wink and a deep bow. "The lads have unloaded all your luggage. Let me know if I can be of service in any capacity."

Amy drew a fan and circulated air over her heated face. Cara hid a laugh behind her tea cup as the rogue disappeared again.

The fire crackled and silence settled between the two old friends. Cara put down the cup and frowned across the table. "Now you're here, you can confess all. What happened?"

Amy remained silent, but her hands took flight. She picked up a cushion and turned it over and over before setting it on her lap to stroke the worn velvet fabric. "We called it off. We were not compatible."

Cara took a deep breath to stop herself from blurting out the words at the forefront of her mind. John Burke made his distaste of Cara clear on their first meeting. "You were so excited, you shone when you talked of the wedding plans."

"He did not like you," Amy whispered.

Cara bit back a snort. "That's irrelevant, he wasn't marrying me. I thought him keen on you?"

A sigh and her face turned to the fire. "He did not like any of my friends. Or my family, my activities or even the way I dress." Her hands stilled on the cushion. "He was so charming at first and then as time progressed he changed. He said the sole purpose of a wife was to ensure his daily comfort and pleasure."

A chill crept down Cara's spine and she rose to sit next to Amy. She removed the cushion and took Amy's hand in hers. "Amy, what happened with John?"

"Every day began with a letter from John, telling me what to wear, where I could go and what he expected me to do before we met that afternoon." Unshed tears shimmered in the eyes of a trapped doe. "Then one day I decided to escape and read one of those dreadful penny romances. Silly I know, but a harmless way to fill vacant hours. He thought it a waste of time and didn't have it on my list of approved reading material. We argued, not for the first time. He threw my book on the fire, then he——" One tear slid down her cheek. "He struck me."

Cara swore and moved to her friend and drew Amy into an embrace. "I'm so sorry I was not there."

A tiny smile. "I do believe you were busy helping your husband escape from the Tower of London at the time."

"Nate's a big boy and he wasn't going anywhere. You should have come to me." Cara pressed a handkerchief into Amy's hand.

"He said I deserved it, that I drove him to it." Her voice dropped to a whisper. "He said he had to educate me about how a wife was expected to behave. I was so foolish. Everyone thinks John is such a wonderful catch. He is putting it about he broke it off because I was at fault. Now they all whisper about me behind my back."

She bit back her anger. "He didn't deserve you, Amy. No man should raise his hand to a woman. Don't ever, not for one instant, think it was your fault."

Her friend cried and Cara plotted. She intended to ensure John Burke learned never to raise his hand to another woman.

CHAPTER 3

Lowestoft, Monday 16th December, 1861

NATE led Jackson down a long corridor through the middle of the house that turned into a narrow staircase. As they descended, lights glowed softly at regular intervals and cast their path in shadow but illuminated the step in front. The stairs opened out to the old wine cellar deep under the estate. Two walls covered in a wooden honeycomb contained bottles that told the alcoholic history of the house above. Dust and spiders had long ago claimed the small oblong flagons, like tiny corpses at sleep in their alcoves in a crypt.

Nate had spent the last ten years in London and abroad, leaving the house to its ghosts and servants. The queen's decision to appoint him and Cara as her artifact hunters meant they would need to spend part of the year at the country mansion, playing museum attendants. The new career breathed fresh life into the old structure and gave direction to the staff long used to an empty house.

As promised, Queen Victoria supplied the funds for the construction work undertaken on the Lyons estate. Her pockets proved to be as deep as the catacombs running back to the cliffs. The most obvious sign of the recent expenditure was the impressive set of shiny new metal doors in the back wall of the cellar. Using dense layers of metal, the doors were reminiscent of the structure used in the Pit under the airship hangar. This particular set was bolted and riveted as though expected to withstand a charging elephant, or to keep the equivalent sealed within.

The middle of the doors held a wheel to draw back the securing bolts. Nate dialled the combination and then Jackson turned the wheel until a deep clunk sounded. The men pushed the heavy doors open and were greeted by a blast of polar air.

"Christ," Jackson muttered and pulled his jacket tighter around his body.

Labouring deep in the cold ground, a handful of trusted workers had made the old smuggling tunnels safe. Metal brackets held back the surrounding rock and earth at six-foot intervals. Electric lights sat in metal cages attached to the ceiling. Thick copper pipes ran from one light to the next, connecting the oversized Christmas ornaments. The yellow light flickered on and off with minute power surges.

"What's the situation with the lights?" Nate asked as they walked down the corridor.

"We've set up turbines along the ridge to power the electrics, but the supply is dodgy. We're dragging the cables further than anyone's done before. Got some bloke workin' on it," Jackson said. "But the tech is still experimental and we're trying to figure it out as we go."

The floor under their feet angled downward as they headed deeper into the ground.

Nate thrust his hands into the pockets of his heavy blue frock coat. "It's like Siberia down here. What about heating?"

"We've fired up the boilers to heat the house. You should have warm air wafting up your arse by the time you return top side. We looked at riggin' the pipes down here, but dollface said some of the objects were better in the cold. She thinks that's why her old man kept them in basements and banks with underground vaults. She said the cold would keep them asleep." He paused for a moment and flicked a glance to his boss. "She's joking, right?"

A smile rippled through Nate's body, but his lips stayed straight. "The theory could hold true, like a reptile in the cold becomes sluggish and hibernates. Personally, I'd rather not heat the place to find out what happens if they all became hyper-active."

Jackson gave a shake of his head and blew into his hands to warm his flesh. "I hope you know what you're doing," he muttered. "This new lark is like stuffin' the basement with gun powder and then playing with matches."

The tunnel stopped at another set of doors identical to the first. Nate entered the second code and Jackson swung the wheel in the middle, disengaging the lock. The doors opened to reveal the large catacomb that used to be the centre of the Lyons smuggling operation. Now the cave housed a secret department of Victoria's regime.

Shelves lined the walls and held metal containers of various sizes. Within one lay Hatshepsut's Collar, the artifact that pushed Victoria to the brink of madness and stole the life of her consort, Prince Albert. Other boxes were larger, some the size of dog crates capable of holding a Great Dane. These were bolted to the floor, waiting for their occupants.

From Cara's research they knew some objects were small, like Boudicca's Cuff; others were far larger, needing their own rooms. Each container or room was triple lined with copper and steel with a space between the layers. They hoped in the future to circulate a liquid between the layers to suspend the artifacts in a type of stasis. Once they figured out what would work. Nate put out the word, searching for a scientist to bring into their little group, but he had yet to find one who had the necessary background and whom they could trust.

A large L-shaped work table dominated the centre of the room. The surface crowded with rows of test tubes in pristine racks and clear glass bottles held over shiny Bunsen burners. Everything gleaming and brand new. The equipment waited for the person who would labour to unlock the secrets of the artifacts, to learn how they functioned and how to keep them silent.

Nate contemplated the work done on the cave, now turned into a cross between a bank vault, morgue, and laboratory. "It looks close to completion."

"This room is done." He waved a hand at two other doors set in the stone walls. "There's a route out to the cove if needed. Plus we can kit out one of the other sub caves if you need the extra space." He leaned back against a tall set of shelves. "Any idea how many toys you're planning to store down here?"

Nate shook his head. "I have no idea. This line of business is new to all of us."

"And more lucrative. The queen has deep pockets. We'll have made a tidy profit while upgrading the house; that's if these things don't get us all killed."

A smile tugged at Nate's lips. "We've come a long way, you and I."

Jackson laughed. "When I met you, you were a wet behind the ears whelp of a noble on his first trip from home."

"And you were a boxer with a bad attitude and no future." Nate remembered those early days, when he set off determined to earn his fortune. One hand drifted to his stomach. "I took a knife to the gut saving your arse in Barcelona."

Jackson's eyes crinkled with laughter. "Never said you weren't handy in a fight."

"We hauled ourselves out of a riot and onto an airship and never looked back." Nate grabbed a wall shelf and gave a tug, testing how securely it was attached to the rock behind. "Our lives are no longer what they once were, Jackson. Times and circumstances change."

The large bodyguard gave a snort of air. "Like all this lovey dovey stuff with you and dollface. It turns a man's stomach after a while. Never thought I'd see you go soft."

Nate leaned against the shelving, crossed his arms over his chest and met his second's gaze. "It's time you moved on with your life too. We all miss Angelique and Sarah. We didn't just avenge them, we stamped our message so deep no one will ever hurt what is yours again."

The bodyguard turned and walked toward a stairway made of metal drawers that curved up the arch of the cavern. He laid his palms against the cold metal and took a deep breath. "It ain't that easy. They were my world."

Both men fell silent, neither accustomed to discussing the emotional turmoil that raged deep inside. They had worked alongside each other for over ten years, faced enemies back to back and dug bullets out of one another. But their courage faltered and baulked at talking about their feelings.

Nate ran a hand through his black hair and skirted around the topic. "I have a proposition for you. I need you to take an active role in acquiring and protecting these cursed objects. I am being spread thin these days, and you and Loki have access to different realms. You can do on the ground what he can do amongst the air leagues."

Jackson's head shot up and his eyes narrowed. "You don't want me as muscle anymore?"

"You have more skills than that, let's use them. Miguel has great potential, but he needs time. Loki has taken him on as crew. Give the lad five years, a couple of tattoos and some hardening off and we'll bring him back in. In the meantime, I need you to take a greater role than just watching my back, and I would prefer if Cara had a dedicated watcher."

A grin broke over Jackson's face at the mention of the woman who lived to torment him. "Would get me out from having to hold her handbag while she shops for underwear. There's one lad I would trust to watch dollface, let me check with him before I hand her over."

Nate slapped the man on the back. "You'll consider my offer?"

"I'm always open to more money." A grin broke over his scarred face. "The new job does come with a pay rise?"

Nate gave a rare laugh. "Let's talk details upstairs over a brandy."

They left the slumbering artifacts and headed back up the tunnel, toward the warmth of the newly steam-heated house.

Cara stretched her arms over her head and relished the warmth washing over her body. Jackson's contacts and Victoria's money worked a miracle and breathed heat throughout the old mansion. Piping ran behind the walls and under the floor and was connected to two enormous steaming behemoths in the basement. Fed on a diet of coal, they puffed heated air and steam back through the pipes, which wafted through ornate brass grates set in the floor of all the rooms. From the outside the house might look like a mausoleum, but inside was now as toasty as the kitchens or Nate's conservatory back in Mayfair.

Amy fanned herself with a wallpaper sample but refused to remove her jacket in the presence of the men. Although Cara didn't know if it was the steam vents or Loki that made her friend run hot and bothered.

Nate was buried in papers and aethergram tape at the desk, while Cara read one of her father's diaries. Amy's plans to redecorate were in full swing and she poured over sample books she brought up from London. Loki assisted by holding up the book to the wall, while Amy stepped backward. She flicked her wrist to signal the pirate to turn the pages to a different sample.

Cara wondered how long Loki would last as a decorator. He looked ready to chew his arm off to escape. "Loki, when Amy is done with you for today, could you jump in the Hellcat, head over to Leicester and bring back Nan and Nessy please."

Loki tried to keep his face impassive, but she saw relief flare before he regained his bored look. "I'm not a hansom cab, you know, ferrying people back and forth."

She gave him a wide smile. "No, but I would trust no one else with those most precious to me."

Questions swirled in his dark eyes. "All right, but before I go, what is the deal with your grandmother and her companion?"

She looked up from her book, a frown lining her forehead. "What do you mean?"

His brows knitted as his mind sought the required words. "They seem awfully … close."

Cara snorted. "You have no idea." She tossed the diary onto the end table. "Nessy's mother was Nan's wet nurse, so they two have been inseparable since they were born. Men have come and gone, but their friendship has endured. The two of them have always been there for each other." Cara watched Amy as she said the words, wishing she had been there for her friend, and vowed to make up for the deficiency.

Amy gave a wave and dismissed her assistant.

Loki closed the sample book and dropped it back into the large chest from Liberty's. "But your grandmother was married for years to the Earl of Morton."

Cara could see Loki's mind working hard. "Yes, quite happily. What's your point?"

"My point, my luscious peach, is was it a ménage a trois?"

Amy turned. "What do you mean ménage a trois?"

Loki licked his lips. "Three a bed, did they share the lucky earl?"

Amy gave a startled yelp and dropped the sample swatches in her hands.

"Ewww," Cara said. "You are talking about my grandparents. But I dare you to ask Nessy that yourself. Now get off your arse and go collect them before they scamper off on their own in search of adventure."

CHAPTER 4

London, Friday 20th December, 1861.

HAMISH Fraser reached a hand into a paper stack clinging to the edge of his desk and

grabbed a file. He gently eased the target away from the unbalanced
tower and dragged it to the middle of his desk. Then he stared at his mug
of tea. Once again he had ignored the refreshment for too long and it
now contained a lukewarm mix of fluids. As the internal temperature of
the drink dropped the milk grew a skin and attempted to expand large
enough to touch the edges and possibly plot its escape.

With a sigh he pushed the mug to one side. He dreamed of a world
where tea came hot and on demand. Perhaps in some sort of insulated
cup so it didn't matter if it lay unattended for a short period, the drink
wouldn't turn treacherous and tepid. *Utopia.*

Flipping open the file cover, Fraser stared at the black and white
photograph of Nigel Fenmore. Or, more accurately, the space Nigel Fenmore's body once occupied, staining the mattress in a black outline. The
demise of the elderly gentleman unsettled him. Burning was such a slow
and grim way to die and nobody even noticed, not even the victim. If
it weren't for the foul odour sinking to the floor below, the death might

have gone undiscovered for several weeks. He wondered if his end would be similar, alone and with no one to remark upon his passing. Perhaps he should make a greater effort to talk to his neighbours.

He closed the file and tossed it back with its companions, causing the delicate structure to lurch to one side. Christmas approached fast and full dark settled over London hours ago. Rising from his chair, he grabbed his overcoat. This winter seemed colder than anyone could remember, or perhaps the queen's intense mourning for Prince Albert cast a pall over the country.

Closing his office door, he decided to head down to hear Doc's report before finding his way back to his cold and empty house. The upper levels of the Enforcers Headquarters were an ant hill of activity, with people scurrying back and forth. Even this close to Christmas they didn't slow down; in fact the approaching holiday saw a marked upswing in crime, as a certain segment did their gift shopping in the homes of others.

The press of uniformed men thinned as Fraser took the stairs below street level. He passed the cell level and the rowdy inmates shouting their innocence. Once he dropped to the second level into the ground, he found himself alone. Very few ventured this far, where death took up residence.

As he pushed through the heavy steel doors, he noticed that for once the morgue did not feel chilly, as the winter temperature outside plummeted due to the heavy layer of snow blanketing the city. Underground and above ground conditions met and mirrored one another. They were both frigid.

"Hiho, Doc. Much on?" He halted on seeing the limbs arrayed on the table.

Doc leaned his knuckles on the cool stone, his attention absorbed by the small collection in the middle of his autopsy table. "Nigel Fenmore was a physician, you know, and a tutor at medical school. He once served the Duchess of Kent and ushered our queen into the world. Now look at him." Doc fell silent, his attention held by the head, foot, and hand. With the red and white striped cap removed, the head revealed a bald pate. A few long white hairs clung to the outer perimeter of the skull. Nigel had combed each strand over with care before donning his nightcap. His eyes were closed in eternal sleep and his face held a peaceful expression.

Fraser stepped closer. "No family has claimed him yet, but we'll wait until after Christmas in case someone shows, if you can spare the room."

Doc let out a deep sigh and raised his gaze. "I am filling up fast with those who wish to permanently escape the good cheer, but at least my fellow surgeon does not occupy much space. I will find a quiet corner for Doctor Fenmore."

The suicide rate jumped mid-December and did not settle again until after New Year's Eve. It revealed the dark side to the festive period. Fraser and Doc would be kept busy cataloguing the deaths of those who felt most alone during the holiday season. Loneliness was an unrelenting pressure, too much for some to bear when surrounded by happy families.

The cleaned bone of the ankle caught Fraser's attention. "Is it a genuine case of spontaneous human combustion?"

Doc slid his hand under the arch of the foot and thrust it at Fraser. "Look at the edge. If someone attempted to dismember the body we would see straight cuts or striation marks in the bone. This is rough and ragged, as though it were chewed off."

Fraser took the limb and turned it in his hands. The exposed bone ended in a jagged line and splinters where the fire had eaten through and severed the connection to the body.

Doc moved to his work bench and fetched a small steel box. Returning to the table, he picked up the head and placed it within, along with the curled fist. Fraser added the foot to the strange and sad package.

Doc closed the lid and rested his fingers on the metal surface. "As far as I can ascertain there is no foul play involved. From my examination of the room the fire appears to have originated in his torso. There is no evidence of any accelerant. The body had not been moved, so he burned in situ. So to answer your question, yes. A highly unusual but dare I say *natural* death."

An icy finger traced a path down Fraser's spine. *Horrible way to go.*

"Thank you, Doc. That's one less case to worry about. I'll see you in the morning."

The little doctor gave a wave as he turned, box in his hands, to place the guest in one of the numerous chilled steel drawers.

Fraser headed back upstairs and slipped through the main doors, into the evening. A man huddled under the eave of Enforcers' headquarters, his hat pulled low over his ears and his scarf pulled high. The inspector paused on the top step to loop his woollen scarf around his neck, and then he noticed a man move in the shadow.

"Inspector Fraser," the man called out, dropping the warm covering from his nose and mouth so he could speak. "Do you have a moment?"

Fraser's body ached and every cell longed to lie down and surrender to oblivion. His mind needed to erase the day before the cycle began all over again in less than eight hours. "You may have a moment."

The man stepped from the dark into the light and extracted a notepad from his jacket. He fumbled to hold a pencil between mittened fingers. "Roger Thurston, reporter with the Daily Times, I wanted to speak to you about the horrible death of Nigel Fenmore. Is it true his body was cremated in his own bed?"

"Correct, Mr Fenmore was reduced to ash." Fraser started a mental countdown. The reporter would only have another sixty seconds of his time.

The reporter's eyes narrowed; the vulture sensed a fresh kill to delight his readers. "How is that possible without burning down the entire building? Do you have any leads as to who committed such a heinous crime?"

"There is no crime, the deceased succumbed to a natural phenomenon known as spontaneous human combustion. Very rare, but there is no foul play unless you wish to implicate God. Now if you will excuse me, this has been a rather long day." He stepped down to the pavement and set a brisk pace along the road, not wanting to be followed. Large flakes of snow swirled around his face and he pulled the striped scarf higher, protecting the end of his nose.

As he approached the bustle of Covent Garden, women called to him from the shadows and narrow alleyways he passed. Some used his name. His body gave a tug when he heard a familiar voice.

"You look all done in, Hamish. Why don't you let me revive your spirits?" A throaty laugh accompanied the words.

He paused on the cobbles. His blood heated thinking of the soft reception waiting beyond the reach of the streetlights. *How long has it been?* He could not remember, but tonight his mind needed relief and his physical appetites would wait until another day.

"Not tonight, Lilith," he called. "I'm afraid I am far too tired and I would be a disappointment to you."

"You'd never disappoint me, lovey," the woman replied with a deep chuckle. "Someone needs to take care of you with Faith gone. Perhaps tomorrow night I'll help perk you up."

He waved and kept his feet moving. His mind drifted with the snow, darting back and forth chasing specks of light. Plumes of deep purple smoke rose up into the sky from the massive apparatuses digging the tunnels for the new subterranean train tracks. Men and machines laboured night and day, unceasing as they crushed rock to circle the inner city from below.

He skirted one scar in the earth where a digger bellowed and belched smoke. Men fed coal into one end and removed carts of dirt from the other. Temporary railings stopped pedestrians from falling into the black pit. He wondered at the ingenuity that came up with the idea of transporting citizens below the ground. The newspapers speculated it would be an expensive fad; who, they asked, would want to be trapped under the earth in a train?

With no awareness of passing time, he soon stood on the rough paving of his little row. He lived close to the St Giles Rookery, a desolate area others avoided. For him, he liked being close to the birth place of so much work for the Enforcers. Although the Rookeries were distinctly quieter and cleaner since a certain viscount stamped his mark on the residents.

He pushed through the door of his small terrace. Fraser once toyed with taking rooms, but wanted the privacy of knowing no one resided above or below him. The solid little houses kept noise at bay between the residents. He closed the door on the world and made his way through the pitch black to the parlour. His fingers sought the switch to the one extravagance he installed in the house. The spinning turbine on the roof powered electric lights in the parlour, bedroom, and kitchen.

He ran his hands over a tired face and through his hair. The dull ache took up residence in his brain and bones. One day he would escape it all and re-join Faith.

The maid had reset the fire, and striking a match he tossed the flame into the pile of paper and tinder. His gaze watched as the tiny flame devoured the paper and grew, swallowing up the tinder. He fed the fire larger and larger pieces of wood.

Is this how a flame devours a body? Too fast for a man to react, and extinguished before the room bursts into flames? Or does it lick at flesh slowly, with leisure, like a well-paid courtesan?

He removed his winter layers and laid them over the back of the sofa. The bowler hat rested on top of the pile. In three slow, tired strides he crossed the room and pulled open a tall wooden cabinet. From within he retrieved a bottle of whiskey and a short tumbler. He dropped the glass onto the mantle and worked the cork from the bottle, and then poured a generous finger of amber liquor. Replacing the bottle, his free hand went into his jacket pocket and extracted a small purple glass vial. He undid the dropper and sucked up a tiny portion of liquid. It took all of his concentration to steady his hand and count the drops he squeezed into the whiskey.

He swirled the laudanum into the drink and settled into the armchair in front of the fire.

In quiet moments like these, the absence of Faith gnawed the most. He didn't miss her. 'Miss' was too small a word for the yawning chasm her loss opened up within him. If people knew of their relationship they never understood it. The gently bred inspector and the common prostitute. But she was far more than the companion of his body and heart, she saw into his soul. The blackened mass in his chest covered by rot and decay never deterred her. Piece by piece she chipped away at the layers he spawned to protect himself from dealing in death on a daily basis. She brought a sliver of warmth and joy into his world and something wholly unfamiliar to him——hope and longing. And then in the summer of 1860, the Grinder snatched her away and the darkness claimed him.

There were days he believed he would never surface from the dark. Faith had been his only lifeline and without her, he was untethered. Only work and the pursuit of Lyons gave him a rock to cling to, a touchstone to centre him when the swirling vortex threatened to pull him under. He would achieve his life's purpose and then surrender to the waves.

He tossed back the glass and waited for the familiar haze to cloud his mind and wipe away the stress of the day. Gentle fingers massaged his consciousness and beckoned for him to follow the wisps, to escape to another world where the cold fingers of death could not touch him. To linger in a world where Faith still breathed and her laughter tickled his skin as her naked form slid over him.

CHAPTER 5

Lowestoft, 22nd December.

THE delicious aromas of bacon and coffee tickled Cara's senses and woke her from sleep. She cracked one eye open and, in the sliver of light breaking through the curtains, found Nate standing by the bed. A silver tray in his hands contained the source of the delectable smell making her stomach rumble.

"Happy birthday," he said, placing the breakfast tray on the side table and sitting on the edge of the bed.

A black velvet box with a silver bow lay nestled between bacon and coffee and seized her attention. She pushed herself to an upright position, dragging the blankets up to cover her naked chest. She picked up the long rectangle and stroked a finger along the plush exterior, enjoying the speculation of what might lay within.

"Open it," Nate said.

She didn't need to be told twice. She slid off the ribbon and cracked the lid. Her breath left her in a gasp. Her eyes widened as she stared at the contents shimmering on black silk.

"It's beautiful," she whispered, lifting out a diamond collar. The gems caught the morning sun that escaped through the drapes. Sparks of red and gold flashed around the room and threw flames against the walls. "I'm holding fire." Never had she seen diamonds respond to the light like these.

Nate placed a hand over hers and turned the necklace over. "Your little friend is shedding and contributed something special. Look closely at the setting."

She peered at the gems. Each diamond had an unusual backing, roughly circular in shape and the source of the brilliant colour. *A dragon scale.*

"The light refracts through the diamond and bounces off the scale, making them blaze with living fire."

She let out a breath. "You've given me dragon diamonds for my birthday." She held up her hand and stared at them in wonder, mesmerised by the play of colour.

He strode to the large window and then pulled the curtain open. Watery sunlight rushed into the room and turned the necklace into molten lava in her hands.

Cara laid the gems back on their silken bed and watched Nate's shoulders bunch under his jacket as he tied back the curtain. The movement of muscle under skin was something else she could never tire of admiring.

"As much as I love my present, I thought I ordered a pirate wake up call for my birthday. Over the knee boots, sword, open shirt." She gave him a slow smile as she mentally divested him of clothing and then redressed him more appropriately for her birthday. "Maybe a pirate with a spot of ravishment on his mind?"

His gaze darkened and with great care he removed his jacket and draped it over the chaise. He stalked back to the bed as his fingers undid the buttons on his shirt. "Just so you know, it's not the clothes that make a pirate, it's the exploits."

His shirt hit the floor by the time he reached the bed. Cara's breath caught in her throat with the intensity of his stare and the emotion surging along their common bond. He heated her from within and without simultaneously.

Mentally she traced patterns over the smooth flesh of his torso; she itched to follow them with her fingers.

Kneeling on the end of the mattress, he grabbed the blanket. She gave a yelp as he pulled the bedding from her grasp and left her naked to his hungry stare and grateful for the warm heat emitted through the newly installed steam ducts.

"If it's ravishment my lady wants," he said as he curled his fingers around her ankle. He pulled her down the bed, sliding one slim leg on either side of his waist.

Cara cast a glance to the tray by the bed and a thought flitted through her mind as warm breath tickled over the inside of her thighs.

Nate growled. "Don't even think of making a grab for the bacon."

Cara stood on the threshold of the dining room and could scarce believe the transformation Amy wrought in just over a week. Her friend arrived in desperate need of a distraction and she fell upon the challenge presented by the gloomy old house. The first room attacked was the impromptu breakfast room. She painted the dark panelling a soft cream and complemented the shade with cream wallpaper scattered all over with bronze dragonflies flitting amongst lotus blossoms. Even the large dining table seemed a pale gold under its fresh linen cloth. The silk drapes reminded Cara of buttercups scattered over a field and framed the French doors out to the patio and garden. Or what would be the garden, once spring arrived and Cara managed to chase the sheep and several goats out from the overgrown maze and weed-ridden beds.

"It's lovely, Amy," she said to her beaming friend. "So light and cheerful and I do believe you have vanquished every spider in the room."

"Lachlan and Mr Jackson removed the spiders, when they weren't shoving them down each other's shirts like a couple of school boys." She gave Cara a hug. "Consider this my present to you, since I have nothing else to give." A slight frown crossed her face at her newly cut-off status.

Cara squeezed her friend's arm. "I'm sure you'll work magic on the house. You seem to have brought a treasure trove with you in those chests from Liberty's."

A shy smile crept over Amy's face. "I have a delicious chintz I am thinking would look perfect in the evening lounge."

A rumble vibrated through Cara's body, setting sensitive nerves alight. Nate shot her an accompanying look. "We may have to negotiate on the chintz," she murmured.

"I'll show you the samples later. But whatever took you so long to get dressed? We have all been waiting for you, breakfast is practically over." She gestured to the assembled family, all in the throes of finishing their breakfast.

"Nate was giving me my present," she said.

Nessy and Loki both gave a snort of laughter from the back of the room. Nessy stared at Cara's tousled hair and flushed skin and then she elbowed Nan. "I'd be late too if he were giving me something first thing in the morning."

"Do tell," Amy said, oblivious to the swirling innuendo. "What did he give you?"

"Diamonds." Cara shot a look to Nessy, willing her to hold her tongue in front of the less worldly Amy. She knew Loki was a lost cause, but she did chuckle to see the pirate preoccupied with reaching the sideboard for seconds while keeping Nessy in his line of sight. He had the look of a man confronted with a python who would draw him into a fatal embrace if he dropped his guard. Which Nessy no doubt would; she made no secret of her desire to wrap herself around the much younger man.

Nan rose from her place at the table and gave Cara a hug before kissing her cheek. "Happy birthday, my darling girl."

"Quite." Amy gave a shake, brushing off her thoughts. "Twenty-two years old today and a married woman. Who would have thought it?"

"I would never have imagined such a scene a year ago." Cara took a seat on the newly covered chaise by the large glass doors. The view outside revealed a grey day with clouds threatening to drop their burden of snow.

"Where were you a year ago?" Amy asked as she sat next to Cara.

A smile lit her eyes. "Pouring drinks at a saloon in Texas."

Loki perked up, having successfully fended off Nessy and heaped more sausage onto his plate. "You were a saloon girl? Why have I not heard this story before?"

"Another time," Cara laughed. "I think it's more of an evening story."

Nate carried a stack of gaily wrapped parcels from the sideboard, and laid them next to her. He picked up the top one, wrapped in stark black and white tissue. "From Helene."

She took the small package in her hands and gave a squeeze. Hard, with a familiar indent on one side. She pulled the black ribbon and slipped the paper off, revealing a squat, thick book.

"*Suetonius' Secrets.*" She ran a hand over the gold work on the cover. "It's said to contain the myths and stories surrounding unnatural objects that he learned about in the ancient world. From what I read in father's journal, many scholars doubted the book even existed. Yet somehow, some medieval monk found his scrolls and made a copy."

"Or a forgery," Loki pointed out, seating himself with his back to the wall and keeping his eyes on the marauding python. "If the book's existence is doubted, how do you know what you're holding is real?"

She met his gaze. "Simple, because it comes from Helene's collection. I swear that woman has the ability to conjure books from thin air."

"She has gypsy blood, so very possibly does exactly that." Nate rearranged the pile of presents.

"Gypsy, really? I can see her reading fortunes." Cara filed away the titbit about Helene. "This book will be a fascinating read, and will aid our work for Victoria." She cracked the book open toward the middle and scanned the ornate calligraphy and embellished drawings. Her mind turned the assorted letters to words and her heart plummeted. "Oh, that's not fair."

"What?" Nate leaned over her shoulder his breath feathered over her neck and reignited embers.

Cara regarded the little volume. "It's all in Latin. I hate Latin, I can only make out every fifth word." She glanced sideways at Nate, hoping he would jump to her rescue.

"Don't look at me. My Latin is rusty, my skills are in oral languages not long dead ones." He kissed her neck, before straightening to take his coffee from the butler.

Amy burst into laughter. "Bet you wished you didn't skive off from so many lessons now."

Cara resorted to the only witty reply that came to hand: she stuck her tongue out at her friend. "Why do I feel like I have been given extra school work?"

Loki's black eyes danced with humour. "You obviously need to practice your linguistic skills."

Amy blinked. "But Cara only needs to understand written Latin, not spoken."

Loki's eyes widened before he laughed. "Oh, kitten, you are so innocent."

A frown settled on Amy's brow and she turned, a question written over her open face.

Cara bit back her laughter. "I'll explain it to you in private, Amy," she said, before returning her attention to the pile of presents and bright ribbons.

Cara treasured each gift, lifting ribbons and paper with care to ensure the experience lasted as long as possible. When no more boxes remained she looked around the room with a soaring heart. She never dreamed to have such friends and family. Even the gruff Jackson earned his place in her affections. Although he absented himself, among the pile she discovered a gift from him, a small brooch of a mechanical unicorn head. The eyes whirled when the tiny horn was pressed.

She closed her eyes, afraid to ruin the moment with the tears that threatened. She took a deep breath and Nate gave her an internal caress, as intimate as a thumb grazing across the pulse in her wrist.

She opened her eyes to meet his pale blue ones. "Thank you, for everything."

"I would do anything for you, *cara mia*." He raised her hand and brushed a kiss over her knuckles.

After breakfast everyone vanished in separate directions, leaving Cara and Nate alone. Bundled up in wool and fur, they trod overgrown paths through the forest to one side of the estate. Cara thought she walked a nightmare world full of bare and twisted trees reaching out to grab her and suck her down to Hell. A raven cawed and flapped large black wings, casting a shadow that made her soul shiver.

"This winter is so unnatural, like the sun has abandoned us." London suffered far worse. Although the city normally saw a few inches of snow in February it came harder and faster this year. The city was buried in an uncommon abundance of snow and despair.

Nate's fingers tightened on her gloved hand. "It came with the discharge from Hatshepsut's Collar. Let's hope the effect fades with the arrival of spring, now the thing is buried deep in the earth."

They had a growing collection down in the cavern. Piece by piece Cara gathered the remains of her father's artifacts and moved them to the new location. "I need to do more research. In many ways we are walking blind with these artifacts. Who knows what they can do? I gather what information I can from ancient texts but little of it is practical." She touched a hand to her chest. "Like how Nefertiti's Heart works."

"That one lets you breath underwater." He flashed Cara a wide smile. "You need to write this down in plain English, to warn those who come after us."

There was something she never contemplated. Who would inherit all those triple-lined boxes after them? "There's a cheery thought, I had hoped we were immortal."

The smile stayed on his face and melted the ice forming inside her due to the frigid conditions. "Mine for eternity, *cara mia*."

Twigs snapped under foot and birds circled in a grey sky. A sheep broke from under a shrub, bleated at them and pelted off in the opposite direction. Finally the path opened out and the view drew the eye down to the lake. Naked weeping willows surrounded the banks, bare arms dangled in the water. Their slight motion stopped the edges from freezing over. Toward the middle, small ripples touched the mirrored surface where fish played and fed below the surface.

"There's good fishing here during summer," Nate broke the silence, his words visible on the chilly air as each exhalation curled from his lips. "And we used to swim here." He pointed to a narrow jetty stretching out over the water.

Cara tried to drape the scene in vibrant green and sunshine but failed. "I'll have to take your word for it." She wondered if she needed coins to pay the resident ferryman.

Another path stretched from the water's edge back to the place Helene called home for twenty years, while syphilis became a squatter in her body and mind.

Cara's imagination had conceived a tiny rundown cottage with only a couple of rooms. *Got the rundown bit right.*

She now stood in front of a modest two-storey home constructed of rough-hewn pale stone. The insipid sunlight lit the brickwork. It glowed like honey and emitted a visual warmth, drawing her closer. The entire structure oozed a charming hand-built appeal. Boston ivy rampaged up the walls and reached arms around to embrace the windows. Winter stripped the plant's frame bare and the scattered leaves formed a dense blanket over the frozen earth below. A banksia rose refused to acknowledge winter and clung to the little portico with a profusion of dark green leaves, waiting for the slightest provocation to burst forth in a profusion of toffee-coloured blooms.

"This would be beautiful in summer." The image before her was far easier to imagine swathed in spring growth than the Styx at her back.

Nate stood on the narrow path behind her. "This whole spot is, despite the fact you think my family home is fit only for firewood."

"Having seen where you grew up I can only assume you modelled your demeanour after its dark exterior." She still dreamed of torching the house and starting from scratch in a more modern and welcoming style.

Silence descended, broken only by the rustle of dry leaves captured by a faint breeze. For one beat Cara's heart stood alone, without its constant companion as Nate withdrew into himself. She reached out a hand to him and with a sigh he reopened the bond. She moved closer to his side, aware she scraped an old wound deep in his soul.

"I learned to guard my emotions by watching my family and it's been a valuable skill. It doesn't pay to show your cards in my line of business, or to let the *ton* spot a weakness."

He squeezed her hand and then released her. Stepping forward, he put his shoulder to the heavy door, cracking it open on protesting hinges. A gust of wind caught the pile of leaves on the doorstep, swept them inside and scattered them down the hallway.

Cara stepped into the gloomy interior. Entering the first room on her left, she discovered the charming exterior hid a rotten core. Once bright chintz wallpaper gave up vertical hold and slumped to the floor. Leaves and dirt littered the floor and piled up in corners and along the skirting. Spiders were so large in the corners they looked like they dined on lost birds. The only furniture was a chair, left in the window overlooking the lake.

"Clean this place out and it will make a lovely home again." The cold ate through her fur-lined coat and seeped into her bones. "Especially if you add a boiler and those heating pipes Jackson had installed in the main house."

"The men have been up on the roof and say she is structurally sound." Nate rapped on a wall. "Jackson is going to move in, he is taking on the role of running this branch of our empire."

Cara's gaze roamed around the leaf-littered rooms. Broken glass in the window allowed the wind to push leaves inside to dance around the floor. A mouse darted out and disappeared through an opening in the skirting. Above their heads, the cast iron arms of a simple chandelier hung on an angle, as though a large creature roosted every night and threw off the balance. Looking underneath she spotted the tell-tale pile of excrement, but she couldn't tell if it was bat or gargoyle.

"It does bear a striking resemblance to places he likes to frequent in London."

Nate moved on silent feet beside her. "Tread lightly there, he lost everything."

Grief washed over her and she cocked her head to regard her husband.

"I saw the house behind the hangar." She thought back to Jackson's movements down in the dusty kitchen. The way he handled the embroidered apron hanging by the cold range and the caress he gave the wooden high chair. "What happened?"

Nate strode to the window and leaned on the side, looking out over the still water. "It was four years ago. My influence started to be felt by a certain individual. Turf wars erupted between my men and the leader of the larger rookeries, but we didn't shut them down fast enough. I made mistakes as my business expanded."

His voice drifted away and Cara moved closer, to nestle into his side, waiting for his story to continue.

"Saul Brandt, the leader of the St Giles Rookery, sent men to slit their throats and left them in the kitchen for Jackson to find. It was a warning. I was expected to run and hide in Mayfair."

Her arms stretched around his torso, tears welled in her heart for all the bodyguard lost. "Did you go to the Enforcers?"

He gave a snort. "And what would they have done?"

"So what happened to the men responsible?"

"We found them. Nobody touches those we protect." His tone chilled her, his voice as cold as the nearly frozen lake. "A few men and I took down thirty of Brandt's men in a single night and brought the

Rookery under my control. Since that night nobody has ever doubted my position. It's also why your Inspector Fraser hates the sight of me."

Cara's heart raced. "Thirty men?" she whispered, and took a step back. "How?" Her voice trailed away as her mind processed the new information.

He let her retreat to the far wall; his cold blue stare never left her face. The valve closed, leaving her alone with her turmoil.

"If I donned a uniform, went off to war, and killed in the name of England would it make my past easier to bear?"

She shook her head, no, it didn't make it easier. Killing an enemy on a battlefield was different. "This was no war—"

"Yes, it was. It was a war that erupted on English soil and under the noses of impotent Enforcers."

Uncertainty skated through her mind. War happened when countries clashed, soldiers fought for freedom, to protect, not for territory and profit.

"This wasn't the slaughter of innocent people, Cara. Military warfare is indiscriminate, it kills children and women. We targeted each and every man because of their involvement. They all had blood on their hands. They used their positions to abuse those without protection."

"You make killing them sound like a humanitarian act." Nausea broke in waves through her gut. She put a hand on her stomach, hoping she wouldn't lose her lunch.

"Do you know how many people died each week in the Rookery?" His tone softened.

She didn't understand his question. She knew he had killed in his past, but thirty men in a night was slaughter. "What do you mean? People die all the time in London."

"Exactly. Is that not worth fighting for? Can those dwelling in poverty not have a better life?"

She frowned, trying to puzzle out his motives. Was he a crime lord motivated only by profit, or a philanthropist?

"Since I took control of the Rookery, children are no longer deformed by their parents to make better beggars. Women can walk the streets without fear of rape. I set up kitchens to provide one hot meal a day to whoever needs one. Victoria was not amused with my method, but she damned well approved of the result. After that incident she agreed to stay out of my business as long as the gutters never ran red again."

Would she ever understand how his mind worked? He married her to save her and took on the Rookery to feed starving children. "And what did you get in return?"

"Loyalty."

They stood in silence, each lost in reflections of the past. *When is a war not a war?* Did the deaths of thirty men justify saving hundreds of women and children from the shadow of abuse and murder? Her stomach settled and she let out a slow breath. *I don't know the answer.*

She pressed a hand to her forehead. "Victoria knew?" Would the queen let a cold-blooded murderer walk the streets, or did she see this as an act by one of her soldiers? *There's something to ask next time we're hauled in for an interview.*

She wondered how so many broken people could come together and heal each other. She needed time to process her thoughts. "After Christmas I'm going back to London. Alone. I need some time to think."

His hand curled into a fist at his side. "You knew what I was the day you stepped into my carriage. I have never hidden the nature of my activities from you."

She gave a small smile. "I'm not saying I don't love you, but this—" She waved her hands trying to conjure the words but none appeared. He killed thirty men in cold blood; it was no sky-high battle between pirate airships. She didn't know how she felt apart from conflicted. "Let me go, Nate, to think."

He gave a terse nod and she turned and headed out the door on her own.

CHRISTMAS was a subdued affair. Cara saw the shades of murdered men loitering against the dark wood of the dining room. She found herself fixated on Nate's hands as he carved the turkey and she wondered how much blood he had to scrub from under his blunt nails.

On Boxing Day she planned a quiet exit and packed a small bag before saying goodbye to Amy, Nan, and Nessy. Bag in hand, she descended to the main entranceway and waited in the hall for Nate.

He strode through from the front parlour with an enormous man on his heel. "Cara, this is Brick. Jackson suggested him as his replacement and he will accompany you to London."

Cara's gaze started at steel-riveted work boots and rose up, and up. The man stood at least six foot six and could barely squeeze through the door frame.

"You call him that because he's built like a brick sh—"

"Yes, he does bear a striking resemblance to an outdoor convenience."

The man's eyes stayed locked on the middle distance, not meeting her stare. Like all of Nate's men he kept his hair military short, so an opponent had nothing to grab. Tree trunk arms folded over a barrel sized chest. *He's a flesh-covered automaton.* Although a well-dressed flesh-covered automaton. Nate's standards dictated all the men wear suits and waistcoats, handmade by his own tailor to conform to the large and muscled bodies. This one wore a wide green pin-stripe. Black leather peeked out at one cuff, holding the blade strapped to his forearm.

She walked around the man, spotting various bulges, and tried to guess what weapons he concealed about his person. "Where do you find them, Nate? Big and brawny?"

He kept his hands in his pockets. Over the last few days he found other things to keep them occupied rather than reaching for her and honoured his word to give her space, both physical and mental. "Many of the men are pugilists looking for better employ. I recruited Brick five years ago. He normally works the machine room, but Jackson hand-picked him to protect you."

Cara remained to be convinced; knowing Jackson selected her new shadow made her suspect an underlining joke. She just didn't know what the punchline was yet.

"He tells me you won't be giving Brick the slip." The faintest smile quirked his lips and then vanished.

Cold dread formed in her gut. *What has Jackson lumbered me with?* Raw power and menace rolled off Brick like he doused himself in eau d'lethal. She gave a sigh. Nate would let her go, but he would make sure someone had her back. "The airship is waiting, let's go."

Nate searched her face, after a pause he reached out and took her hand. He stroked his thumb over her skin. "Be safe in London, I will join you after New Year's."

The Hellcat made short work of the trip back to London and she avoided her new tail the entire time. Cara stood at the bridge and stared out the window, watching the patchwork of fields below turn into houses and streets. They descended and landed on the ample lawn of the Mayfair mansion. Cara trotted over the frozen snow and headed straight inside.

She paced in the familiar warmth of her study while she pondered what to do. She cast a quick glance to her new personal guard and tried not to let the knot of worry chew all the way through her stomach. "I have a few things I want to do in town. Starting off with an expedition to the St Giles Rookery."

A frown carved deep lines in his brow. "I don't think you want to go there."

"Oh, I'm going there, you either do your job and tag along or I go alone."

His eyebrows shot up. "Jackson said you got into more scraps than a nosy kitten."

"Nosy kitten?" She gave a snort. "Remind me to use him for sparring practice next time he's in London." Her plan for the next few days took form in her head. If she was going to reconcile herself to Nate's actions she first had to understand why he became involved in the Rookery. She couldn't imagine anything further from the Mayfair mansion and society events he frequented.

"After I drag you through St Giles I have an even bigger challenge for you."

He puffed out his mammoth chest. "I can handle anything you throw at me."

She gave a sly smile. "I need to go see my modiste. I expect you to hold fabric swatches." Jackson hated the dressmaker's studio and she was certain he would rather face a charging rhinoceros than a bolt of silk. However, the threat of shopping didn't elicit the expected reaction.

A smile cracked over Brick's face and he clasped his hands together. "Oh, lovely, I've heard all about Madame Levett." An animated brown look rested on her and an open expression transformed the man. "God, I'm sick of working the exoskeletons and being covered in grease all day long. What I wouldn't give to have a nice chiffon in my hands instead of rough spun cotton."

Cara blinked, unsure of what she just saw and heard. "Pardon?"

A frown settled on Brick's face and his eyes resembled a puppy caught peeing on the good rug. "Did I say something wrong? Jackson said I could be myself with you, that you wouldn't judge me for who I am on the inside." A meaty finger tapped his chest.

Her mind whirred, making sure she understood the subtext before she burst into laughter. "Oh, Jackson, you are such a crème brûlée." She linked arms with her bodyguard. "You are most certainly free to be yourself around me. I suspect we shall get on swimmingly."

Cara decided on a direct approach for the issue keeping her awake at night, and walked down New Oxford Street that cut the St Giles Rookery into two halves. If you drew a medieval map of London, the Rookery would be a blank space with the narration *here be dragons*. Londoners considered it the birth place of crime and vice and skirted away from its overcrowded streets. The government sought to clean it up by laying a new major road through the middle, but the residents weren't so easy to budge. Like water they parted and flowed around the obstacle.

Why did Nate get himself involved here? she pondered as she walked the visible face of London's notorious underworld. The streets were busy with vendors and pedestrians despite the snow and cold. Faces pressed to dirty windows above her head and watched her progress. The buildings were worn with chipped facades and dirty brickwork. There were no turbines on the roofs here to power electric lights. Even the gas company stopped at the boundary and lanterns flickered in darkened interiors. The cries of infants drifted through cracked windows along with the laughter of older children. A hundred eyes bore into her as they walked the pavement.

Her mind catalogued all she saw but none of it made sense. The area was poor but seemed no worse than any other poor neighbourhood. If anything it seemed slightly better. The drains were clear and she hadn't seen a single body lying in the street. She needed to talk to people, to understand their daily lives.

"You're scaring people away," she muttered to Brick at her side as another woman closed her front door after gawking at Cara.

He gave a snort of laughter. "I was born here, I'm not the problem."

She stopped to look up at him. "What was it like?"

He gave a shrug and gestured for them to continue walking. He manoeuvred her down a side road, this one narrower and the overhanging buildings offered some protection from the weather. "You know what people in the Rookery are really good at?"

"What?" She heard it was drunkenness and licentiousness, which would Brick pick?

"Dying. That's why I got out." His gaze swung back and forth, checking out the environment. Occasionally his attention would be caught by someone and he gave a tiny nod of acknowledgment.

Up ahead she spied a small group of children playing in the shelter of a wide porch. Sitting on the ground they took turns to toss knuckle bones into the air and catch them. The children had dirt-smeared faces but wore smiles that revealed gappy teeth. Their clothing was worn and second-hand, but the holes were darned or patched. They all wore heavy socks and boots to keep the cold from nibbling at their toes.

An idea tumbled into her mind and she approached the group. "Can I play too?" she asked, crouching down to their level.

Suspicious looks swung her way. One child scowled, another snatched the knuckle bones as though they thought she would steal them.

"Why?" the scowling child asked.

Cara shrugged and sat on the cold wood of the porch. "I only had one friend growing up and her idea of playing knuckle bones was to stare at one under a microscope."

"What's a microscope?" one child lisped between missing front teeth. She was also missing an arm and rested a stump on one knee as she leaned toward Cara, unconcerned by the stranger in their midst.

Cara tapped her chin as she thought how to explain the device. "It's a piece of glass that makes something little look very big."

The child frowned. "That doesn't sound like fun."

She gave a soft laugh, remembering Amy bent over her microscope while she disappeared out a window. "It wasn't. I much preferred climbing trees since I could do that on my own."

The child held out her hand to the scowler in the corner. The knuckle bones changed hands and then she slid them over to Cara. "You can play if you want."

"What's your name? Mine is Cara," she asked as she picked up the yellowed bones.

"Rachel," the little one said. With her stump she pointed to the girl wearing the frown. "That's Sarah and those two are Timmy and Jimmy. They're twins." She imbued the word twins with a sense of wonder, as though they were a world oddity.

Cara didn't have to pretend to be bad at the game, she had lost the knack of how high to throw to scoop up the bones on the ground. They kept raining down around her and soon the children were giggling at her efforts.

"What happened to your arm, Rachel?" Cara picked up the bones and tested the weight in her palm. Around her the children fell silent. They exchanged glances between themselves. The unspoken question shot around the group, how much to tell the new person?

"Poppa did it," she whispered.

Cara missed her throw with the bones and they scattered over the porch timbers. "Why?" she asked as she picked the pieces up.

The girl wet her lips. "We didn't make enough begging. Brandt said we would get more if I was a cripple."

Her heart crumpled for the life these children lead. She would have pulled Brandt's heart out herself if he materialised in front of her.

"A pleasure to have your company in St Giles, Lady Lyons," a soft Irish brogue addressed her.

Cara turned to find a man on the street watching her. He wore a heavy wool cloak and a scarf wound around his neck. His head was bare and revealed tousled black hair. Laughing brown eyes watched her.

"You know who I am?"

A wide smile crinkled the corners of his face. "Not too many pants-wearing, gun-toting women wander into the Rookery dragging little Patrick behind them." He waved a hand in Brick's general direction on the last part.

"I guess when you describe me like that it does narrow down the available options. But what do you mean little Patrick?" She laughed and glanced at Brick who frowned at the new comer.

The Irish gent gave a wink. "Ask the runt yourself."

The curious child with the missing teeth elbowed her. "That's Liam, he's in charge around here."

"Is he?" she whispered back.

"Liam O'Donnell, I guess you could call me the mayor of the Rookery." He doffed an imaginary hat and executed a bow.

"You're Nate's man."

"I'm my own man, but Lyons holds my loyalty. Would you care for the guided tour?" he asked.

"Yes, thank you." She rose and dusted off her knees and bottom from where she had been sitting. She gave a wave to the children and promised to visit tomorrow, before she joined Liam on the street.

He fell into step next to her and Brick followed behind. "As lovely as it is to have you grace our streets, might I enquire as to the purpose of your visit?"

She made a gut decision to tell the truth with the self-proclaimed mayor of the Rookery. "Curiosity."

He laughed. "I have heard that about you."

"Oh?" She frowned, who exactly was talking about her? Her mind considered chasing that rabbit, but gossip about her wasn't the reason for visiting the poorest part of town so she hauled her dog back to the original scent. "I want to know why Nate seized control here."

He gave her a steady look, his head to one side as though assessing her, and then he made a noise in his throat. "You don't think he was motivated by altruism and the desire to give us a better life?"

Cara laughed. "I love him and I have seen him do selfless things, but they also advance his own goals in some way."

"Doesn't matter if people make their living on their back on their feet, we all pay our tithe to the overlord, whether it's Brandt or Lyons."

"Then what's the difference?" she asked.

"Ah." He tapped the side of his nose. "The difference is what they do with it. Brandt lined his own pockets and squeezed us for more. Lyons cleaned out the drains, organised gangs of men to check every building had a roof that could keep out the weather and then he set up kitchens to provide one hot meal a day."

Cara stood on the edge of understanding. On the surface his motives still seemed like the noble philanthropist helping the less fortunate. Scratch the surface and there would be a deeper reason that advanced the Lyons empire.

"Look around, Lady Lyons, and what do you see?" Liam asked.

As they walked she scanned the faces on the street and saw a predominance of men standing on the corners. The older ones talked and joked. The younger ones sparred with each other, their moves critiqued by their jeering friends. Young men with idle hands and no direction in their lives.

"Men." She breathed the syllable as the purpose behind Nate's altruism hit her. "Men loyal to the person who puts food in their stomachs and gives them something to do with their hands." Nate had an army at his fingertips, should he ever need one.

Liam nodded. "Now you get it." He escorted her to the edge of his territory and then shook hands with Brick. "It's been a pleasure, Lady Lyons." Another bow and he headed back down the street, whistling.

CHAPTER 7

Nan & Nessy

1809, twelve years old.

SUMMER warmth filled the study and the elderly tutor at last succumbed and slumped over his desk, fast asleep. The soft snores rose and mingled with the drone of the bumblebees surrounding the lavender outside the window.

Nan set down her pen and crept out the room. Free at last from her lessons, she escaped and went in search of her best friend. She dashed down the servant's stairway to avoid meeting her mother on the main stairs. Her feet ached to run across the meadow, not mince in the ballroom to the latest dance. She burst into the sunlight and paused to take a deep breath of fresh air after so long in the stuffy nursery. Rounding the side of the house, she heard Nessy's laughter ring out around the courtyard.

Curiosity aroused, she sneaked toward the stables and peered around the side of the old stone barn. Her constant companion stood chatting with the stable boy, Roger. Tall, lanky, and handsome, the stable lad was nearly eighteen. Nan had decided he would be the one, her first kiss, if she could only work up the courage to broach the subject. He never showed any interest in her, despite her persistence and constant presence in the stables. *Such a gentleman, worried about my reputation.*

He displayed no such reservations with Nessy. The two stood so close their arms brushed as they talked. His skin darkened by the sun, Nessy as pale as moonlight. The intimacy kept Nan hidden in the shadow, even as it grated that flirting came naturally to her friend. It wasn't fair, no one worried if the common girl talked with the stable boys or gardening lads. She even practiced on the tinker pedalling his clockwork devices. Nan was wrapped in protective layers and barely allowed to say a word to anyone. Some days she was convinced she lived in a glass bell jar and, scream as loud as she might, no one ever heard a whisper from her lips.

Roger couldn't tear his eyes from his buxom companion. With the arrival of spring, her figure blossomed in all the right places, giving her petite frame curves and enticingly rounded parts.

Nan glanced down at her own body. Tall and slender, the advance of puberty gave her only straight lines and awkward angles. Even her corset failed at its job, making her torso more rectangular, like the books she carried everywhere.

Nessy tapped his forearm as she said something. He laughed aloud. Then his head lowered, one hand resting on Nessy's hip, large fingers pulling her smaller body even closer.

A cold lump settled in Nan's stomach. She liked Roger, Nessy knew that, why was her friend flirting with him? They had spent countless afternoons talking about him, especially when the warmer weather meant he removed his shirt to muck out the stalls and strap the horses. They both hid in the hay loft, peering down as he worked. They watched the movement of muscles under his taut brown skin. They traded whispers about what it would be like to run a finger along sweat-slick flesh.

Nan watched as Nessy tilted her head to stare up at Roger, the two youths lost in their own world. Nan bit back a squeal as he placed a finger under Nessy's chin.

He's going to kiss her. How could she! The trollop.

Nan had declared her intent for Roger to bestow her first kiss and now she couldn't believe what played out before her. Right there, in the yard, that little blonde hussy with the bosom was about to be kissed first.

His head dropped lower and his sun-roughened lips covered small pink ones. Large arms wrapped around Nessy and pressed her to his chest. One hand ran up her back to tangle in long locks, holding her head in place.

With a sob, Nan picked up the corner of her skirt and ran all the way to the orchard. She threw herself on the grass. Tears welled up in her eyes and she blinked them away. She liked Roger. It wasn't fair. Nessy was supposed to be her friend, but she had thrown herself at him. How could he refuse when she thrust herself at him?

Betrayal wound through her heart, squeezing the delicate organ. One cry after another built in her chest. She pulled at the front busks of her corset, trying to loosen the grip around her torso but gave up, the lacing too tight at the back and beyond the reach of her fingers. Sobs came in shallow gasps and tears rolled down her face. She tore up frustrated handfuls of grass and threw them away.

Through narrowed eyes she watched fluffy clouds drift overhead as sparrows flitted in and out of the foliage, feasting on the ripe fruit. Nature ignored her pain and the glorious day continued unmarred. It wasn't fair, life hated her.

It should rain, I am broken. Why does the sky not cry with me?

"There you are!" a breathless voice exclaimed. Nessy dropped on the grass and leaned against the trunk of the apple tree. "I have something to tell you."

"Let me guess, you are madly in love with Liam and the two of you are going to marry and move into the pig sty?" Nan muttered, without bothering to sit up. She wiped a hand over her cheek, swiping away the tears.

Nessy frowned. "I thought you had your sights set on Liam. Or have you changed your mind?"

Nan pushed up on her elbows, to find an easier pose to glare at her friend. "What hope do I have now? I saw you kissing him." Another tear dangled from the edge of her lashes, waiting for a chance to roll away.

"I did no such thing!" Nessy punched her in the arm. "He grabbed my hair, slobbered all over me and when I wriggled free I slapped him. Anyway he's not interested in me. His eyes never met mine once, he just kept staring at my titties." She stared down at her emerging bosom, as though wondering what about the new appendages generated such rampant interest in boys. She placed a hand under each and stared at them.

"They are hard to miss," Nan pointed out. Her friend resembled the succulent apples, while she looked more like the branch they hung off.

"I would give them to you if I could, honest." Nessy's lower lip drooped and then quivered a little. "Please don't be mad at me. I didn't ask for them, I pray nightly that your chest will erupt. Maybe it's all that scrubbing they make me do while you have lessons? I think using my arms so much made my dumplings grow, like extra muscle."

Nan considered her friend's words. She knew her mother set Nessy to help the maids while she was trapped learning French, history, and mathematics. Her attention fell on Nessy's chipped nails, red fingers, and emerging calluses.

Was a bigger bosom worth ruining her hands? She held up her long tapered fingers and white nails. Would she trade her silken skin for something rounded and soft to press into Roger's palm? *Perhaps, for a chance to touch his lips?*

She needed more information before she traded dance lessons for scrubbing the hallway. "Did you like it when he kissed you?"

Nessy looked thoughtful for a moment. "It was kind of nice, but his lips are quite rough. Like they are sunburnt from being outside all the time and they were scratchy. Then he stuck his tongue down my throat, and I swear I tasted horse manure."

A giggle burst from Nan, her decision made. "Eww!" She had no desire to learn what horse manure tasted like. She would stick to dance class and hope nature woke up and did something about her lack of a figure.

"I bet he licks the horses." Nessy stuck a finger in her mouth and ran it along her tongue. She pulled it out and frowned at the digit. "Look, horse hair." She held up the finger to show the coarse hair lying over the tip.

Nan shuddered; Nessy had sacrificed herself, saving her from that horror. Perhaps she should stick with noble boys, who wouldn't taste of their beasts or shed in her mouth. "Do you like him? I promise I won't mind if you do, you can have him." It was the least she could offer as her friend picked another hair from the corner of her lip.

"Oh no! Not after the way he treated me. He tried to put his hand down my dress and squeeze my boob. I told him that wasn't appropriate; I am her ladyship's companion after all, not some common trollop." She gave a wink.

Nan laughed; there was no betrayal to break her heart. Nessy had shown Roger for what he was, a boy trying to get his hand under a girl's skirt. Reaching up, she pulled a tortoise shell comb from her hair. With her thumbs in the middle, she snapped it into two pieces and then placed one in Nessy's hand. "Let's make a promise, that we will always be friends. No matter what. No boy will ever come between us. We are two halves, like this comb, complete only when they are together."

Nessy stared at the delicate comb and then nestled it within her pale tresses. "I will keep it as a constant reminder of our friendship. Pinky swear?" She held up her little finger.

The girls linked fingers. "Friends, for ever, no matter what," they said in unison.

London, Saturday 4th January, 1862

INSPECTOR Fraser worked through Christmas, preferring to

spend his time buried in his case files rather than eating turkey. Connor invited him to his family's festive dinner, but he declined. Those who are blessed during the holidays are unable to see how their offer of inclusivity only highlights the outsider's separation. Being alone amongst others was like lying on the bottom of a frozen lake and staring up at events through thick ice. He could watch the touches between husband and wife, hear the laughter of happy children, but he would never be a part of it. Far better to be alone on your own than have each second in company carve a reminder into your skin.

He heaved a sigh and stared at his nemesis sitting to one side on his desk. Fate decreed the mug of tea would forever stand undrunk. Or so it seemed as every time he stretched out his hand in the mug's direction, someone barged through his door and demanded a slice of his precious attention. Reports needed signing, criminals needed his casual approach, and his Super wanted his opinion on what to wear for his reunion mess dinner.

All I want is a cup of tea and a biscuit. A ripple through his body reminded him of other, more primal needs and he remembered Lilith calling his name from the darkened alley. *Perhaps slightly more than a cup of tea.*

Sergeant Connor's heavy boots shook the landing and caused ripples on the fluid in the cup moments before his body squeezed into the crowded office. Papers, reports, and photographs fought for space and attention. A large board covered one wall and held scribblings of names, places, and dates connected with arrows and question marks as Fraser worked visually on a number of cases.

"Grab your coat, we've got another one," Connor said.

Using his index finger, Fraser pushed his glasses back up his nose as he looked up from an open file. "Another one, what?"

"Burned body, not much left, was found this afternoon."

"Spontaneous human combustion?" He looked up, the furrow in his forehead deepened. "The phenomenon is extremely rare, it would be highly unusual to find another case just weeks after the first."

Connor gave a shrug. "I leave that bit for you to figure out, or take it up with Him." He pointed upstairs.

Fraser kept the frown in place. "The Superintendent?"

Connor plucked the bowler hat from the top of the stand and threw the object at his inspector. "Higher up the chain than him. You know who I mean, the one who does the smiting with fire."

Fraser caught the hat and popped it on his head, a small smile on his face. "Well, let us go see the latest victim of Divine Justice."

The Enforcer's dark blue vehicle waited at the bottom of the steps. Thick black plumes of smoke rose from the funnel at the rear. The still London air gave the smoke no room to escape so it clung to the vehicle and forced tendrils back through the windows, no matter how tightly they were wound shut. Fraser gave a cough and wished command would stump up with the funds for a mechanical vehicle before they poisoned somebody.

The little blue box bounced its way past Hyde Park and into Bayswater and rattled over the cobbles so hard Fraser feared for his teeth. Out the window he watched mechanical horses glide past on felted feet. He spotted a new battery-powered horseless carriage with high suspension that let its occupants pour champagne without spilling a drop. Sometimes he wished he pursued a career in the private sector, where the higher salary would have afforded him a taste of such luxuries. But his mind tugged at him to hunt down criminals and his body preferred to find release in darkened allies, even if his chosen path might cause him to die of smoke inhalation.

The engine gave a burp and halted. Fraser descended to the footpath and gave a shake, letting loose limbs tensed from the constant jarring. He breathed the cold air, waiting for his brain to revive after the noxious fumes in the cramped space lulled him half to sleep.

"I hate those things," Connor muttered from his side. "Makes a man miss his horse."

"Quite."

The house sat in a respectable middle class area. On tippy toe one could glimpse Hyde Park, which gave the area added charm. Fraser took the stairs at a slow pace, thoughts and ideas churning in his mind.

A small crowd gathered on the footpath, huddled together for warmth as they murmured and whispered, watching the Enforcers. Fraser spotted the reporter standing off to one side, his gaze keener than anyone else's with his attention fixed on the building. Fraser ignored him and followed the trail of blue uniforms.

They paused in the building's hallway and Connor held out a small metal tin. Fraser swiped a finger through the thick white paste, and smeared it over his top lip. Menthol zapped up his nasal passages, sliced into his brain and dispersed the last of the coal smoke. Prepared, he pushed open the panelled door and stepped into the parlour.

The sweet, cloying odour battled with the menthol and tried to overwhelm his olfactory sense. He took several shallow breaths and let his body find equilibrium with the smell, so he could do his part of the job. Retching out a window was not a productive use of his time.

The hallway looked freshly scrubbed. The mat under their feet showed signs of wear, but was beaten and clean. A few sprigs of winter sweet stood in a tall vase, giving off their spicy aroma which mingled with the other, pervading scent. The parlour showed a long life and gentle retirement. Stretched linen in a frame held the beginnings of needlepoint. Brightly coloured silks spilled from a basket on the floor, waiting to be picked and used. Pictures and paintings hung from the top rail, each depicting some sort of ocean theme, from fishing to naval. Fraser made a note to ask the husband's profession.

Two brown wing chairs sat on either side of the fireplace. One chair was empty, at the other resided two feet in thick green felt slippers. Their soles were flat to the ground, skinny calves rose above once shapely ankles, and stopped mid shin. Charred flesh and white bone was a stark relief against the blackened leather of the chair. Light shimmered on the sticky ooze coating the surface. A hand rested on the arm, fingers curled around the end, as though the owner gripped the chair for support about to rise but never made it to a standing position. Purple flannelette fibres clung to the exposed wrist bones and were all that remained of what the person once wore.

The thick drawn edge of a body sitting in the chair was filled by tiny pieces of bone stuck in a soup-like sludge of ash. The grim outline revealed the head once rested in the crook of where the chair back met the high arm. Now only a few strands of grey hair lay over the edge. Nothing but the pair of feet and a hand remained.

"There's no head," Connor muttered. "I hate it when they don't have heads."

Fraser examined the area surrounding the deceased; the soot trail spiralled up the corner of the room. The black cloud spread outward and faded to grey at the centre of the ceiling. "You didn't like the last one who still possessed his head."

The large Enforcer turned to stare at a painting on the wall, the azure ocean which lapped at the small boat now smeared a menacing storm grey. "That's because there's supposed to be something connecting the head to the feet."

Fraser bit back a huff of laughter. "So your problem is not so much the lack of head, as the lack of anything in between. That would explain why you kept throwing up on me while we investigated the Grinder."

Their eyes met and there was a pause in conversation as they both remembered the street girls who ended up as mincemeat one hot summer. Their butchered limbs stuffed down sewer drains, the flesh carved from bone. They saw enough to fuel thousands of nightmares and each man sought his own oblivion to lighten the burden he carried. Violent death marked each of them in its own invisible way. No one escaped.

Connor turned and shook his head at the cremated remains. "I hope this combustion thing isn't catchy. It'll drive up church attendance if people think God is back in the swing of smiting sinners."

Fraser stood back from his inspection and clapped his hands together. "Right, while we wait for Doc to arrive, fill me in on the pertinent details."

"Penelope Stock. Sixty-four years old. Her daughter found her." As if on cue, a high pitched hysterical scream from further down the hallway punctuated Connor's statement. "The boys have their hands full trying to settle her down."

Fraser cast around and pointed a finger at a nearby uniform. "Tell one of them to give her a few drops of laudanum. That should reduce the screaming so we can get some work done."

A nod and the lad disappeared on his errand.

He turned his attention back to Connor. "I assume the daughter confirmed identity, despite the missing head. We don't have some poor unknown here?"

"Mole on the inside of her ankle." Connor pointed with his pencil at the detached limb.

Fraser swung around and crouched by the chair. His eyes narrowed at the small dark smudge above the ankle bone in the rough shape of a flower head. Two short black hairs protruded, like stamens. "Always handy when they have distinctive birth marks." Rising he gestured to the paintings around the room. "Was her husband a seafarer?"

"Navy. Died about ten years ago. Penny here worked her way up in service of the old duchess, kept her busy while he was at sea. Daughter says she started off as a chamber maid and rose to be the housekeeper."

Fraser's head snapped up. "Which old duchess?"

Connor flicked back a page in the notebook. "The Duchess of Kent."

Two separate pieces of information collided in Fraser's head and exploded in a shower of sparks. He breathed out a long sigh. "Nigel Fenmore, our first man to die by this divine touch, was the Duchess of Kent's personal physician."

Connor scratched an eyebrow. "Odd coincidence."

He shook his head. "I don't like coincidences, especially not ones involving strange ways to die. Or unusual ways to kill somebody. Two elderly people die in extremely rare circumstances and both are connected to our queen's mother." His body froze as his mind chased threads. Like a kitten at play he sought to grasp the end of something tangible. "I think there is something larger afoot here."

"Yeah, but look at the old bird." Connor's large hand gestured to the slim remains of the woman. "This is some freak of nature; you can't kill someone with Divine Fire."

Fraser's eyes lit up, possibilities and connections rocketing through his brain. "Can't you? Do you know that for sure? There is more in this world than what we can explain."

"You've got that look," Connor muttered. "I hate it when you get that look."

They catalogued the scene and made notes on the evidence of Mrs Stock's life in their notebooks. The photographic technician arrived first and took his exposures. Just as he packed away his equipment, excited chatter heralded the arrival of the doctor.

Doc stood on the threshold, hat in his hands. "Well I never. Another? God is very busy this holiday."

CHAPTER 9

Mayfair, Wednesday 8th January, 1862

CARA sat in her study, the ancient books on her desk. She stroked a finger over the fat notebook that belonged to her father. The one Nate asked Jackson to steal. That encounter set her on this path. She knew what he was and that he harboured a creature that dwelt in the dark. Nate made choices that cost some lives and saved others. To find peace, Cara needed to find a way to put her own mark on the aftermath. To take Nate's decisions into her life. Every day she went to the Rookery and played with the group of children. She decided to teach them to read, to open their minds to the world beyond London through books. If she could encourage one girl to spread her wings and fly, she would add something of value to what Nate started.

Voices announced Nate's return to London as he walked through the house issuing orders. Cara rose from her desk and left her study. With a firm decision in her heart she could now face her husband.

He stopped on seeing her, his hands clasped behind his back. "I have missed you."

A tiny smile tugged at her lips. It melted her heart when he momentarily lost his cool composure and the small boy peeked out. "I have missed you too," she said.

He arched one dark eyebrow. "You seem … content."

"What you did was before I met you and cannot be changed. I understand part of why you took down Brandt." She thought of wee Rachel with one arm and she could remove Brandt's spleen through his throat for what he did. "But promise me now nothing like that will ever happen again without me knowing beforehand. I want, demand, to be involved."

He nodded. "Full disclosure, remember? But I cannot change events that have already played out."

She had learned much on each of her visits to the Rookery, like how the annual death toll of fifteen hundred dropped to under a thousand since the change of regime and continued to decline. She found comfort by focusing on the positive outcomes. "I met Liam; apart from the divine accent I think he's very gallant." She fanned herself with one hand as she remembered her guide.

Nate's dark brows drew together in a scowl. "He's a rogue, watch him; but he cares deeply for his people." He sent a caress along their bond before he reached for her physically.

She took his hand in hers and ran her thumbs over his palm. "I'm going to teach the little ones to read, I want them to have choices."

Nate relaxed his pose under her touch and a smile quirked his lips. "Just what the world needs, more smart women who can fight their way out of a corner. I'll talk to Liam about finding space for you to use."

"Thank you." She just had to find a way to make learning fun now, so the children didn't wise up to her too quickly.

He held his arms open and she went to him. As he held her tight she let loose a sigh and her body hummed. She was learning that relationships were hard work, but these moments of quiet peace made it worthwhile.

Later that day

"What plans do you have?" Nate asked as he pushed around the papers stacked on his desk, looking for anything urgent. A paper caught his attention and he extracted it from the pile.

Cara perched on a corner of the desk. "I need to go see McToon and decide what to do with my Soho house. It's evicted the only tenant we could find."

His gaze flicked from lines of text up to her. "You talk about that house as though it lived."

"I think it does and it has always hated me. In hindsight perhaps it has absorbed an artifact? My father buried the Heart in the basement, who knows what might have leeched into the brick work." She chewed her bottom lip. "I know I searched the house, but I can't help thinking there is something else there."

He dropped the memo and brushed a thumb over the back of her knuckles. "Are you all right to go back?"

She gave a shrug. "Yes. I'm not fond of the cellar, though, after what happened down there."

He gave a brief smile. "Weaver tried to cave my head in with a dock exoskeleton, so I understand the sentiment."

"I shan't go alone, I have Brick and I'll hide behind him if the house gives me any trouble. On the off chance it does try to electrocute me, I would be grateful if you kept me alive."

"Always," he whispered, and dropped a kiss on her hand before releasing her.

Nate folded Cara in his embrace and his lips slid over hers in a gentle tease, somewhat placating her concern. She sighed and leaned into the kiss, over far too soon.

He pulled back from her. "I have several meetings today, including one with Victoria. I'll tell you all the details over dinner."

Late that night she awoke to find herself alone. She pulled a velvet robe tight around her naked figure and padded down to the study on bare feet. The household slumbered except for Nate and one lone man standing guard in the entrance way. They dimmed the lights at night and the bulbs threw long shadows, illuminating the face of the man who stood watch outside the study door.

She gave a nod as she pushed the door open and crept into Nate's domain. The deep green walls absorbed the light and gave nothing back, the only illumination the dance of firelight and the single beam from the desk lamp.

He sat at the desk, papers scattered around him, a small red box open in front of him and his head in his hands.

She padded closer. "What's keeping you awake so late?"

He looked up and his hungry stare roamed her body for a moment. Then he sighed, pushed back the chair, and beckoned for her to sit on his lap. "I am kept awake by a surplus of possibilities. Like a general faced with a war on many different fronts, the time has come to pull back, regroup and pick a direction to strike."

She nestled into him and he slipped his arms around her. "You're playing general now? Does this mean you have a plan for the army sitting in St Giles Rookery?"

He gave a short laugh. "No, that is my contingency plan. Like when you wear your pistols, you might never use them but there is a comfort in knowing they are within reach."

A chill of premonition shot down her spine. *He will use his army, one day.* "So start at the beginning of what is preying on your mind. Full disclosure, remember?"

His voice rumbled through his chest as he spoke. "The long range airships have been tested and are ready to go. We can open up trade routes to the farthest corners of the earth, such as Australia and Asia."

The behemoths rivalled a naval frigate in size. Their construction dominated time, money, and gossip in the Lyons empire for the last six months. On the first test run the massive ship blotted out the sun and nearly caused a panic in the rural village where Nate had it built. "Will those routes be financially viable?"

"Not just viable, lucrative. We could transport emigrants who don't want to spend three months in a leaky ship's hold and bring back a wealth of stock and gems from the new countries."

Her hand rested over his heart. She found comfort in the single beat resonating between their bodies. "So definitely worth pursuing. What else is worrying you? Problems in Lowestoft with the local thug?" Her hand played with the buttons on his waistcoat as they talked.

"No, he's a gnat and Jackson will squash him." He paused as though reluctant to breach the next subject. After several heart beats he pointed to the red box. "That contains the prime minister's idea of a joke. Palmerston has sent me papers concerning Poor Law reforms along with a Writ of Summons instructing me to take up my seat in parliament." His hand stroked her back through the thick robe. "I think I'd rather take up residence in the Rookery than play politician."

She remained silent, lost in thought about the night he claimed St Giles as his own. A brutal business and one she would gladly see him relinquish. He called it war, but she saw the blood spilled on the ground when he struck like a beast in the dark. The only way to alleviate the unease in her mind was to concentrate on the good the change wrought rather than the profit.

"Unfortunately Palmerston has Victoria's backing on this one. She called me in today to tell me it's time to take up my family seat in the House of Lords."

Having pushed open his waistcoat, she turned her attention to the tiny shell fastenings on his shirt. "Why this push into the realm of politics?"

He gave a sigh. "As you know my endeavours have always been on an individual, rather than national, scale and based on pure self-interest. Victoria thinks it is time I grew up and took an interest in the land that gave me my title."

She looked up; a smile danced over her lips. She could imagine the queen gave Nate a proper scolding about his activities. "I can't imagine you discussing law reforms with a bunch of stuffy old toffs."

"Neither can I, but there are those complaining about the seat remaining empty when I am in town. I have a potential excuse though. Victoria has offered to expand my intelligence role. She would give me a diplomatic posting, which would explain why I am absent from the House."

Cara's mind jumped to the obvious conclusion. "She wants you as spymaster?"

He nodded.

Cara tapped a fingernail on his chest, thinking. "Spymaster would give you the freedom to travel and would also give us a cover for gathering the artifacts."

"My thoughts exactly. But there is only one of me. Taking up such a role would mean pulling back from other areas of business. I can't afford the time to establish the new trade routes."

They sat cut off from the world in the small pool of light, as though nothing existed beyond them. The deep of night, while the rest of England slept, was the best time to ponder plans for the future.

An idea sprang into her mind, one that would solve two problems. "Then give Loki the responsibility. Send him off to the Pacific Ocean, I'm sure the women there would appreciate his presence."

Nate gave a rumble of laughter. "Loki and responsibility don't normally belong in the same sentence."

Her fingers undid the last button on his shirt and she slid a hand against his warm flesh. "Give him the chance. You might be surprised what a bit of responsibility does for that one. He's smart and can think on his feet, he'll do well if you expect more of him. Plus he's always looking for a chance to show off his linguistic skills. He can talk his way into trade deals."

Nate pulled the tie on her robe and slid the velvet off her shoulder; his lips trailed fire over her collar bone. "I could bring him in as a full partner and increase his percentage in Lyons Cargo, see what he does with the opportunity."

Cara arched her neck to give him better access. "See, a problem discussed is a problem halved."

He scooped his arms under her body and stood, lifting her to his chest. "Now, I have another problem we can discuss upstairs."

Thursday 9th January, 1862

Cara sat once more at the desk with her father's notebook spread in front of her, along with the two ancient volumes given to her by the mad Countess de Sal. The small collection of books had become her guide to identify and find the unusual artifacts. What worried her was how many were out there that her father never located but merely alluded to. Where were they and who held them?

Nate stood behind her, and ran strong fingers along her tight shoulder muscles. "How goes the collection?"

She closed the book and tossed it on to the growing pile of reference material. "We're nearly done."

Week by week she worked her way through her father's coded entries. Once she located a piece, Nate uplifted the artifact from its hidden resting place, and they locked it away in the secure underground chamber, far below their feet at Lowestoft.

"There are only three more to hunt down, including Boudicca's Cuff, which you need to retrieve from its purchaser." She dropped her head forward as he massaged her stiff neck.

"I'm working on it, but the man has the luck of the cuff on his side and I cannot win a bet against him."

"If you can't win it, why don't you just steal it back?" She turned to stare at him, wondering who this man was, that he could bring the most notorious breeding ground of crime under his grasp but baulked at stealing a trifle they needed.

"My wife is recommending larceny?" He arched one eyebrow.

"Use the skills you have at your disposal." She batted a hand at him. "The next artifact is strange. If I have decoded Father's notes correctly it's hidden in the opera house in Covent Garden, but that can't be right. He concealed them in bank vaults and cellars. Places where they lay in the dark, cold and quiet."

"And this is the complete opposite, light, loud, and crowded." He ran a hand down her spine as he ran over the options. "Perhaps this particular artifact is better hidden in confusion and would draw attention to itself alone in a basement or vault."

She chewed her bottom lip, the change of location had to be significant. "The home of the royal opera is a strange place to conceal an artifact, but it makes sense when you put it like that."

He returned to massaging the kinks from her body after long hours at the desk.

She hummed as he worked magic with his fingers. "I assume we'll break in when the theatre is empty?"

Fingers moved up to the base of her skull, thumbs working through her hair. "Where would be the fun in that? Let's make an evening of it. What are we looking for?"

"Helen of Troy's fan. According to the book it is said to attract admirers, inspire love, and make men your willing supplicants." Cara imagined having such an object might be handy. *That would shake things up around here.*

"Well, she certainly did that. How did it end up at the theatre?"

She forgot the book, her eyes closed as Nate massaged her scalp. A purr welled up in her throat. "Father was unclear on that. Reading between the lines, he had his eye on a singer and perhaps planned to gift it to her."

"Given he placed it in such a public spot, I wonder if it's still there."

"I guess we'll find out. The notebook says it's concealed in a box he used to frequent. Behind one of the decorative roses is a small panel at the front that can be removed. Behind that is a coded safe that should contain the fan. If it hasn't already been discovered." She picked up a tiny gold key. "This was stuck to the page about the fan."

"Good. It will be the perfect opportunity to show off my viscountess." He laced his fingers around her neck. "Wear your dragon diamonds with that new red velvet dress. I want to see you wrapped in fire."

CHAPTER 10

London, Friday 10th January, 1862

THE horses trotted along Bow Street. Moonlight slid over bronze rumps and gave off golden flashes against the passing buildings. They joined the queue of carriages waiting to discharge passengers under the portico of the opera house. Cara craned her head out the window to watch as some poor noble decided to beat the crowd by being lowered from airship onto the roof. She watched the woman in full evening gown sway back and forth with the slight wind. Her ostrich feather head piece disappeared on a gust and her skirts blew up around her waist to reveal lacy drawers. Cara couldn't help the laugh that welled up. *Probably not the entrance she planned on making.*

Nate shook his head. "They are far too high. What were they thinking trying to drop passengers from that height? Their captain must be an idiot if he can't hover lower than that."

As Cara stepped to the pavement, screams came from above as staff tried to winch the woman to the flat roof. A crowd gathered to watch the impromptu show and ruin the woman's reputation by discussing her undergarments.

"So we won't be doing that next time?" she asked.

He gave a huff. "I think we shall, just to show them how it should be done."

"Well, you don't have to worry about the wind lifting my dress and showing my drawers." She leaned in close to him. "You know I don't wear any."

"It's one of the many reasons why I love you," he whispered. He took her arm and escorted her up the wide stairs into the foyer.

The roof was three stories above their heads with rose-coloured marble columns to hold it aloft. Chains lowered chandeliers closer to the patrons. Thousands of tiny lights and crystals glittered and threw sparks around the soaring space.

Nate slid Cara's cloak from her shoulders, revealing the deep red velvet dress clinging to her form. Embroidered gold-thread flames licked around the hem of the train and then reached up to encircle her waist and side. The perfect complement to the dragon diamonds around her neck. The scale backing threw molten claws whenever the light caught the gems.

Curious and hostile glances alike followed them as they wound their way up the stairs. Brick the bodyguard trailed behind, resplendent in formal wear and enjoying his change from working the docks strapped in a metal exoskeleton.

Nate's box was positioned close to the stage and Brick swung the door open. He did quick visual sweep around the plush interior before he stood back to admit them. The box was furnished in deep red, from striped wallpaper to curtains, and even the velvet on the chairs. The little room had two rows of three chairs at the front. The back half held a sideboard for serving drinks and food. A champagne bucket stood in a tall steel frame. "I could disappear in here," Cara said. "I match the curtains and walls." She ran a hand down the heavy drapery held back with a golden cord.

"Oh, I would find you." Nate poured champagne into two flutes and offered one to Cara. "Brick will wait until the show is underway and then see if the box your father used is occupied tonight."

"What if there are people in there?" she asked, sipping her drink.

"He will inform them the box is unavailable."

The orchestra below played a few bars, alerting patrons that the show would soon begin.

"Bodyguards really are handy." Cara took her seat at the front of the box, aware of curious eyes glancing their way. She was grateful for the way each box was angled, giving the occupants a degree of privacy from those around. They could see out, but only those directly opposite could see in, and even then only the front row of chairs was visible. Those seated below could only see her when she stood or leaned over the railing.

The curtain rose on stage and *La Traviata* began. Cara watched with rapt attention as the story of the famous courtesan unfolded. Brick slunk back in during the second act. He whispered that he moved on the box's occupants during the short intermission and stayed a while longer to ensure no one slipped back in.

"Are you coming to retrieve the item?" Nate asked from beside her.

Below the curtain dropped on the empty stage, the only way they could prise Cara from her seat. "Yes, I could do with a stretch."

They strolled down the corridor, ignoring the other nobles who didn't know quite how to cope with their presence among them. Nate ignored them and Cara practiced her poker face. The press of people thinned as they reached the end of the hall. Nate opened the door while Brick stood guard.

This box was further back, smaller and seemed somehow sadder and less polished. The wallpaper not as opulent, the carpet cheaper and the champagne bucket tin instead of silver. The front still had the same ornately carved roses with their central emblems.

Cara knelt on the carpet in front of them and Nate sat back on his heels next to her.

"Which one?" he asked as they looked over the row of four.

She ran a finger over the wooden petals. "I don't know. Try them all until we find one that opens."

The climbing roses encircled an oval shield with the opera house emblem of the lion and chained unicorn. She let the pads of her fingers run around the edge, trying to find a hidden catch or hinge. Then she pushed, although that seemed clumsy as anyone who bumped into the side would trigger the catch and open the hidden compartment.

Nate experimented with his shield and after several long minutes they each moved to the next one along and tried the whole process again. Cara muttered about her father under her breath. When she watched his casket dropped into the earth she thought she washed her hands of him, never expecting to be following the clues left in his notes. In a small way he still controlled the path of her life and it grated.

"Ah." Her nail caught on something. A tiny depression hid under one side of this emblem. She pushed a fingertip into the groove and pulled. With a soft pop the unicorn and lion swung open to reveal a tiny locked metal door.

Nate dug into his pocket and handed Cara the gold key. She turned the lock and the next door gave with a click. Within a small safe lined with green velvet sat an ordinary looking fan. Cara pulled the object out; the now familiar tingle of electricity ran over her skin as she touched an artifact of power.

"Said to make men do your bidding." She turned to Nate with a smile on her face.

"I already do your bidding, wench." He took the delicate fan from her hands. "Stop getting ideas right now."

She screwed up her face. *Spoilsport.*

Nate turned the key in the lock and shut the hidden panel. He escorted Cara back to their opulent seats just as the curtain rose for the final act. As she settled, a knock sounded at their door and murmured conversation washed over her. Nate returned to her side. "I need to take care of some business."

She waved her fan, the mundane one, not the powerful one in Nate's jacket pocket. "I'll be here." The unfolding drama below held her attentive captive. The courtesan had given up her life to live in the country with her lover.

Nate dropped a kiss onto her forehead. "I'll take Brick, but we won't be long."

Cara clasped her fan close to her chest and leaned forward, enthralled by the emotion of the opera below. Her entire focus centred on the woman on stage and the drama of Violetta's life. The fallen woman now on her death bed.

Sometime later came the snip of the box door shutting.

"Did you find it? You've been gone for ages," she called without turning. Below, the ill-fated woman lamented that she reunited with her lover too late, her death now imminent.

"That's a pretty necklace, miss. I'll be having that. I've never seen diamonds flash so red before."

She turned at the unknown voice to find a man dressed in a brown street suit, not tails like the evening demanded. One extended hand held a knife. Nate's encouragement to wear the unusual diamonds apparently attracted a little too much attention. She reached up to touch the row of dragon scale-enhanced gems around her neck. "I'm rather fond of this necklace myself."

He waved the knife at her head. "Let's do this quietly, eh? Don't want to interrupt the performance."

She rose from her seat and pointed to the champagne bucket. "Mind if I have a drink before you rob me? I find I am suddenly parched and need to quiet my nerves."

He inclined his head. Cara rose, picked up the bottle and then topped up her glass. She placed the bottle back on the side table and ran a finger along the metal edge of the cooler while she sipped champagne. She played for time, knowing Nate and Brick could not be far away. Plus he would respond to her increased pulse rate and burst of alarm.

The man took a step to close the gap between them. She sat her glass down and contemplated her options. A rattle from behind and the intruder turned his head, his attention caught by the turning door knob.

Cara curled her fingers around the lip of the cooler and seized the momentary distraction. With the bucket in both hands she spun and connected the solid object with a less solid skull. The man's eyes widened in surprise and then rolled up into the back of his head as his knees crumpled and he keeled over. Ice cubes rained down his body from the upturned container.

The door swung open and Nate's body filled the void. He stared at the downed thief. A trickle of blood oozed from the wound in the man's head and dripped to the carpet beneath his body. Nate gave a huff. "Damn it, woman, at least allow me the pretence of rescuing you."

She dropped the dented bucket back in its cradle and a smile played along her lips. She raised her hand to her forehead. "Help," she whimpered. "Somebody help me." She glanced at Nate from under half-closed lashes as the music rose from the orchestra below and spilled into the box.

"That's better," he muttered. He gave the prone man a prod with the tip of his shoe.

"Business concluded?" Cara asked, watching Nate inspect the intruder.

"Yes, for now." He patted his jacket pocket. Satisfied by the lack of response from the thief, he stepped over the body and then pulled loose a curtain tie. The lush velvet drapery tumbled free slid along the front of the box. With the cord in hand, he advanced.

"Oh, good thinking," Cara said. "Let's tie him up before he comes around."

Nate walked past the unconscious thief. The silken rope slid between his fingers. "He's not the one I am interested in restraining." The devil smiled.

A tingle started in Cara's toes and crept up her body as Nate's intentions blazed over her.

"You can't be serious." She took a step backward but heat already bloomed over her skin. "We're at the opera in an open box with an unconscious man on the floor. Plus you will miss the ending." She waved a hand toward the stage where the soprano began her climatic song.

"You started this by telling me about your lack of undergarments. I find I cannot wait until the ride home." He stepped closer and pulled her hands toward him, making a loose loop with the cord around her wrists. "Besides, he won't wake for some time, you made sure of that. No one can see in here because of the loose curtain and I'm certain the singer will cover your cries."

Cara's back touched the plush wallpaper and the first few strains of the aria flooded the box. Nate raised her hands and hooked the cord over the light bracket. She tested the bonds; if she wriggled her hands she would be free. Her restraint was an illusion. Nate bound her but would never imprison her. A charge pulsed through her body as she surrendered control of her own volition.

He claimed her lips in a languid kiss as the music rose beneath them. Her body responded as though he were the conductor, setting the tempo with his hands. As he stroked her through the velvet of the gown, liquid heat ran through her and pooled in her core. Each musical note washed through her as Nate coaxed her higher, her desire building with the song of the soprano.

He unbuttoned his trousers, then his hands drew her skirts up to her waist. He lifted her and settled her knees over his hips. She gave a sigh as with a single thrust he claimed her. They stilled for a moment, bound together as the violin played, drawing out each note before plunging once more into the desperate composition.

Cara flicked her hands from the light and dropped them over Nate's neck. She grasped the silken cord and stretched it over his back, using it to pull him closer as he began to move. Their bodies followed the cue of the music below, each ebb followed by a higher and higher peak. The final crescendo played; she gave a cry as release crashed through her and pulled Nate over the edge.

NATE did use the curtain tie on the thief. Eventually. The gash on the man's head had stopped bleeding and now sported a lump the size of a small egg.

"He'll have quite the headache," Cara said.

A smile spread over Nate's face as he looked at the silver cooler with the large dent on the side. "Champagne will do that to you."

The man stirred and moaned as they lashed his hands and feet together. A check of his pocket found a choker made of rubies and a pair of diamond cufflinks. Cara was not his first visit of the night, but definitely his last.

"Brick is outside. He can take this fellow downstairs for a chat about how business is conducted in London." In the corridor, Nate gestured for Brick to enter the box. "Are you all right to navigate these waters solo, while we clean up?"

Cara kissed his cheek. "Give me a champagne bucket and I can deal with anything. Plus I haven't been slipped a plea for help from anyone in a while. I'll circulate and see what troubled birds I find."

Well-dressed nobles emerged from their boxes; the men in black tails with snowy cravats, the women in brilliant silks and satins and dripping with jewels. Cara touched a hand to her neck; none had diamonds that flashed as brilliantly as hers, nestled against the fire dragon's scales. The modiste draped her form in ways that other women did not dare replicate. They preferred their crinolines and stiff skirts.

She headed down the stairs and out into the foyer. The grand entranceway was a crush of bodies. Her skin was still overheated from her encounter with Nate and she longed for a blast of cool air. Automaton waiters circulated as refracted light from the overhanging lights played over the polished steel of the mechanical servants and clothed them in ever changing hues, their plain forms elevated to gliding paintings.

She passed the lone men, waiting for partners freshening up in the Ladies' Room. They looked like they were lined up for neutering. Each darted nervous glances at the others, hoping not to make eye contact with anyone they knew, as they clutched delicate shawls and throws, and tiny reticules in rainbow shades.

Long-ingrained instinct made her turn toward the assembled noble ladies. They stood in a loose group, gossiping behind their fans. The older matrons formed the head of the shape, their minions ranged out around them. One spotted Cara and curled her lip in a sneer. She turned to her closest companion and nudged her. The warning shot along the row of women like an electrical current dancing from head to head. One by one their eyes narrowed.

She froze in place. If she continued to advance they would turn their backs and deliver the ultimate public cut. Cara's breath caught in her throat; even married to Nate with a title to add to her name, they still would not recognise her or give her the time of day. Never in public. Only in private would they approach her with their sordid problems.

The unloved child deep inside curled further into a corner. *I should have grabbed Helen of Troy's fan out of Nate's pocket, then they would have liked me.*

Her brain whirled, trying to locate an escape route that would minimise the oncoming humiliation, when a hand slid through her arm and arrested her disastrous course.

"Don't give those boring old toffs the satisfaction." A soft feminine voice whispered from beside her. "A moment of your valuable time, Lady Lyons," her rescuer continued in a louder tone, audible to the matrons and ladies poised to deliver their killing blow.

The newcomer continued to swing around and Cara was forced to follow. She now stood with her back to the assembled ladies. She met the warm gaze of a petite woman with vibrant red locks.

She gave a wink and continued in a hushed tone. "Now they are staring at you, unsure what to do. They titter amongst themselves. They were about to cut you down, but if you're not looking they cannot deliver their insult. Whatever will they do?" Laughter burned in the woman's eyes.

"Who are you?" Cara asked. The woman's face itched at a vague memory.

"Catherine Walters, but you can call me Skittles, everyone does."

Ah. The infamous courtesan and current darling of half of London.

Her focus slid over Cara's shoulder. "The old birds are abuzz now, the vultures have seen their feast snatched away from their claws. You didn't want to talk to them anyway."

Relief ran through Cara's body at the offered lifeline. "Thank you, but why are you rescuing me?"

"They don't want you and it's their loss. Come to our side, where you can tell us what desperate acts your delicious viscount lets you perform upon him. He has not given any of us so much as a second look since you arrived in London last year." Skittles looped her arm through Cara's and drew her into the brightly lit world of the birds of paradise.

"Surely you don't want all the sordid details of our life." Cara made a mental note to find out all the sordid details of Nate's dealings with the courtesans.

Skittles laughed. "We most definitely do. Don't we girls? Who wants to hear what our villainous viscount has been up to since abandoning us?"

Women laughed and surrounded her and Cara heaved a sigh. These women accepted her for who she was, not for any title or endowment. Sparkling women pressed her with scandalously intimate questions and welcomed her into the world of the demi-monde.

"I see Nate still has quite a bite," one said, tapping a hand to the side of her neck.

Cara raised a hand to the spot on her body and flushed. Nate had bit down on her skin to stifle his cry of release. *Trust this lot to notice.*

Laughter rang out and the questions became even more impudent. Men circled the group, eager to participate in the conversation or to be cast a favour. The more seasoned men, who had proven the depth of their pockets, were admitted to the inner circle. The young bucks looked on with envious eyes. They had yet to buy their way into the glittering world of pleasure.

"You have more titles surrounding you than the old matrons can drum up," Cara said, casting an eye at the cream of society vying for attention. Fragile noble girls stood tethered to their chaperones and could only sigh as the most eligible bachelors preferred the company of the vibrant courtesans.

"Even royalty waits upon us." Skittles pointed out one tall and wan-looking gent. "That's Edward, the Prince of Wales."

"He looks forlorn, like a child no one wants to play with." Two uniformed men stood at his back and made him seem even more out of place, his every move watched and guarded.

Skittles took a champagne flute from a passing tray and pressed the drink into Cara's empty hand. "We are not sure of him yet, he is young and unproven. This is his first season out in public. We will probably admit him, he is royal after all and is in want of someone to help him spend his allowance."

Cara shook her head at the power these women wielded. Common born, yet by their position they could cut the Prince of Wales. She looked around at the variety of shapes and sizes before her. Even the plainest demimondaine glowed with a vibrancy that proved irresistible to the men fed a diet of bland and shallow beauty. Their worth not based on physical appearance; although that was an advantage, men valued their wit and intelligence. These women sparred with the men, cutting them down with choice words, and the wounded lapped it up and crawled back for more.

"Ah," Skittles said. "Here is one who is most definitely not of our group, but he looks like he wants a word with you."

Cara turned and found Inspector Hamish Fraser, out of place in his day suit. As usual he twisted the brim of his bowler hat round and round with his long fingers. She wondered if tormenting the hat was a form of nervous twitch and how many a week he destroyed with the constant fidgeting.

"Inspector."

"Lady Lyons." He gave a stiff bow. "Could I trouble you for a moment?" He glanced around at the curious stares his presence drew and gestured for her to follow him to a quieter corner.

She broke away from the gay group. "I'm sure it will be trouble coming from you, Hamish."

He rocked back on his heels and gathered his thoughts before proceeding. "There have been two recent deaths in London, of rather unusual circumstances."

"Oh?" She arched an eyebrow, wondering where he was leading and hoping she hadn't raced to the top of his list of murder suspects. Or Nate. She glanced around the busy foyer. Still no sign of her husband.

"It is called spontaneous human combustion. The individual is completely burned and rendered to ash while the surrounding room and furnishings remain untouched."

Vague facts surfaced from a newspaper article. "I do recollect seeing a report in the newspaper. Divine Justice, I think the reporter called it."

"Quite." He gave a soft smile, the one that lured you in, thinking a gentle demeanour lurked beneath, when actually a barracuda sat with bared teeth ready to strip your flesh from bone. "But spontaneous human combustion is so rare, to have two such deaths in the last few weeks is highly … unusual."

Fraser and Cara's history seemed to meet and clash over artifacts of power. He wouldn't want to quiz her about a random natural death. If he sought her out, it was a safe bet he thought the deaths were beyond his realm of expertise. "You think something else is at play?"

He gestured with his hat. "I wondered if the circumstances meant anything to you, with your knowledge of things beyond the understanding of mere Enforcers."

Cara ransacked her brain, thinking of her father's notes and the two ancient books. Nothing leapt to the forefront as matching the circumstances. "I cannot recollect anything that would generate such an effect and nothing has passed through my hands that would match. I would have to study my books in more detail to be certain."

The smile remained in place. "If it wouldn't be too much of a hardship, Lady Lyons. I would value your input."

She catalogued away spontaneous human combustion for later reading. "I'll let you know if I find anything."

He nodded and replaced the bowler on his sandy locks. His line of sight moved beyond her and he froze, the polite smile dropped away as he exposed the point of his canines and gave a snarl. A quick eye lock and he turned, removing himself from the busy atrium and disappearing among the crowd.

Nate's breath feathered on her bare skin. "What did he want?"

"I think he is my broken sparrow that needs help."

"Nate," Skittles called. "You have been too long from our circle." The courtesan kissed his cheek. "What did you think of the opera?"

"I think Cara and I should use the box more often. There's nothing like a standing ovation after a grand performance." He stroked Cara's wrist and removed a stray gold thread from the curtain tie.

Her mouth opened and closed but nothing came out. She snapped open her fan and stirred a breeze around her face. *Infuriating man, why do I let him seduce me in public?* Memory stirred within her. *Because he's so damned good at it.*

CHAPTER 12

Nan & Nessy

July 1815, eighteen years old.

AFTER years of battle and thousands of lives lost, a combination of British army and airship superiority defeated Napoleon. While the emperor sat imprisoned on Saint Helena England rejoiced, until a far greater extravaganza erupted on the social scene——the coming out ball of Lady Annette Edington.

Society whispered for months about the unknown young woman, kept by her reclusive father on a country estate. Those few who met her commented on her beauty and wit. At last, tonight, the *ton* would be able to judge for themselves.

Nessy fussed with the diamond pins adorning her friend's brunette locks.

Nan reached up and stilled her fingers. "It's fine. Leave it alone."

A frown marred her face. "I want everything to be perfect for you."

"How can it be? Mother and Father won't let you attend." Her eighteenth birthday, the most important night of her life and her best friend was not allowed to join her on the dance floor. Her mother wouldn't even attend, her malady meant she could not bear crowds or public appearances. Instead she stayed shut in her rooms in the London residence, so why did she care if Nessy danced or not?

"I don't mind. I'd much rather be here than trapped with a bunch of stuck-up toffs. All I need is some company." She gave a wink to Nan.

She laughed and gave her lifelong companion a hug. "I'll find someone fitting for you and send him along with a bottle of champagne." She stepped out the door, and took the arm of her father, waiting to launch his daughter upon the marriage market and hoping for a quick contract offer.

They paused at the top of the stairs for the Master of Ceremonies to announce her. Her fingers tightened on her father's sleeve as a hush descended over the ballroom and all eyes turned. Poised on the step, she became a product for sale; matrons appraised her looks and made assumptions about her child-bearing abilities, rivals dissected her hair, dress and accessories while bucks speculated about the size of her dowry.

With a fake smile on her face she stepped down and into society. Her father cut her loose at the bottom step as the gazelle wandered amongst the lions. She was now out and fair game. She could hear the other girls sharpening their knives as she passed. Before she became trapped by the subtle warfare employed by women, she needed to ensure Nessy had an enjoyable evening. She cast around the packed ballroom, evaluating and discarding young men in her mind, trying to find one who would appreciate her friend. Her attention fell on a particular tall lad who came from a rural estate and a pragmatic upbringing.

"Sir Henry," she held out her hand and smile wide at the youth.

"Lady Edington." He clasped her hand and bowed. Large brown eyes and an open countenance regarded her, awaiting her command. Sun-bleached hair curled around his face and disclosed his love of being outside. His pragmatic upbringing meant he took people as he found them without regard to station, and his down to earth appeal would be a perfect match for Nessy——or so she hoped.

"I have a favour to ask, Sir Henry." She cast around and gave him a wink, drawing him into her plot.

"For you, dear lady, anything." One hand went to his heart.

"I have a beloved friend who is unable to attend this evening. She is all on her lonesome in the Jade Room. I promised her a bottle of champagne. Would you be so kind as to deliver one to her?" She gave her best endearing smile as she reached out to squeeze his arm.

"Of course." With one hand he snapped a bottle from the tray of a small mannequin circulating on a set track around the outside of the room. With his other hand he lifted two delicate stems. He clicked his heels and headed in the direction of the languishing Nessy.

"One task accomplished, now on to the next item on my list," Nan muttered.

Compliments from well-wishers rained over her and she brushed away the barbs of rivals. With practiced skill she murmured thanks, commented on the gowns of other women and flirted with the older men. All the while she assessed the gathered cream of the *ton*, all present to celebrate her eighteenth birthday and all keen to see where she would lay her favour.

Nan spent months doing her research, from Burke's Peerage to the gossip sheets and military reports. She narrowed her field and investigated her chosen candidates, learning all she could of their lives and personalities. Finally she spied her target and approached the group of older men in military uniforms. All but one broke the conversation and turned to bow at her intrusion. One kept his back to her.

"Lord Morton, I believe you owe me the next dance," she informed the broad back in the rich red of his cavalry jacket. Gold trim hung from the shoulders and the shine on his knee-high boots rivalled that of any mirror hanging about the room. A ceremonial sword hung from his side, the hilt decorated with a tasselled cord larger than those used to hold back curtains.

"I believe you are mistaken, milady." The lord turned. "I do not dance, due to a war injury."

She cast her eye over his tall and well-muscled frame in the exquisitely tailored uniform. He wasn't classically handsome like the dandies, but strong in features and character. A man unafraid to express his opinion and who valued the same in others. *A good choice.* "Unless I am gazing upon a remarkable trompe l'oeil, I understood you lost an arm, my lord, not your legs."

Laughter broke from the other men. A square jaw ground as she met a clear grey gaze and issued her challenge to the renowned war hero. His right hand tightened on a glass tumbler, the left sleeve of his jacket rolled and pinned at his elbow.

She arched an eyebrow and smiled. "I know I have a reputation as something of a handful." Laughter from the men surrounding her. "But I thought given your reputation on the battlefield, you could show the others that you only require one hand to hold me captive."

His steady look bore through her and for a moment she wondered if he would turn his back. The earl had remained apart from society since his return and Nan ensured many of his fellow officers and friends were invited to lure him out this evening.

A broad smile split his face and he gave a bark of laughter. "You have spirit, I'll give you that. Very well." He thrust the tumbler at one of his friends, bowed, and extended his hand to her.

Nan placed her gloved hand in his, her fingers curled around his larger palm as they walked to the dance floor. He pulled her close and she inhaled a warm musky blend of whisky, cigars, and pure male. A thrill shot through her body and heated her blood.

"And what have you chosen for us to dance to?" His voice brushed against her skin as he leaned close.

"The waltz. No silly changing of partners so we have a chance to converse, and no hand waving. You have only to slide your arm around my waist and hold on for the ride." She spun to stand in front of him and placed her left hand on his shoulder. With only a momentary hesitation she rested her right hand on the stump of his left arm and raised her eyes to meet his.

"A handful, you say?" he murmured. He slipped his arm around her and pulled her closer to his chest.

His aroma enveloped her and a sigh escaped her parted lips. Nan knew exactly what she wanted and she intended to get it. She would pursue Lord Morton with the same focus he pursued Napoleon. It would be an all or nothing battle and she would use every weapon in her youthful arsenal against the much older and seasoned soldier.

The slow music started and he guided her around the floor.

"What shall we talk of? The latest fashion in gowns? Musical theatre? I will confess to knowing nothing of needlepoint or how to breed small and annoying dogs."

A smile touched her lips. She didn't pick him to talk sewing. Her mind thirsted for real conversation about the world and politics. "Three years ago the King offered you charge of the new airship fleet. You would have been the Nelson of the skies, admiral of the fledging Aeronautical Service. Why did you refuse?"

She held her ground as he appraised her. "Are you always this forthright?"

"I have a mind, I intend to use it. Does that intimidate you?"

Laughter rumbled through his chest. "You are a spirited filly." A new appreciation crept into his eyes along with something primal that licked along Nan's skin like an open flame. "I didn't want to hover above the battlefield like a vulture, waiting to pick over the carcasses. I needed to be amongst it with dirt on my skin and smoke in my lungs. My unit led the charge. I may have lost my arm, but I would do it all again if given the choice. Have I shocked you?"

He waltzed her to the edge of the floor and away from the other couples.

"Not at all. I could apply the same analogy to the *ton*. They hover above the rest of society, keeping their hems out of the muck, yet like the vultures they circle. Waiting for one of us to falter, then they will tear into our still warm carcass."

"Don't you want to take your place among them?" Curiosity simmered in the swirling depths of his pale eyes as they approached the open doors to the wide terrace.

"No." Heat coursed through her body as she pressed herself closer to him. "I want to live and be amongst the action, whatever the consequences."

They slipped out into the cool night air and he kept his arm around her. "Even if living is with a cripple?" He raised his stump.

She curled her fingers around his upper arm. "A man's strength does not lie in his hands, but his heart and mind.'"

"You are an incredible creature." His head dropped closer, his breath mingled with hers. "If you stay out here you will be ruined. The entire room saw us waltz out the door."

"Not ruined." She rose up on her toes and met his lips. "Saved."

CHAPTER 13

London, Wednesday 15th January, 1862

CARA stood at the window of her study, sipping coffee as she watched fat flakes of snow settle on the rear lawn. The aethergram jumped into action, vibrated, and hummed for several minutes and then spat out a stream of tape. She ripped off the paper, read the message and then chewed her thumb nail.

Need medical supplies for estate. Please ask my father to order a standard hospital kit.

Brick sat in the corner with the newspaper. The front page ran another scandalous story about the decades old rumour of a supposed love affair between the Duchess of Kent and John Conroy, her secretary. Cara had hoped they killed that story when the queen executed Duke Nolton, but the public exhibited an insatiable appetite for gossip about the royals. She heaved a sigh.

Brick's head lifted from the scandal rag. "Problem?"

"I hope not. We left Jackson to look after a dear friend of mine and now she is requesting medical supplies." She hoped the henchman used kid gloves to handle Amy. Her friend still smarted from her broken engagement and the cad's attempt to besmirch her reputation. "I told her to treat him like I would, now I'm wondering if she shot him."

"He seems to inspire that response in women." Brick gave her a wink. "Whatever is happening, his heart is probably in the right place."

She crumpled the message and tossed it into the waste paper basket. "It better be, or I will remove it with a spoon and then Nate will deal with what's left of him."

Her new bodyguard gave a huff of laughter. "Any plans for today?" He closed the paper and tossed it on the end table.

"Yes, I have work to do here. I need you to run to Madame Levett's. She has a new gown for me, and your suits and waistcoats."

The brightest smile lit the man's face. "They're ready?"

"Yes. Not that there is anything wrong with Nate's tailor, but he doesn't understand the needs of a budding Beau Brummell."

If possible the smile became even broader before a frown darted across his enormous forehead. "Promise you won't sneak out on your own."

Cara patted his tree trunk arm. "I promise, I wouldn't dream of depriving you of the opportunity to wear your new clothes out this afternoon. I suspect you would throw a worse sulk than Jackson."

"I won't be more than a couple of hours," he said, and left singing a popular tune in a melodious baritone.

Cara collected the books for her morning's work. She sat at the desk and pulled open the first volume. She reached for more coffee as her brain swam in the unfamiliar Latin sea. Two hours later the coffee pot had sacrificed its last drop and the book only yielded two pages.

"How did I end up as a scholar?" she muttered, tossing aside one old dusty tome to pick up another. On the other corner of her desk sat a stack of neatly folded newspapers. Each article about the recent unusual deaths was circled in red ink. With two deaths by spontaneous human combustion, the reporters ran stories full of lurid speculation about what supposed crimes the poor unfortunates committed that made God resort to burning their presence from our world with Divine Fire. As a consequence church attendance went up. Others seized on the fear of the weak-minded to peddle charms against God's wrath, and advised keeping curtains closed in a bid to escape the all-seeing eye.

In the open book Latin and medieval English warred across the pages in spider scribble that made her squint. Her fingers caressed a page end as she scanned each sheaf. Her linguistic skills were rudimentary and her brain deciphered only the occasional word of Latin in the beautiful ornate script. Miniature oil paintings embellished with gold and silver were her best guide to what she would find described in the text if she took the time to laboriously decipher each word and phrase. Even then strict translation often failed to convey the true meaning of the sentence.

Amy is right, maybe I should have spent less time up trees and more time in class.

She thumbed open *Suetonius' Secrets* while her short interview with the inspector played over and over in her mind. Two deaths of apparent spontaneous human combustion. A coincidence so unusual Fraser suspected something other than mere coincidence. It still seemed quite the mental leap from horrible natural death to murder by fire, but Cara gave up trying to figure how Fraser's mind worked. A mind that conceived of using her as bait to catch a killer. Shame he pegged the wrong man as responsible.

She rubbed the long faded scar over her chest as she turned the pages of the book. Images of cups, blades, and various items of jewellery passed before her vision. Her sluggish caffeine-deprived brain caught the flash of red and orange, but her fingers already flicked past. Her eyes widened and her breath hitched as her hand stopped and lifted the previous page. Cold dread slithered down her spine as she peered underneath, before laying the leaf flat.

"Oh bugger."

Flames licked outward from the centre of the little book, the colours glowed with metallic paint lovingly rendered by some long dead hand. God's holy fire consumed the body in the centre of the gay conflagration.

Flesh melted from bone to reveal a screaming skull, the horror of the moment forever captured in the tiny likeness.

She tapped a fingernail on the poor individual, his limbs in the process of being devoured by flame. As long as the volume existed he would suffer the horrible death, he would never know peace.

"Got you." She turned the page holding the drawing to scan the following text then flicked back and forth. "This doesn't make sense." What few words she could translate mentioned fertility and birthing rites. The polar opposite of the picture holding her captive.

Lifting the book, Cara risked cracking the delicate spine to hold the book flat. She hissed out a breath just as the door to the study opened.

Nate crossed the floor to stand opposite her, his head cocked at his wife's careful examination of the object in her hands. "Find something?"

She turned the book to show him the double spread holding her interest. Leaping flames danced around outspread arms and legs. The illustrator captured the moment of one limb turning to ash, the outline filled with black soot up to mid-calf.

One black brow arched and the cold blue gaze met hers. "An artifact can do that?"

"I don't know." She angled the book, prising the pages as flat as she dared. "The relevant text is missing."

Nate leaned close to examine what made his wife hiss. Someone had removed the pages with a very sharp blade; only a sliver of paper showed where the knife severed the leaf from the spine.

"Any chance it's some sort of Roman fire ritual? Or a bonfire out of control?"

She laid the book on the desk and pointed to the fiery corpse's leg. "One that devours flesh leaving only ash? Fraser was right. Two deaths are far too coincidental, they were deliberate if this is caused by an object."

A frown settled over Nate's face. "I don't like it."

Cara continued her inspection of the ancient book, trying to imagine what was missing and why someone would go to such effort to remove the relevant pages. "I don't like it either, I'm all for being toasty warm, but I prefer not to be crispy fried."

"Actually I meant Fraser being right."

Her head shot up. Nate stood with his arms crossed over his chest and a frown settled between his brows. She would have to keep the two of them apart. Putting them together was like mixing baking soda and vinegar, things could turn volcanic in the blink of an eye. "There's no good end to things between you two."

"There's a good ending the way I imagine it." His face remained dead pan.

Boys, Cara sighed. Perhaps she should lock them in the Pit until they worked it out or they ran out of oxygen. Although that wouldn't work with Nate. "First things first. Since the book came from Helene, I need to visit her and find out if she knows what happened to the missing pages. The picture is a start and tells us there is an artifact at play. Then I need to tell Fraser his natural deaths most likely just became murder."

He moved behind the desk and his large hands played over her collarbone. Fingers splayed up her neck to stroke the skin behind her ear.

An idea popped into her mind. "Do you have access to photographic equipment?"

His lips trailed a blaze behind his fingers. "Want to pose for me?"

"I rather thought I would send something to Fraser."

A growl came from Nate. "Tread carefully, *cara mia*."

She tapped a finger on the open book. "I want to photograph this and send it to him."

His teeth nipped her skin. "I'll sort it for you."

"Thank you. Once I do that little chore and Brick returns, I need some fresh air. Latin is clogging up my brain."

They took a photograph of the image in the book and once the paper dried, Cara popped it into an envelope for Inspector Fraser. She handed it off to one of the men to deliver and gave Brick the good news that they were heading out to the park. On foot. Unlike Jackson he didn't grumble, but he did need ten minutes to decide which hat to wear.

Cara grabbed a long wool coat with military buttons and fur trim and soft kidskin gloves. Brick wore a new outfit with a green velvet frock coat and green and cream striped waistcoat. He grumbled to the other men about Cara forcing him to wear the clothes but grinned once out the door. His awkward posture transformed into something fluid. The clothes became a new skin, one he was unafraid to don in her presence.

He held out his arm to her. "Come on then, milady."

She hooked her hand in the crook of his elbow. "I hope you don't mind too much that we walk? I hate being trapped inside by this gloomy weather."

He swept his hand down his body. "And hide this in a carriage? I don't think so."

Outside the main gate to the house a man stood on a barrel. Bundled up against the cold, he waved a placard urging Nate to repent or suffer the hot wrath of God. "Sinners!" he yelled when he spotted Cara and Brick. "God's fire will strike you down." He waved his board with renewed vigour now he had an audience.

"Doesn't God have other things to worry about?" she asked. "Shouldn't he sort out the civil war in America, or does he condone slavery?"

God appeared to strike down his supporter with apoplexy as the man choked on his words under Cara's watchful stare, unable to explain why God would smite an elderly physician and a housekeeper but allowed some people to keep their fellow men as slaves.

"You shouldn't toy with them," Brick said, pulling her along the pavement and away from the confused man.

She enjoyed Brick's company and their conversation always covered a raft of topics from fashion and literature to politics. With his background as lower class muscle, Cara didn't expect to find an active mind hidden under his fashionable hat. As they walked he expressed his opinion about the ongoing civil war across the ocean.

"Fighting affects economies around the world. Famine is biting already in Lancashire, the war has restricted baled cotton imports. Horrid business to watch children starve."

She tightened her grip on his arm. "Which explains all the missives Nate receives about the Poor Law reforms and relief for the textile industry. I think legitimate business causes him more headaches than smuggling."

They continued discussing the effects of the war as they crossed over Park Lane and into Hyde Park and struck out for the river. Only a few souls braved the frigid conditions to escape the confines of their homes. Children screamed and played, throwing snowballs at one another, oblivious to the dropping temperature. They found the Serpentine frozen and ducks and children alike skidded across the surface.

A pair of horse riders appeared at the end of the lane and passed close to where they sat. A man rode a placid looking horse whereas the woman sat a high spirited stallion, in perfect balance with the animal. Her hands restrained him without being harsh as he listened to his mistress's commands. A tremor of impatience ran over the horse's flesh as he stood still.

The rider's habit revealed every contour of her body. Warmth sacrificed for fashion. Only one woman in England rode so well and wore such tight habits. Catherine Walters. Some said she was without equal in all of Europe for her skill in handling a stallion.

I wonder if she is as skilled in handling men. Might be why she is so popular.

The two women made eye contact and recognition passed between them. Skittles beckoned a finger to Brick and tossed her reins to her companion. He stood at the horse's shoulder and held out a hand, to help her down. She picked up the loop at the back of her skirt to make walking easier and passed it over her wrist. Her companion tossed Brick an ermine lined cloak and he draped it over the courtesan's shoulders.

"Cara," she said, as she kissed her cheek. "You have been on my mind, how fortunate to find you in the park."

"Skittles." Cara couldn't do it. She couldn't hold her tongue, she had to know the truth behind a famous piece of gossip. "You must satisfy my curiosity about something."

A dark eyebrow arched. "Oh? What is that?"

She contemplated the tight melton cloth habit under the cloak. "Is it true you have your seamstress sew you into your habit?"

The courtesan gave a chuckle and tucked her hand into Cara's. "For someone in my position it always pays to keep the men speculating."

Cara laughed. "Well, you certainly do that."

Arm in arm, they started along the path. Skittles' companion took the reins of the stallion. Brick dawdled behind, at a sufficient distance to allow the women to talk in private.

"What brings you out on foot in such chilling weather?" Skittles asked.

"The cold clears my mind. I find myself plagued with thoughts about society and its expectations." A squirrel found a forgotten acorn in the snow and scuttled across their path. Cara watched him dash up the trunk of an old oak tree.

"Something we don't worry about in the demi-monde, it really is quite liberating." Skittles swatted at a drift of snow with her long side-saddle cane, using it like a golf club. "What in particular is worrying you?"

Cara paused, wondered how much to burden the courtesan with. "Noble men are expected, even encouraged, to seek lovers among you. But does it happen in the reverse? Do noble women seek pleasure outside the vows of marriage?"

Skittles let out a whistle between her teeth and startled a sparrow above their heads. "Please don't tell me you are unhappy with Nathaniel? You will devastate my sisters."

She gave a huff of laughter. "There is only one man who will ever possess my heart and body. I'm thinking of another."

They walked in a silence Cara could not fill. Skittles pulled her to a stop. "Do you know what quality men value the most from us?"

She had some inkling of what drew the men like moths to the flame. "Your wit?"

"No, our silence. They confide in us with their deepest and darkest fears knowing we will hold them safe."

"The newspapers are stirring up the ancient story about the queen mother again. Do you think the duchess took her secretary as a lover?" Cara pulled on the public example of infidelity while she considered a far more private situation.

Skittles gave a shrug. "There was a substantial age difference between the duke and duchess, perhaps they were mismatched in more ways than one." She cast a glance at Cara. "I doubt that is the issue preying on your mind, though. Something closer to home, perhaps?"

Cara took a deep breath. There was a niggle in her mind that she dared not say aloud. She never said it to herself, could she tell the courtesan? "You really are good. I'm considering telling you something I can't even say to Nate."

Her companion laughed. "Think of me as your confessor. Sharing it will lessen the burden for you and I vow to take your confidence to my grave." She crossed her heart.

Cara dove in before courage deserted her. "I know nothing of my parents as a couple. I don't know if they were happy or if it was an arranged marriage. In my darkest moments I wonder, what if my mother took a lover and Lucas was not my father?" The words sounded surreal, she couldn't believe she allowed them free from her swirling brain. Ludicrous to think a noble woman would pass off another man's child as her husband's. But it was exactly what the gossips said about the Duchess of Kent.

"If he were not your father, would it make it easier to hate him, or forgive him for selling you?" Skittles asked.

A sharp gasp rose and fell from Cara's chest. How could a father sell his daughter? But if she were the child of another man did his actions become easier to understand? Did it ease her burden? "As a child I thought it was my fault, that I was not a good enough daughter and that

I somehow failed. As an adult I know he alone was responsible for my fate, whatever his justification."

Skittles squeezed her arm. "Seek the answers if the truth will ease your mind. Did your mother keep a diary?"

She shook her head. "I don't know, not that I have ever seen." Or did the house hold one last secret?

CHAPTER 14

London, Friday 17th January, 1862

FRASER

looked up as his office door bumped, shuddered, and then gave. Connor pushed through, sliding his shoulder over the wood to hold the door open as he backed into the crowded office. One beefy paw held a mug of tea, the other a stack of letters and reports. A heavy black boot kicked the door shut as he ambled farther into the chaos. He held his breath as he sidled by the chalkboard so he didn't brush against the notations and end up with crucial linkage stuck to his cuffs.

The mug dropped into the middle of the desk and the spicy fragrance of bergamot wafted toward Fraser's nose. His fingers curled around the heated metal and he dragged the liquid closer. A fresh brewed Earl Grey with just a dollop of milk. *Perfection.*

There was only one drink that calmed his nerves faster than tea—— whisky with a few drops from the small bottle in his jacket pocket. There were long days when his hand shook and he nearly succumbed to taking laudanum while at his desk. His will prevailed and so far he managed to trudge through each minute until he reached home and could take his oblivion in peace. But each week the craving grew stronger. Yesterday his fingers caressed the vial and the poppy extract called to him like a siren.

He removed his glasses and squeezed the bridge of his nose before donning the spectacles once more. His gaze went to the deposited pile of papers and one envelope drew his attention, large yet slim, the heavy cardboard a pale blue colour. The front bore his name embellished with feminine swirls and flourishes. The black wax on the back bore the Lyons crest. He glanced to Connor before casting around his desk for a paperknife. His fingers groped under a haphazard tower of folders.

"Ah." Something cold and narrow butted against his grasp and he drew it from the stack.

With the plain silver grip in his hand he slashed through the wax seal, cutting Lyons' symbol in two. A smile twisted one side of his mouth at the action and then he drew out the contents. A photograph fluttered to the desk. Even in stark black and white the flames consuming the man leapt from the image. The melting flesh and bone evident as the fire ate the extended limbs.

On the back a simple message from his newest assistant.

The effect. Still hunting for the cause.

He blew out a long whistle. "My suspicion may be correct. Lady Lyons is on the trail of an artifact that produces Divine Fire."

He placed a fingertip on the image and swung it around to face Connor. The sergeant picked up the photograph to peer at the man being devoured by flame.

"What will you tell the Superintendent?"

"Nothing until I know for sure what path we are pursuing. The fire may be divine but there will be a terrestrial hand directing its course." He rose from his desk and stalked to the enormous board covering one wall. Picking up the duster, he wiped half the space clean and took up a piece of chalk. "If these deaths are intentional, we need to look what connected Nigel Fenmore and Penelope Stock. A retired physician and a trusted maid to our queen's mother."

He began scribbling on the board, their names, dates of birth and death, locations the bodies were found, and, connecting the two, *Victoria, Duchess of Kent*.

"The queen's mum died last year." Connor crossed his arms, trying to keep up with the mad writing. "And those two were old, really old. You've got to hope they weren't sneaking around having an affair or something."

"God doesn't smite adulterers, too many targets." Fraser stood back as far as the cramped quarters permitted. The chalk dangled in his fingers. "Murder always has a reason, Connor. We just have to dig deep enough to find it." No pattern emerged from the scant details so he tossed the chalk back onto its small ledge. "We need more information."

The sergeant rubbed the back of his head. "How far back do you want to go?"

"Back to the beginning, I want to know when these two first crossed each other's path and we work forward from there." Fraser clapped his hands together and cast around the office, wondering where his top coat ended up. The coat rack in the corner sat forlorn, its outstretched arms empty.

Connor stepped over to the spare chair and lifted up a large box, underneath lay the crumbled coat. He gave the box in his hands a rattle and something heavy rolled side to side and collided with something equally dense. "What's in here?"

Fraser slid his arms into the coat and pulled the collar around his neck. "Two heads."

Connor dropped the box back on to the chair and gave it a scowl.

"Evidence from the McGinty case. It's the two skulls we found in his wardrobe. I need to drop it down to Doc to see if he can match them to any unclaimed body parts currently in residence."

"Why would you want two heads in your office?" Connor followed his inspector out the door.

"Two heads are better than one." Fraser slapped his sergeant on the arm as he disappeared out the door and down the stairs. Once past the main doors they stood under the slim eave, eyeing up the weather before heading into the biting cold.

"Where to?" Connor asked.

"Bayswater and Penelope Stock's daughter. I want the overview of her career in service to the old duchess. No family has claimed Mr Fenmore, so we will have to rely on other sources to piece together his life." Fraser pulled his scarf tight and tucked the ends into his jacket. "Damn it."

"What is it now?" the sergeant asked.

Fraser headed to the Enforcers' steam carriage. "I forgot to drink my tea," he said over his shoulder.

Connor laughed and followed Fraser to the waiting conveyance. He spoke with the driver before he climbed inside. The carriage swung back and forth on its springs as he manoeuvred his bulk to one of the seats.

They chugged past Mayfair and Hyde Park. It seemed each corner sprouted a person waving a placard to repent or bear the wrath of God, and people braved the cold and snow to pray for their immortal souls. The church coffers soared and attendance numbers swelled.

Their vehicle passed another black scar on the landscape where the land opened up for entrance to the new underground. Workers swarmed the site. An airship hovered low, an enormous chain attached to take away a skip laden with soil and rock.

"Do you think anyone will use this new underground train?" Connor asked, his nose pressed to the glass to watch the swaying load of earth hoisted high.

"It can't be any worse than this contraption," Fraser said, coughing on the incoming fumes.

They headed to Bayswater and the middle class row of terrace houses. The victim's daughter showed them through to the little parlour. Fresh orange striped wallpaper brightened up the gloomy room. Fraser glanced at the redecorating. Connor look relieved, although he avoided the new chair in one corner of the room, opting instead to stand by the window.

The woman caught their exchanged looks. "The black wouldn't scrub off the walls. We had to tear the old paper off and put up new." A sob choked off her words and then she grabbed a hanky from her apron and blew her nose.

"How terrible for you," Fraser murmured. "I wanted to ask a few questions about your mother's distinguished service with the duchess."

"Why?" The hanky was shoved back in the apron's pocket.

"Excuse me?"

"I have nosy reporters wanting the gory details and all the time the neighbours are gossiping behind their curtains that she must have done something really evil for God to do this. It was a horrible tragedy, Mam was a good woman. Why do you need to ask more questions and keep feeding the gossips?"

Fraser donned his calm smile while inwardly he cursed reporters with nothing better to do but rack over a family's sorrow. "We want to understand her life better. Plus we need to ascertain if she ever encountered Nigel Fenmore."

"That's the man that died the same way, isn't it?" She cocked her head to one side, as though trying to see his purpose.

"Yes. Another terrible tragedy for his family." Not that any had come forward, perhaps too concerned they would be struck with the same fate by association.

The woman's eyes widened as her brain made some connection. "Do you think my mam caught something from him? You don't think this burning is contagious do you?" She tapped her chest. "Will I catch it?" Her voice went up an octave as panic set in and she scanned the room, perhaps for a water source in case of any flames.

"No, no, of course not." He held up his hands to placate the woman. "We just want to be thorough. Two such terrible deaths, we need to do all we can to reassure you."

"Well." She walked to the table, picked up her tea cup and then took a noisy slurp. "She started as a chamber maid back in 1815——"

The woman droned on into the afternoon, recounting her mother's work in the royal household. Time would have passed quicker if she narrated amusing anecdotes about the Duke of Kent and his wife, shame she didn't know any.

They escaped after forty five years, or so it seemed. The interview took three hours but the bereaved woman had no gift for storytelling. Fraser took brief notes of key events. He jotted down when Penelope changed roles and who she may have encountered. Fenmore attended the duchess on a regular basis and the little maid would have seen him a number of times over more than four decades in service.

He stood on the pavement and heaved a great sigh. "Forty five years to dig through. What does our killer know, Connor? What secret might have passed between them that someone deemed it worth taking their lives?"

Back in his office, Fraser contemplated the dead end. If someone deliberately targeted the two victims of spontaneous human combustion he could not discern the underlying cause. He needed something more substantial; he was the bloodhound without a scent chasing his tail instead.

He stood in front of the filing cabinets and his hand sought one in particular. He pulled a metal drawer open and stared at the stuffed files competing for space. His eye went to a familiar one. The sharp edges of the cardboard roughened and dog eared by the hours he spent running his fingertip around the file.

Deep in thought he wandered over to his desk and dropped the bundle of papers, newspaper articles, and photographs. On the front a cream label stood out against the dark grey background. In a neat precise hand a name identified this particular open case.

Nathaniel Trent. Viscount Lyons.

He flicked open the cover. On top sat the latest gossip sheet clipping, detailing the shocking news of the viscount's secret marriage to Cara Devon. The reporter viewed the entry in the marriage registry, revealing the two had been wed for over three years. The *ton* erupted in a furore for missing that juicy snippet. The eligible bachelor suddenly whipped off the market.

He laid aside the article and turned to a particular section.

An incident report noted that date and location. 1858, St Giles Rookery. Over twenty dead and who knew the real number murdered that night. He began leafing through the few notes and photographs he managed to gather that day.

Chaos reigned for a few short hours in the Rookery until the new order exerted its control. A tiny window of opportunity that let the Enforcers in. They saw the bodies and managed to take photographs of a few. None made it out of the tight knit community. Family claimed the fallen, some were stolen off the back of the Enforcers' vehicles, his uniforms powerless in the face of the grieving mob. They counted twenty dead by looking at bodies, blood stains and the absence of well-known faces. Whispers on the street said closer to thirty fell. Nobody would talk. Nobody saw anything. It was as though the grim reaper himself wielded his scythe under the cover of invisibility.

Saul Brandt, the leader of the St Giles Rookery, was stabbed in the chest in the middle of a crowded pub. Saul stood at the bar, drink in his hand conversing with his men and the next moment lay in a pool of his own blood on the floor. Not a single witness. Every last one was either staring at his beer or looking in the opposite direction at the precise time the fatal wound was delivered and missed the entire incident.

Fraser didn't have to witness the murder to know whose hand drove the blade into his rival's heart.

He let out a sigh. He planted his seed, it simply needed time to grow and bear fruit. "You will fall. I shall see to it."

London, Sunday 19th January, 1862

CARA fell into a routine living with Nate that always involved a large breakfast, just in case she got kidnapped, stabbed, or otherwise detained during the day. Plans were discussed over coffee and bacon. The English could keep their kippers, once she visited America and discovered the joys of bacon for breakfast she wasn't going back to small fish.

"We're still plotting the route to Australia and New Zealand, and the supplies needed." Nate said, sorting through the dispatches that arrived overnight. "We don't think they will have to land anywhere, but we're planning a stopover just in case."

He tossed several papers to one side and several more straight into the bin. "We should have Loki in the air soon with an airship full of people wanting to escape England for more temperate climes."

She watched the never ending snow piling up outside. "Can't say as I blame them. Rather tempted myself to journey to somewhere tropical."

Nate looked up from the letter in his hands, a smile quirked his lips. "Tahiti for a second honeymoon? Very few clothes required, you wouldn't have to pack much." He folded the letter and slipped it into his pocket.

She rose for her morning kiss. "Let's deal with Fraser's mysterious deaths, then we can discuss heading somewhere warmer and my lack of clothing. I'm off to see Helene this morning and find out if she knows what happened to *Suetonius' Secrets.*"

Snow fell outside and Cara took the carriage and mechanical horses to Belgravia. Each day winter deepened and the Thames froze. People speculated if the ice would thicken enough to hold people, stalls, and animals. There hadn't been a frost fair since 1814, when elephants walked across the Thames. Bookies were taking bets that 1862 would see another festival held on the river. The mechanical workshops were open late into the night as the craftsmen laboured to make enormous metal creatures to rival, and surpass, elephants. This frost fair would see gryphons, unicorns, and dragons glide over the ice as soon as it reached sufficient thickness.

Cara stepped from the warmth of the carriage and stood on the footpath. Looking up, she wondered what she would find behind the house's façade today. Split paint and cracks ran down the door as though trying to escape what lay beyond. She glanced upward at the dust and soot coated windows. Clinging to the sills, abandoned boxes contained the remains of long dead plants and one held a desiccated pigeon that looked like it died on the job.

Snow settled on ledges and water dripped to freeze mid-fall, but even the pristine tear drops became tarnished by contact with the house. Soot puffing from steam conveyances and chimneys left a grimy dark layer over everything. The entire structure gave off an air of decay and abandonment.

Bet this house is related to my one in Soho.

She pushed the door open and stepped into the gloomy hall. Dust motes floated in front of her face and she batted them away. Brick cast a curious glance around and took up position by the main door. His back rigid, he didn't risk lounging against the wall and being contaminated like the snow outside.

"Hello!" she yelled, and waited for any sign of life, ears pricked to catch the faintest noise to give her search direction. A shuffling from the hall drew her attention and the elderly butler appeared and squinted at her.

His rheumy eyes passed over Brick and failed to register the hulking man as anything other than a statue. He gave a hrumpf of vague recognition at Cara, waved his hand in a dismissive manner and then shuffled back down the hallway.

"Warm reception," Brick quipped from his corner.

"He's always like that. I swear he's an automaton on a set route." She stared at the ceiling, checking the plaster for any sign of leaks from the old roof. "Stay here, it only gets worse depending on what sort of day Helene is having."

A bark came from upstairs. On the trail of the pug, Cara placed a hand on the end newel post and a piece of the ornate barley twist broke away in her hand.

"Bugger," she muttered, and dropped the wormwood-infected timber over the side.

At the top of the stairs she struck off left, to Helene's suite. She studied the dark paintings on the landing and lining the corridor as she walked past. Helene liked to use her ancestors' portraits for target practice and many sported bullet holes in the foreheads, testament to the countess's excellent aim.

Cara considered having a portrait of her father hung in the Soho house so she could kill two birds with one stone. Or more accurately, shoot the two sources of pain in her life with one bullet.

She stopped at the painting closest to the double doors to the master bedroom.

"That's new." A cross bolt jutted from the bridge of the man's nose. "What did you do, I wonder?" she asked the executed man.

She pushed open the dark doors and stepped into oppressive heat. Summer or winter, Helene kept the drapes tightly closed and the fire stoked, trying to sweat the demons from her mind.

The countess reclined on the bed, sinking into a mound of decorative pillows. The four pillars of the bed were made from tree trunks, their branches spread outward holding the flimsy curtains. Helene resided in a forest bower, like a mad fairy queen. Minnow gave a happy bark and shot off the bed. Today he wore deep blue taffeta.

Cara bent down and scratched the little pug's ears. "Hey boy." Reaching into a pocket she pulled out a piece of beef jerky and slipped it to the mutt. His curly tail wagged and he disappeared under the bed with his treat.

"I see you have a crossbow." Cara drew back the leaf-embroidered organza and twisted the swag of curtain around an end post. She sat on the bed and searched Helene's face, wondering how lucid her friend was today and where she hid the crossbow and bolts.

"I got it special for Henry. He's been taunting me at night and won't let me sleep." Deep blue circles ringed the woman's eyes, red seeped into the irises and echoed the rot eating through her brain. "He says he knows things, important things, and teases me that I cannot guess."

"Would you like me to move him?" *When did this become my life?* she pondered. Pouring drinks in Texas was far simpler, although to be fair, that life involved just as many bullet holes.

"Oh no, don't move him, then he would talk to the others. No, I need him close, so he doesn't rally them against me. He will, you know." She lurched forward and grabbed Cara's arm, pulling her closer. Her once beautiful eyes locked on Cara's face, but her mind remained miles away. "You believe me, don't you? You won't let him overthrow me with his whisperings? I only have you and my little canary on my side. No one else believes that they come to me at night, invading my mind with their constant chatter."

She remembered Nate's comment about Helene's gypsy blood and their fabled ability to see through the veil of death. She wondered if the syphilis drove her mad, or her inability to sleep with the ghosts crowding around her bed.

She took Helene's too thin hand in her own and gave a soft squeeze. "I'll not let Henry plot against you."

Helene gave a sigh. "I hold them back you know, on the other side. My mother taught me how."

"You tell me what you want me to do and together we will thwart him."

"Yes, yes, if we work together we can silence the screaming. Then I can sleep." She fell back on the pillows and a cloud of dust rose up around her and danced on the heavy air.

The fire crackled, munching came from under the bed, and Helene's eyes stayed closed. Cara chewed her lip; she needed to pick her friend's brain but today looked like there was little to poke through. She chewed a nail while wondering how to nudge the conversation in a more rational direction.

"You have a question, ask it now." The voice much stronger, clearer.

"*Suetonius' Secrets* has some pages removed. Unfortunately they happen to be the very pages I need, about an artifact that generates fire."

"Fire." The syllable whispered over Helene's lips. Her eyes flung open and she sat bolt upright. The red receded from her eyes and sanity paid a fleeting visit. Their time together often followed this pattern. Cara would tempt lucidity forth with a bait of tantalising clues and questions. Helene would give her cryptic responses and then sink back into the darkness within her.

Saloon girl, much simpler job than this caper.

Cara pulled the volume from her satchel and held the book open. "Look." She pointed to the tiny fragment of shorn paper. "Someone cropped the pages out."

Helene's fingers wrapped around hers and she dropped her head so close to the book she seemed to be gazing at the individual fibres in the rough paper.

"Malachi," she breathed over the pages as though uttering a word of power to resurrect the lost text.

"Who is he?" Please don't let it be a painting or someone who died years ago.

A smile spread over the countess' face. "You have been there before. He owns the little bookstore that you once visited and then he sent you to me."

"Do you think he removed the pages?"

"Doubtful. Malachi would never harm a book. But he once borrowed my edition to transcribe it for a collector. If he has touched a page he remembers the text. He absorbs the words through his skin. He will know what you are missing."

Cara remembered the ancient store with its equally aged owner. He set her after *Magyck of the Gods*, the volume that became her guidebook to the strange artifacts.

Helene's fingers tightened around her hand. Meeting her gaze, Cara watched the madness slink back into her friend's eyes. She wished she had known the young Helene, the one full of life and vitality and not the shell that remained.

"Make sure my little birdie finds happiness. He has dwelt too long in the darkness with me, he needs a creature of light."

Cara placed the fragile hand over the sunken chest. "I'll try and find somebody willing to take the grumpy bugger on, I promise." *God knows who though, Amy has the patience of a saint and she can't stand him.*

A smile touched Helene's face. "Angelique promises to help, she knows who will heal his heart." She slumped back against the pillows and within moments heavy snoring filled the air.

"Fantastic, on top of everything else I have to find a woman who comes with a ghostly endorsement."

Cara stoked the fire and placed the guard close to the bricks, making sure no wayward spark would escape while Helene slumbered. Minnow appeared from under the bed, dragging the strip of jerky, and plonked himself in front of the heat. He turned large brown eyes to Cara.

Checking Helene slept, she reached down and removed the taffeta dress from the dog.

He gave himself a shake and returned to the treat.

She stroked his wrinkled head. "Look after her, little one."

Leaving the bedroom, she confronted Henry. He appeared to be from the seventeenth century with his enormous wig of powdered ringlets and a painted heart on one cheek. A cold light in his eyes belied the dandy image and a chill shot down Cara's body.

"What do I do with you, Mr Conspirator?" she addressed the painting. An idea came to her mind and with a suppressed giggle she headed downstairs to the library, to find the supplies she needed.

Rummaging around in the desk, she found glue and a roll of crepe. Borrowing a knife from Brick, she sliced off two short strips of fabric and took her supplies back up the stairs. A few minutes work and she stepped back to survey the results. Henry now had his mouth bound shut with bandage, stopping him from muttering a word and disturbing Helene's sleep.

"That's Henry silenced. Time to tackle the rest of my tasks for today."

That afternoon, Cara stood on the doorstep in Broadwick Street Soho and pulled a key on a chain from her battered satchel. She unlocked the door and pushed it open. She peered in as though expecting an ambush. She kept putting this day off, but McToon wanted to know if anything could be done to make the house not so much habitable as more hospitable.

She resisted the urge to cross herself as she stepped over the threshold and into the empty entranceway. Brick crowded behind her and shut the door. Gloom enveloped them.

Bugger. I'll have to turn on a light.

She reached out a hand, took a breath and activated the switch. The barest tingle of surplus charge ran back through her fingers. The bulb above flickered a few times before deciding to go and cast its yellow light.

"House is mellowing," she muttered, trying to decide where to start.

Brick laughed. "It's a house, what do you think it will do?"

She turned to face him. "It extracts a blood toll from the occupants. I spilled a fair amount on the floorboards, women died in the basement and the only tenant I found managed to slit a wrist slicing bread because the house played with the lights."

She waited for a smart reply. Proving how smart he was, Brick didn't have one. He did touch the knife on his arm as though checking it remained safe in its sheath.

"So what exactly are we looking for?"

"I don't know," she whispered. "But something is here."

He cast around the half empty house. "How can you be so sure?"

"Have you ever stood outside during a thunderstorm? Before the rain, when the sky turns black, thunder booms from above and lightning arcs through the clouds. The air becomes charged and it skates over your skin. These objects we seek give me the same response when I am near one." She pulled back the sleeve of her jacket and showed the goose bumps on her arm. "That's how I know something is here."

"Where do you want to start then?"

She placed a hand on the newel post. "Upstairs. You can wait in the parlour, there is something I have to do alone first."

He raised an eyebrow and gave her a hard stare.

"I don't plan to jump out a window." She gave a weak smile.

"All right." He tapped a pocket in his jacket. "I've got a book, take all the time you need." Then he crossed to the front room.

Cara trod the stairs with a heavy heart and turned down the hall to her mother's suite. An interconnecting door led to her father's more masculine rooms. This softly feminine room was painted in palest cream and yellow with hints of rose and green. A few pieces remained untouched; the whitewashed bed and matching dresser. A cream cane chaise in front of the window.

The decoration and furniture were all Cara had of her mother. Bella laboured and died in this room. She never paced the floor to walk her newborn daughter to sleep. Never brushed Cara's hair while she sat at the dresser. She never curled up and watched her mother dress for an evening out.

"Were you happy here?" she whispered to her phantom mother. "Or did you seek happiness with another?" A vain hope perhaps, but Skittles set her mind in motion. Once she gave the idea life she couldn't let it go until she knew one way or the other. If her mother kept a diary surely it would be hidden in her room. Or had her father found it years ago?

She examined the dresser, pulled out all the drawers and checked for hidden compartments. Next she gave the bed frame the same thorough going over. Nothing. In the walls? She ran her fingertips over the walls and skirting looking for joins or cracks. After an hour she admitted defeat and returned downstairs.

"Any luck?" Brick asked, looking up from his book.

She shook her head. "It was silly really, I thought my mother might have left something hidden in her room."

He slid his book back into a pocket. "Want to look for whatever else might not be here?"

She laughed. "Sounds stupid when you say it like that, but yes. I just want to wander around slow, see what tingles."

They spent the next couple of hours walking from room to room. Two rooms made the hair on the back of Cara's neck stand up. The basement and the library.

"Do you think something is hidden in the walls or floors?" Brick asked.

She chewed her lip. "No, I think the blood soaked into the floor is giving me the shivers." Except the house toyed with her long before she spilled her blood in the library or her father hid Nefertiti's Heart in the basement. What was she missing?

CHAPTER 16

Nan & Nessy

1816

FOR three days Gideon, Earl of Morton paced back and forth in the corridors, listening to his wife scream. With each passing hour the strength of her cries diminished, by the time dark closed on day three, the shrieks turned to sobs for mercy.

Events unfolding behind the closed door tortured him far more than when a cannonball blew his lower arm off in battle. He used his belt as a tourniquet and severed the dangling tendons with his knife in between fighting off French soldiers trying to finish the job. Although he couldn't put his arm back together he could at least do something, here he could do nothing. Except wait, listen to the screaming, and pace.

Annette. He remembered that night she raised her eyes to his and dared him to dance with her. He knew a rare gem when he saw one, he married her that night. Every day since, his love grew deeper for the woman who invaded his life.

The midwife exited the bedroom and pulled the door closed. Her heavy gaze rested on him.

"Well?" His heart sunk, one look at her face told him the prospects were limited and mounting against his wife. A campaign with insurmountable odds and no hope of a cavalry charge or airship strike to save the day.

She shook her head. "We are having trouble getting the babe to turn, stubborn thing, it's facing the wrong way."

His heartbeat slowed and almost stopped. Time suspended as he struggled to say the words caught in his throat. He could make decisions in the heat of battle that would affect hundreds of men, but this choice could end him. "What are our options?"

She wiped a bloody hand across her forehead. "She is a fighter, but her strength is nearly exhausted. We can try one more time to turn the babe, and perhaps help it free. If not——"

The hanging question, asked far too many times of noble husbands, who to save——wife or child?

Within his wife's slender frame lay his heir, the hope for the entire estate and the continuation of his name. A well-bred woman's sole purpose in this world was to provide a male child. Preferably two, the requisite heir and a spare. Their baby struggled to enter the world and draw that first breath and *live*. But what would his world be without Annette? He would be the earth without the sun. The warmth of her caress forever denied him, a land in eternal dark never to see the light again.

He balled his hand into a fist. "Do what you have to. Save my wife." He choked out the words and condemned his child. He knew the tools that lay within the room, waiting to be used in such a situation. Hooks and knifes to severe the tiny limbs in his wife's womb and remove the babe piece by piece.

A phantom appeared before him. A head of dark hair like Annette but with his pale grey eyes. Lanky limbs showed the promise of height and athletic ability. He extended his stump and non-existent fingers ruffled the ghost's hair and then he said goodbye to the imagery child. *Forgive me, son.*

The woman paused for only a moment, before nodding. "We will give her as much opium as we can. She won't be able to fight, but it will dull the pain, somewhat, for what lays ahead." She opened the door and blood and sweat assaulted him.

The smell sent his mind back through time. He remembered the field hospital where he lay after his injury. Men screamed in pain as surgeons cut off their limbs with hand saws, no time or luxury of opium to free their minds from what they endured. Wounds cauterised with fire and bound with dirty cloth. If they survived that they could still fall prey to the slower death of infection.

He turned and with a roar, slammed his fist into the wall. Plaster and chips of paint flaked to the polished floor. Whimpering, like a whipped dog, came from the room beyond. He ground his teeth, never had he felt so powerless. Each second of inactivity peeled a strip of flesh from his body. He led troops into battle where his men relied on him to guard their lives and see them home safely. He always had a strategy to see them through and the king recognised his bravery after the fall of Napoleon.

But how could a man fight nature in a woman's solitary war? What weapon could he raise to protect his family?

God save them both, please, he whispered to the unforgiving night.

Voices murmured and the constant whimper cut through his soul. Moments stretched, the second hand tick on his pocket watch magnified to mortar fire raining upon him. He bit down on his fist to stop tears from forming in his eyes. A scream ripped through the heavy atmosphere and tore through his heart. The cry high pitched and full of suffering and outrage.

Then silence.

Straining his ears, he heard nothing. He held his breath, had he lost them both?

Then came the thin reedy cry of new wet lungs.

The door opened again, blood stained up the midwife's arms and she mopped at her hands with a cloth. "We freed the child. You have a daughter."

His heart stopped in his chest, from beyond the door came only hushed whispers and the exhausted cry of the new born. *Nan.* "My wife?"

Tired eyes met his. "Time will tell. If she continues to fight, she will survive."

"I must see her." He made to brush past the midwife, but she laid a hand on his sleeve, leaving a bloody imprint.

"One more thing. This has been a long and difficult labour and her body is damaged. If she lives, there will be no more children from her."

A single daughter. No more children. No boy to teach to ride, shoot, or fish.

No heir.

"So long as God lets me keep them both, then I do not care." He entered the room, blood and sweat thick in the close atmosphere. Here at last was something he could control. A situation he could command and bend to his will. He would not lose the warmth of his sun. He would fight with all weapons at his disposal, fight to save his wife. The field hospital taught him one thing, men died more quickly when left to lay in their own filth.

"Open the windows and fetch fresh bed linen and hot water. Let us clean and air the room, so my wife and child can sleep more comfortable." *And pray infection does not find her.*

Nessy sat in the bed, her arms supporting her lifelong friend, the other woman's head slumped against her shoulder. "I tried," she said on seeing him, tears pooling in her eyes. "I tried so hard to take her pain, to make it easier for them."

Gideon nodded, his heart swelled at the love the young woman bore for his wife. She had not slept for three days, refusing to leave Nan's side. Knowing Gideon was banned from the birthing room she declared she would be his proxy. "I know, Nessy. Would that I could have borne it for her."

Nan's head raised on hearing her husband's voice. Black shadows haunted her eyes as she turned. Her long dark hair plastered to her face by sweat, an impossibly small bundle in her arms.

"All that trouble, for a girl." She tried to smile, but her body couldn't muster the energy to move her facial muscles. "I'm so sorry." A large tear escaped the corner of her eye and rolled down her cheek. "I have failed you."

"Hush," he sat on the bed and captured the tear with a fingertip. "I love my women strong and opinionated, and I will adore our daughter even more for being exactly like her mother. Fighters, both of you."

"I will deliver you an heir, I promise, next time." Her eyelids dropped closed, her battered mind seeking the release of unconsciousness.

"Sleep and get better. We will worry about that another day," he stroked her hair.

Nessy eased the tiny bundle from Nan's grasp and slid the newborn into his arms. He stared at the little crinkled face. Swirls of dark hair clung to her head. With a fingertip he reached out and dared to touch his daughter. Her mouth opened on reflex, searching.

For the first time in three days he smiled. But he would worry. With no heir, his estate had no future. Should anything happen to him there were few options for his wife, daughter, and Nessy. They would be cast out with nothing, alone in the world apart from each other.

His family would never be secure until he had an heir.

CHAPTER 17

London, Tuesday 21st January, 1862

IF Cara ventured to Seven Dials it was normally to the pub the Prick and Rose, accompanied by an overprotective Nate and a few of his men. Tonight she sat on the bed in a brothel, a distinctly lower class one. She used her association with Skittles to track down this particular patron. John Burke struck her friend and then destroyed her reputation. Even though Nate assured her he would deal with the matter, Cara wanted to deliver a personal message to the reprobate.

She smoothed an edge of tape encasing her knuckles. Brick didn't want any tell-tale bruising to alert Nate later. She closed her fingers over the roll of pennies in her fist and then clenched and released to judge the weight in her grasp.

Her bodyguard stood in the corner, behind the door. Arms crossed over his chest and a scowl darkening his face. "You know the boss is not going to be happy when he learns about his little caper."

"Let me worry about him *after* this little caper." Although the bodyguard had good reason to be worried; Nate walked a line, controlling his over-protective urge when it came to Cara and it mollified him that she always had a shadow. For her part, Cara learned to either lose them like she did with Jackson or talked them into being accomplices in her escapades, like with Brick.

A red shawl covered the only light, washed the room in blood and disguised the stains on walls and floor. John Burke frequented the lower end of the spectrum of pleasure houses since being denied access to the bright lights and clean sheets of the demi-monde. Not just because of his proclivities, but simple economics. He didn't spend freely enough to purchase his place in a better class of establishment.

Laughter sounded in the hallway and the doorknob turned. Brick froze and became a blur melding into the random pattern of the wallpaper.

The door pushed open and a figure filled the space and then lurched to one side. "Damn whore, where are you?" the shape asked.

She rose from the bed and stepped forward. The red glow played over her form, putting her in shadow with the light source behind her.

The man moved closer. He pulled free his cravat and tossed it to the floor. "You can start on your knees." He gestured to a point in front of his shoes then reached down to pull out the tail of his shirt before undoing the buttons on his trousers.

Cara took another step forward. Close enough for him to see her in the gloom.

A frown crossed his face. "I know you." He squinted, memory trying to force its way to the surface through the alcohol sloshing around in his brain.

"Yes, we have met." She kept her hands behind her back.

"You," he muttered. "I suspected you spent a lot of time on your back. I could have protected Amy from your filth, but she chose to embrace your contagion instead."

"Contagion? Is that how you see free will or women thinking for themselves? Or were you talking about reading and scrapbooking?" She moved to one side, so his back remained to Brick, undistinguishable from the long shadows in the room.

He clenched his fists at his sides. "I can give you a much needed lesson in submission. Obviously Lyons doesn't know how to rein a woman in."

She gave a snort. "He has more power in the caress of one fingertip than you will ever understand."

He gave a short bark of laughter. "There's only one way to discipline a slattern like you." He cracked his knuckles and closed the distance between them.

"I'm not the one who needs to learn a lesson, John." Cara smiled. "You see, there's one big difference between Amy and me. I hit back." She swung fast and connected with his jaw. Pain shot up her hand and she bit her lip. Before he could regain his balance she struck out with her foot and introduced her new dock work boots to his face.

John Burke keeled over backwards and into the outstretched arms of Brick.

Wednesday 22nd January 1862

With Brick in tow they wandered to an ancient part of London where roads narrowed and carriages could not travel. Once they stepped off the main street they entered another world.

Goslett Yard lay deserted, as though long forgotten by pedestrians and abandoned after the Great Fire. Tall Tudor buildings crowded the rough brick path and held off the worst of the weather raging elsewhere. The little shop wore her battle scars with the great tragedy, blackened timbers scarred but not defeated. Thick glass windows with a smoky swirl obscured and distorted the interior.

"Do you want me to come in with you?" Brick asked.

"I'm perfectly safe." She patted the shoulder holster holding her custom Smith and Wesson. "But come in and browse, it will be far warmer inside than out." Light snow fell on the city and added to the sludge under foot.

Cara knew what she would find behind the thick door. She had stood in this spot before, on the trail of an artifact and needing an ancient book to aid her search. She pushed open the door and the little bell above gave a faint chime. Stopping inside, she drew a deep breath. Whenever she doubted her new role as a scholar she remembered this moment. Surrounded by the smell of books, beeswax, and lavender. Candlelight cast a warm glow over the quiet volumes.

There was something in the silence, aroma, and presence of the books that soothed an ache deep in her soul. A part of her she tried to satisfy with fighting and action but that only settled with the opposite, the written word and quiet reflection. Like her mind rebelled at the idea of being dominated and yet her body found release under Nate's control. At the thought of her husband a pulse came through their bond and warmed her toes.

She headed down the narrow aisle to the high counter at the end, past the soaring towers of thousands of tomes. Brick slipped in behind her and headed down a row, lost in his own exploration.

A range of ornate pots stood in a row on one edge of the desk. An electric lamp cast a sharp light on the workspace, chasing away the shadows thrown by the candles. A stack of hand cut pages lay ready to receive illuminated words from the idle peacock feather quill.

The ancient proprietor looked up from his work as Cara approached. The cataracts turned his eyes milky and ethereal, as though he saw not just her physical presence but her thoughts and emotions swirling around.

"You're back." He smiled. "Did you find *Magyck of the Gods*?" He continued their conversation of seven months ago as though only a few days had passed.

"Yes, I did, and it was most helpful. But now I am perplexed by *Suetonius' Secrets*."

"Ah." The smile deepened. "Very secretive man, Suetonius, he saw much but wrote little. Unless he was drunk, in which case I am led to believe his tongue ran away with him and he penned some very saucy tales."

"Well, I am after information he wrote, but someone saw fit to remove." Opening the satchel at her side she withdrew the valuable book. She lay it on the desk and revealed the fiery scene. In the changing light of the shop the flames flickered and shone and Cara swore she saw them wrap closer around the central figure and lick higher up his body.

"Someone has removed the pages about this particular artifact." A moment of doubt crossed her mind; with his degraded eyesight would he see the sliver of paper where the knife had sliced off the pages?

He let out a long sigh and shook his head. "Such desecration of an old friend."

"I was told you once copied this book."

"Oh yes, over ten years ago now. An overseas collector wanted this volume, but the countess would not budge. She does not willingly part with a book for just anyone. She did however kindly allow me to duplicate the text." He ran his fingers along the outside edges, reassuring the object that he meant no harm. "We have an understanding, she knew the book would not leave my hands."

Cara's hopes fell and slunk into a corner in her gut. *Ten years ago, he'll never remember what is missing.*

"Nero's Fiddle," he muttered, stroking a long nail down the cut-off paper peeking up from the spine.

"Is that what it's called?" Vague history lessons tumbled through her mind, one line standing out, Nero fiddled while Rome burned. "You remember what the picture is about?"

A smile crinkled the corners of his face like screwed up tissue paper. "I remember every word."

Hope sat up and begged for attention. "Could you tell me?"

He tapped the side of his head. "I'm not as spry as I used to be, give me a few days and I'll write it all down for you. Come back Monday."

She laid a hand over his. "You are a marvel."

He patted her hand and smiled like a benevolent grandparent. "Come back Monday and I will have the missing text for you."

She jumped up the counter to kiss his dry cheek. "Thank you."

"One thing, Lady Lyons. Nero's Fiddle is a dangerous artifact, fuelled by revenge and death. Do be cautious in your handling of it."

She squeezed his hand. "I have learned not to underestimate these objects. I promise I will be careful."

She knew she was in trouble the moment she stepped over the threshold of the Mayfair mansion. One of the henchmen stood in the middle of the entrance, blocking her way. He pointed at Nate's closed study door. "Gov wants a word with you."

She pushed in without knocking and closed the door behind her.

Nate looked up at the intrusion, a frown on his face. "What the hell were you thinking?" He rose and paced beside his desk, taking several short quick steps before he turned and wrapped his hands around the back of his chair. Holding himself in place. The coiled snake about to strike at a sudden move.

Ah. He found out about my little caper.

Cara rocked back on her heels and placed her hands behind her back. Damned man still had to learn she could take care of her own business. "Burke needed to be taught a lesson so I dealt with it."

Nate looked up and stilled. "I was going to deal with it when the time was right."

She balled her hands into fists. "Amy wasn't the only woman he used as a punching bag. His lesson needed to be delivered by a woman."

He rounded the desk and stalked toward her in long strides. He stopped before her and raised one arm with a jerk.

Suppressed instinct made Cara close her eyes and turn her head, even as a part of her knew a blow would never fall. Not from him. "Careful," she whispered.

Nate blew out a long breath. "God, Cara. You know I would cut off my own hand before I ever raised it against you."

"I know." She opened her eyes to meet his blue gaze. "But my demons sleep lightly. I don't want to disturb them."

"You're come so far," he whispered, his hand still poised mid-air. "You no longer flinch when someone touches you."

"You ground me, make me safe." She took his hand and guided it to her cheek as the burst of fear ebbed.

He drew his thumb over her skin. "I just wanted to make sure you are unhurt." He dropped his hands to her shoulders and down her arms to draw her hands to the front of her body. He ran a finger over the back of her red knuckles. One eyebrow arched at the bruise forming on her skin.

"Brick bound my hands and gave me a roll of pennies, but Burke's jaw was damned solid." Hits were somehow softer when they sparred.

He held his breath for a beat and then let it out. "If he had laid so much as a finger on you——"

She gave a snort. "Please, Brick would have torn his arms off. Isn't that why I have him?"

A slow smile spread over his face. "I can't stop you, but I prefer to know someone capable has your back. You made the newspaper by the way."

Releasing her hands, he moved to the desk and picked up the morning paper lying on the corner. He held it up so she could read the headline.

Prominent High Street banker becomes work of decoupage.

"Oh look, they even got a picture." She scanned the article that detailed the strange assault. How the unfortunate Sir John Burke was found beaten, naked, and covered in paper decorations. The accompanying photo showed him wrapped like a Christmas present.

"Are you taking up scrap booking?" Nate asked.

"He hit Amy for her so-called vacuous hobbies, so I thought it would send the appropriate message. We stripped him, covered him in scraps and left him outside his office so he wouldn't freeze. I did the roses, Brick added the bunny motif. He thought it gave the whole thing a touch of whimsy."

Nate dropped the paper, laughter replacing the worry on his face. "This is why you are my number two; you understand the value of tailoring a message to the situation. But next time, please talk to me."

Monday, 27th January 1862.

Nervous energy burned through Cara's veins as she tried to make it through the long days to Monday. Never good with inactivity, she tried to quell her unease by reading up on Nero, and when that didn't work she dragged Brick to the Pit for sparring practice. Brick stood like his namesake while she practised punches and kicks. Only the teeniest quiver of his lip betrayed that he found her efforts amusing as hell.

Nate offered a different sort of oblivion and only with sweat-slicked limbs could she drop into an exhausted sleep in his arms. The nightmares kept at bay by his presence.

By Monday morning she was like a kid with a second Christmas morning, all pent up excitement. Nate cut off her caffeine supply and told the kitchen not to brew any more until she returned and settled down. Keen to get moving and with feet unable to still even without her normal coffee fix, she made Brick trudge the entire way from Mayfair through the gathering snow.

"You grumble about physical activity as much as Jackson," she told her minder once they reached the rare book dealer.

"A stroll now and then is good for a man, but you're ruining the lines of my suit with all this bustling about. I think I should swap with Jackson, flicking through fabric swatches would be much more my style and he can chase you around the back alleys."

They pushed inside and Brick detoured off to browse gothic novels. Malachi conversed with another customer and Cara ran a light finger over spines as she waited. Her attention kept wandering to the unknown man; a faint hum buzzed over her skin and made the hairs on her arms raise under her wool coat.

He stood with his back to her at the high counter. A black velvet cloak enveloped a tall and lean figure. He appeared to be a shadow poured from above. The lilt of conversation rose and fell, but she couldn't recognise any words and her brain couldn't decide what language they used, she only knew it wasn't English but seemed much older. Then the man turned, his hood pulled low over his face. He paused when he reached her, as though on the brink of saying something when Brick stepped forward from between the rows. The stranger shook his head and he continued on his way. He didn't touch Cara as he passed, but a trail of damp air washed over her as though a wave broke on shore and doused a fine mist over her body. She shuddered and watched him disappear through the thick old door.

She rubbed her arms to dispel the chill and approached the high desk. The store owner wore a deep frown that only lifted when his opaque eyes rested on her form.

"Problem?" she asked, indicating with her head the closed door, the bell giving a last jingle.

"That one has many strange requests, most I am unable to satisfy." He gave a sigh.

She gave him a wide smile. "Did you have success with my issue?" She wondered at his mental faculties and hoped they worked far more efficiently than Helene's dodgy mechanics.

"There were two leaves removed, or four pages of text. I have rendered them for you as they would have been. If you like I can repair the book?" He reached under the desk and withdrew two sheets of thick handmade paper.

Cara picked up the pages, thick fibres grabbed the ink and gave the words an added dimension of depth. With hungry eyes she scanned the ornate calligraphy and uttered a moan.

White eyebrows snapped up and his head cocked to one side. "You are not happy with my penmanship?"

"No." She reached out and patted his arm. "It's beautiful. It's just that it's all in Latin."

"Of course, Suetonius wrote in Latin or occasionally Greek." He gave the benign grandparent smile.

By sheer strength of will she resisted the urge to burst into tears and wail how much she hated Latin. She sucked in her bottom lip, well aware she was about to have a tantrum, not unlike what happened as a child when her father insisted she attend her history and language classes.

This is God's revenge for all those times I climbed out the window.

"My Latin is a little rusty." She gave a weak smile, relieved to have the missing pages restored but aware that nights of translation lay ahead before she could offer anything of substance to Inspector Fraser. Unless she could enlist Amy, who loved ancient languages.

"Then I may be of further assistance." He slid another page across the counter. "I took the liberty of translating the text for you."

"You tease," she said, earning a deep chuckle from the elderly rapscallion. She reached out a hand for the English version of Suetonius' commentary about the ancient artifact.

He kept hold of the sheet. "I ask one favour."

Here comes the kicker. "Oh?"

"I am old and my eyesight fails me. Would you perhaps visit me when you are in London? If you could read the passages I am transcribing, I could help with your Latin in return."

Cara gave a soft laugh. "I would like that, I believe Latin is a skill life has decreed I must learn." It truly would not be a hardship for her. Peace washed through her soul in the old store surrounded by thousands of books. This was her church and her place of worship. The tingle at the base of her spine warned her that days were coming when she would need this sanctuary.

"We have a common interest in these dusty old volumes. I may be able to locate others that will aid your research." He passed the English text to her.

She leaned over the desk and dropped her tone to a stage whisper. "You're not flirting with me, are you?"

"Oh yes." The grin never left his face. "I'm not dead yet, you know. What do you say, my dear, want to find out about the vast experience that comes with my age?" He gave her a wink.

Cara kissed his cheek. "See if you can make me blush next time I visit." She tucked the pages into her satchel and headed up the aisle.

Brick stood by the door, trying hard to contain his laughter at the octogenarian who fancied his chances with the wife of the villainous viscount.

CHAPTER 18

London, Saturday 1st February, 1862

AS usual, Connor's heavy tread acted as a type of early detection alarm and announced his approach long before his body manoeuvred through the office door. Fraser looked up as the larger man danced from foot to foot. The collection of gadgets on his bandolier jangled back and forth and produced a musical accompaniment.

"Grab your coat. I've got packed lunches. We're heading off on a day trip." He rubbed his hands together at the thought of escaping grim London for the next several hours.

Fraser frowned. "Day trip?"

"You're wanted in Billericay." Connor rearranged his utility belt and checked his pockets for notebook and pencil.

"That's outside of London and beyond our jurisdiction." His mind raced and snatched at facts; the small town lay nearly thirty miles east of central London. What call would they have for a city Enforcer? The small towns maintained their own constabulary. Usually a couple of well-liked local lads kept petty crime under control.

"Special case, it's all been cleared with him upstairs. It might be beyond our reach, but they have a death beyond their ability."

The cold shiver swam down Fraser's spine. His brain sparked into overdrive. "Which is?"

Connor swallowed and his Adam's apple bobbed above his stiff blue collar. "Woman, lived alone, burned with not much left of her."

Fraser swore under his breath and stood so fast he banged the desk with his thigh and his mug of tea slopped over the side. He pulled out a handkerchief to mop up the stain spreading on a case file. "Another one?"

Connor nodded. "Doc is waiting downstairs, thought it made sense to grab him as well. He's rather excited about the field trip. Had me carting stuff back and forth loading up the carriage. I'm in charge of the scene when we get there."

Which explained the man's impatience to get going, the London sergeant would have the opportunity to direct his country counterparts and be the very large fish swimming in a tiny pond.

It was a tight fit in the Enforcer's steam carriage with four men and assorted equipment. It looked more like Doc intended to set up a field hospital than attend the death of one woman. From reports he barely needed a snuff box for the remains, not the several cartons stacked on the seats with their sharp corners pressing into Fraser's back.

On the slow trip out he wondered if they might not make it at all. Smoke from the small coal-fired engine kept swirled through gaps around the door and windows. He coughed into a handkerchief.

Doc slapped him on the back. "It won't kill you, Hamish, just line your lungs against the cold."

The photographic technician kept his nose buried in a novel and never uttered a word. Connor stuck his head out the window, watching the passing countryside and traffic like a keen dog out on a hunt. After thirty minutes of him lunging out the small space, Fraser halted the carriage and dispatched him to sit up front with the driver, freeing up much needed space inside. The man's enthusiasm was far too much to bear this early in the morning.

Or this sober.

The cobbled roads of London gave way to the earthen laneways of the country and they kept lumbering along their route. Eventually they came to a shuddering halt on a packed dirt road. Fraser stretched his arms up over his head, his body acting as though he had spent days in the cramped space, not two hours. He drew a deep breath of winter air and noted the temperature outside London was far warmer. The city lived under an arctic cloud that sent freezing air down to chill the citizens.

A man approached, his great coat plain but serviceable and a pork pie hat pulled low on his ears. Years of sun damage etched deep lines in his face and they nearly obscured his eyes. "Thomas Fowler." He held out a work-roughed hand to Fraser.

He shook the offered paw and waited for further explanation.

"I'm the local law," Thomas said. "In between working the mill."

"Ah. Well, thank you for securing the scene." He smiled, appreciating the effort. Always best to keep the locals on their side, particularly if they wanted a hot lunch from the local pub.

"I've never seen the likes before. Went and saw Lord Redfern. He read in the paper you had two cases in London, so his lordship said to bring it to you." The man removed his cap to scratch his head, as though thinking made it itch.

London might be a bustling cosmopolitan city but out in the countryside ties of fiefdom remained. Villages still held deep allegiance to their local lord and sought his governance and advice on all aspects of their lives.

The nineteenth century has yet to reach some parts of England.

"We will do everything we can to assist," Fraser murmured, taking in the small dwelling. "And will make a full report to Lord Redfern." Showing deference to their lord would keep the locals happy and the lines of communication open.

The simple cottage before him reflected a life simply led within its mud daub walls. The small garden slumbered through the remains of winter, unaware of approaching spring. The snow melted but green tips had yet to appear on any of the plants. Twisted twig fingers grasped at trouser legs as the men brushed past and crowded on the small threshold.

"I'll leave you to it then. Got to get back to work. Holler at George if you need anything." He gestured to a strapping lad standing beside the picket gate. "He'll keep the gawkers moving."

Fraser nodded his thanks. As he walked up the lime chip path he muttered under his breath, repeating the scant details Connor relayed on the journey. "Claudette Foreman, our youngest victim yet at just sixty-one years old."

He stepped into the small hall and he scanned the space before settling on the remains of the unfortunate woman. Connor remained silent and stared at a pastoral scene hanging on the wall.

Doc bumped into Fraser as he came to an abrupt halt when he caught the gruesome sight on the stairwell. "Good god. It's as though she were struck down while fleeing from God himself."

"Quite," Fraser murmured. Movement caught the corner of his eye as the doctor crossed himself and muttered a prayer for the poor woman's soul.

He moved closer and stopped at the bottom of the narrow stairs. Only Claudette's right hand remained, the fingers curled around a balustrade. The grip was so tight he suspected they would have to either cut the wooden railing or break the fingers to remove the limb. A silver ring glinted on her thumb, the shine untarnished by the enveloping scum. He tried to make out the design but failed from his position at the bottom of the stairs; he would have to wait until Doc finished his examination.

Nothing else escaped the conflagration. With each death the fire consumed more of the victim. At this rate, if there were a number four he doubted they would retrieve anything at all.

"Ain't right." Connor coughed into his hand. "This wasn't peaceful. That first one was still asleep and the second one never rose from her chair."

Fraser agreed; although the body was once again reduced to ash, the stark outline of this one suggested she fled her fate. Limbs outstretched, she raced up the stairs, to what? Was there something above she thought would save her? A bath tub perhaps? Why not run out the door and into the lingering snow? Claudette only made it halfway up before the flames consumed her. So many questions crammed into his brain, each demanding his full attention. Did she fall when the fire ate her legs and grip the railing to drag her torso away?

Pushing the rush of thoughts aside, he moved with slow, deliberate strides through the rest of the lower floor. There were only two rooms, a kitchen and a small parlour. Although items showed the wear of hard use, everything was neat and tidy. Gleaming copper pots stood in neat stacks on the kitchen shelf. The doilies on the back of the sofa were darned and mended but washed and pressed.

"It started in the parlour," he said over his shoulder.

Connor ghosted his inspection. "How do you know?"

Fraser raised one finger and pointed up. Connor's gaze followed the finger and his eyes widened on seeing the scorch mark in the white-washed ceiling. The angry black streak originated over the armchair and fled out the parlour door and across the hall before congealing above the mess on the stairs.

"Oh God." He swallowed several times. "She ran and it followed her."

"So much for the theory of a peaceful natural death. It appears Claudette fought tooth and nail against the flames consuming her body."

"Why up the stairs, why didn't she run outside?" Connor gestured to the front door. Through the open doorway they could see the small pond at the side of the path.

"An interesting question." Fraser focused on the top of the stairs. What was up there? Where was she going, when she took flight?

Returning to the foot of the stairs, he began issuing instructions to the few men assembled. He sent Connor back to their steam carriage for the photographic equipment and a tall wooden ladder.

With brute strength and a few guide ropes they managed to dangle the camera operator over the side of the stairs and hovering above the unfortunate. From his precarious swing, he opened the aperture. Everyone stayed frozen like statues, not wanting so much as a breath of wind to nudge his position and ruin the exposure.

Time moved at a snail's pace as photographs were taken and the plates carefully stowed for the trip back to Enforcers' Headquarters. Then they relinquished the scene to Doc. Working with small brush and shovel and a pair of tweezers, the medic removed all the fragments and ash into small containers. Boxes far too small to contain a long life well lived. One of the men sawed off the railing and then hand and balustrade were detached and laid in their own container.

After three hours Fraser was able to skirt the charred timbers, careful lest the stairs give way under his weight. He made his way up the narrow steps.

He paused on the small landing. With the doors and windows open, the sharp acrid smell dispersed and he drew a lungful of almost clean air. Body immobile, he allowed his mind to roam the space first. The second story held only one room that extended back over the parlour below. A bed with a handmade quilt in tones of red and green peeked through the open door.

A wooden shelf held a deep blue vase. The glaze smeared with soot. The bracts of pussy willow dusted with black. He visually swept the floor back and forth, to then fixate on a point only a hand's width in front of his feet.

A thin veil of soot covered the bare floorboards, except for two shapes at the top of the stair.

Someone stood here. That's why she ran this way. To stop the killer, or perhaps to plead for her life?

"What ya got?" Connor yelled from below.

"Footprints in the ash. Somebody stood here and watched her burn."

An oath drifted up the stairs.

A disturbance in the soot showed where the person turned and strode back through the bedroom and the open window. He went out the back instead of walking through the remains of his victim.

"Fetch the photographic equipment and operator, I want to capture this before the dust stirs and moves."

What sort of killer watched a woman burn to death? And why? Did she know him, was that why she ran up the stairs hoping to stop the celestial fire eating her body?

He muttered to himself, rattling off facts, trying to spark connections in his brain.

"This victim doesn't fit, Connor."

Connor glanced at the grimy smear on the ceiling, the outline singed into the wood of the stairs. "Looks the same to me."

"No." He shook his head. "Ignore the unpleasant method engaged and look at the larger facts. The other two worked for the old duchess, Claudette was a village midwife. She had no contact with life in London or the nobles. These deaths aren't random, but deliberate. What connection does our killer see that we are missing?"

The sergeant scratched the back of his neck, dreaming up motives outside his area of expertise. "Unless there is no connection, and he's just randomly killing people."

"No, they are connected. Otherwise why go to so much trouble to make them look natural?" He had to find the connection. Now he knew the deaths were not the result of fire wielded by a divine hand, but by a far more terrestrial one.

Motive was everything, uncover that and he would hunt down their pyromaniac.

CHAPTER 19

London, Tuesday 4th February 1862

NATE prowled the edges of the bedroom like a caged lion. Cara watched him pace across the expensive silken rug as she finished dressing.

"What has gotten into you? I haven't seen you this pent up since Victoria threw you in the Tower."

"I don't like it." He halted, his icy blue eyes focused on his wife. "I don't like him here, in my house."

"You forgot to add, breathing my air." She inserted the last clip in her short locks, to keep the longer pieces from falling into her face. She refused to let her hair grow out. She wouldn't do anything so conventional when she could horrify the *ton* by sporting a pixie cut. "I doubt Fraser feels any better about the situation, he is entering the lion's den."

"Keep Brick with you." His gaze burned.

"Yes, my lord." She fluttered her lashes, recognising he walked a line between wanting to protect her and giving her freedom. "Anything else?" She didn't understand the competitiveness between males and wondered if on this occasion he would pee in the corner of the parlour to mark his territory.

"Yes," he growled.

A delicious shiver washed over Cara and she parted her lips on a sigh. Nate stalked toward her and undid all her careful work in dressing.

Nate left to spend the day at the dock. The cold weather caused problems with the mechanism they used to operate the arms and unload the airships. But it was more than Fraser preying on his mind, he needed to settle on a course of action that would affect both their futures. She just hoped he didn't respond to the writ and appear in parliament, she doubted being forced to listen to fatuous politicians all day would improve his mood.

Nor did she want to host pointless afternoon teas for gossiping wives. Unless she could invite Helene and her crossbow, that would liven things up.

"I need to have an adult conversation with that man before he does something silly, like take up politics because he thinks I want him to go *that* legitimate," Cara muttered as other voices echoed in the marble entranceway. She settled on her favourite sofa as the parlour door opened.

With a scowl entrenched on his face, Brick showed the uniformed Enforcer and the dapper Inspector into the room. Connor was large, Brick larger still. Cara had no doubt he could handle the sergeant if need be, although he was developing a reluctance to wrinkle his new clothing. Or chip a nail. The ghost of Beau Brummel settled inside the hulking frame and made itself at home.

"Thank you for coming here, Hamish, I'm not overly fond of your office." She wouldn't step foot across his threshold again. Last time they had words he caused her to flee into the path of a maniacal killer.

"I understand," he murmured with his warm smile and inviting hazel eyes. His attention drifted around the parlour and beyond the open door.

"Nate is out." *And thankfully didn't pee anywhere.* She pulled a lilac chiffon scarf tighter around her neck. Nate, with his propensity for biting, left a clear mark for Hamish.

The smile never faltered as he passed his bowler hat to Connor and took out pencil and pad.

She indicated for him to sit on the opposite chaise. Perched on the end, she poured tea into delicate gold-rimmed cups. "I see the papers are full of the third death and speculation about the poor soul's life."

The reporters were gleeful in their views on another death by Divine Fire. Gossips dug hard to recollect any moral infractions the poor woman may have committed in her lifetime. No dirty laundry was safe as lives were laid bare to ascertain what line was crossed and required God to intervene.

Their personal priest at the top of the drive gathered acolytes who all urged the Lyons household to repent. Although Cara thought they just wanted ringside seats in case God did turn up to do some smiting.

"Yes, we have kept certain particulars out of the press. Like the fact this poor unfortunate tried to flee from her fate." He set the pad down on the arm of the chair, as though he were in no hurry to turn the visit into an interview.

"She ran?" Cara imagined a terror-stricken woman trying to outrun the flames licking at her body. A shudder ran through her hands and made the tea slop against the side of the porcelain.

He nodded and took the offered cup. "I doubt she ran from the Archangel Gabriel, probably a far more terrestrial killer." He dumped in three teaspoons of sugar before idly stirring the silver handle. His manner was casual, his shoulders relaxed, but his keen gaze never once wavered from her face. "I found your photograph intriguing."

She played with the handle of her cup, running a finger over the curve. "Your suspicion was correct. There is an artifact called Nero's Fiddle, an item of death used to kill a person's enemies."

He gave a non-committal noise and took a sip from his cup. A sigh of pleasure escaped his lips. "I so rarely get to enjoy a fine cup of tea. In my line of work they are often abandoned and grow cold. Please continue, Lady Lyons."

"Suetonius said that Nero became so enraged at those who spoke out against his authority as emperor that he sought out a mage. He had the man work dark magic over his lyre." She read Malachi's beautiful script and remembered the story attached to the fiery item. "Consumed by revenge, Nero had soldiers steal a hair from the head of each of his enemies and used the strands to string the instrument. He invited them to a feast and pulled out his lyre to play music while they ate. But the song he played was one full of anger and vengeance that caused his victims to smoulder and burn. With the last note their bodies were rendered to nothing but ash."

"Is that how Rome burned down?" Connor asked, speaking up from his position opposite Brick. The two men faced each other, casting glances to measure their opponent but listening to the history lesson. Brick already knew the full story, Cara had read it out to him on their way home while he steered her around other pedestrians.

"If you believe these myths, then yes." She extended a plate of shortbread to Hamish and he took one.

He dunked it in his tea and stared at the biscuit like he held a piece of treasure before nibbling the soaked edge.

He intrigued her, so genteel and inviting on the surface, yet he harboured a ruthless streak underneath. He was the polar opposite of Nate, who projected a cold exterior to the world but she saw the honour and molten heat held in tight control.

What fuels Hamish's anger? What set him on this path against Nate?

She made a mental note to do her own digging about Inspector Fraser and his history. She would find his motivator and then figure out a way for him and Nate to co-exist without one destroying the other. Regaining focus, she continued her story of the Roman emperor. "The burning bodies ignited other material which set off the great fire. And so we have the legend of Nero fiddling while Rome burned to the ground around him."

Fraser's keen mind jumped on the relevant fact that could be the clue to their current killer. "You say he took a hair from each victim?"

"A hair from the target is used as a string in the lyre. As the holder plays the hair will smoulder and slowly burn. When the hair is completely obliterated the victim will also be consumed." She took a sip from her cup, waiting for his next question. "The hair acts as a sort of trigger, telling the Divine Fire who to target."

"That may be how we find him. He would have needed an opportunity to obtain a hair from each victim." He scribbled notes on his pad, while still clutching his biscuit. Then he popped the entire morsel in his mouth so he could turn the page.

"Not unlike searching for a needle in a haystack," Cara said. "Three single hairs from three victims over a large area. Who knows when he may have taken them?"

His hazel eyes lit up as his mind sought to tread the same path as the killer. "These deaths are not random, our killer has a very particular reason in mind. Once we discern why these three individuals were targeted we will know who he is."

There was one thing about the fledgling arrangement that she needed to set straight. "Nero's Fiddle must be found, it cannot be allowed to fall into anyone else's hands. It is an item of death that yearns to be used. From my research, it induces a sort of mania in the holder, the more it is used the deeper it burrows into the mind."

The hazel depths of his eyes hardened and Cara could smell Fraser's cogs doing overtime.

"May I assume, given your new role, that you will be pursue the artifact while I locate the killer?"

Of course he would know. She nodded. "Her Majesty will want the object contained. Fear is spreading through the community. Almost every street corner holds a person calling for London to repent lest we are struck down as one by fiery wrath." Scared people lost their good judgement and did stupid things. The artifact needed to be found and the killer stopped, and spring needed to show up. "I'll work forward from Suetonius and see if I can trace the last owner."

"I do hope you know what you are doing," he murmured, tucking his notebook away in his jacket pocket.

"With Victoria? I do what I am commanded to do." Cara set down her empty tea cup.

He shook his head and waved his hand around to indicate the room. "I mean here. With Lyons."

She stiffened. "I'm an adult, I make my own decisions about people."

"Has he told you about St Giles? The men murdered, wives left with no husbands, children with no fathers." The smile never faltered, just like when he told her Nate was a cold-blooded killer of young women.

This is a man who would smile as he watched you burn. "Tell me, was more blood spilled that night than what those men had on their hands? I understand the death toll has dropped considerably in the Rookery and it is much safer now for women and children. Did you number the innocents killed by your so-called victims or how many they merely maimed?" A gappy-toothed smile sprang to the forefront of her mind.

The smile turned into a sneer. "Is that how he justifies it to you, as a humanitarian act? So many men slaughtered on his command. I don't even know the true number, do you?"

The barracuda broke through the handsome exterior, but he didn't rattle her. "Did the Enforcers investigate the murders of Angelique and Sarah Jackson?" Cara kept her composure, least she send a distress message to Nate. That would be all this interview needed, an enraged husband charging to her rescue. The two men circled each other, looking for an opening or a weakness to exploit. She'd be damned if she would provide the match to light that particular powder keg. "Did you know little Sarah was only eighteen months old when Saul Brandt ordered her throat slit?"

A twitch at his jaw. His fingers froze on his knee. "Their deaths were not considered significant enough to warrant a full investigation."

"Not considered significant? So you weighed the life of a mother and child and deemed them less worthy than the men who killed them." She discovered a deeper understanding of Nate's actions from the time she spent with the children of the Rookery. Far more than avenging the murdered family of a friend, he sought to make the lives better for hundreds of families. *And earned himself thousands of loyal men in the process.* She took a deep breath and fixed her sights on Fraser. What would the dapper man in front of her do to protect his own?

"You publicly went against your Superintendent to catch the Grinder. Many nobles thought he performed a needed duty, thinning the number of street girls. Tell me, Hamish, what was different about the murder of those prostitutes compared to Sarah and Angelique?" Her mouth moved faster than her brain and she didn't know what made her say the next few words. "Did you find release with one?"

The cup clattered to the table and Fraser jumped to his feet. "I think the time has come for me to leave."

Ah, hit a nerve. Must be on the right track. Cara followed him out to the entranceway, curious about the high profile case. He nearly ruined his career to catch the killer. The Enforcer hierarchy and *ton* were quite happy to see the trash swept off the streets and down the gutters. Fraser defied them all to bring the killer to justice. He turned into a one-man crusade to find the man responsible. Gut instinct flashed a cue card for her brain. *It was personal. He knew one of the girls. No, more than knew——loved.*

He took her hand and bowed, and then released her to don his coat. "I must warn you of one thing, Lady Lyons."

"Oh? What is that?"

His fingers played with the brim of his bowler. "One day the viscount will falter and stumble. I intend to be there to ensure he falls. I would hate to see you crushed in the process."

She thought of Nate's contingency plan and held out a hand to stop the inspector from leaving. "Tell me, Hamish, how many men wear the blue of the Enforcers?"

"There are just over five hundred men now, keeping the streets of London safe." He puffed out his chest and straightened his back as told her of their size.

She made a noise in her throat. "And how many men in St Giles Rookery?"

He frowned. "I believe there are several thousand."

She chewed her lip in thought. "If I were in your position, I would add some extra numbers to my side, before I made any move against Nate."

His eyes widened and Cara wasn't sure if she threw the man a much needed warning or if she just poured fuel on his campaign. Either way, he wished her a good day, and then stepped down to the drive, trailed by Connor.

Back in his office, Fraser pulled out the chair and sunk into the hard wooden frame. He placed his hands palm down on his desk and surveyed the chaos of files, reports, and photographs.

In the background of his mind he replayed his interview with Lady Lyons, like leaving a phonograph recording to run. He would pin the Rookery slaughter on Lyons, he just needed the evidence. He only needed a single witness to place him in the pub with the knife in his hand. Just one person who would come forward and say they saw him plunge the blade into the heart of his opponent.

He reached out and picked up a tiny brown envelope from his in tray. "That's new." The front bore the scrawl of Doc. *The item you asked about.*

Ripping open the glue on the flap, he tipped the packet into his palm. A silver signet ring fell out, worn from decades of use. Last seen on Claudette's thumb, on the hand that clutched the railing in her house. He twisted it between his thumb and finger. He knew the rough pattern, a family crest. Why would a country midwife have a ring bearing a noble crest? A man's signet ring at that, which would explain why she wore it on her thumb, the ring too large for one of her fingers.

The outline nagged at him, familiar yet not. A ring showing wear from years of handling and a secret that bound three individuals. Was the secret tied to the ring——a secret as old as the piece of jewellery?

Thoughts ricocheted in his head and a part of him knew the ring was the key.

He had only to turn the lock and the truth would tumble out.

CHAPTER 20

Nan & Nessy

Early summer, 1818

FAT languid bumblebees lumbered from flower to flower. Their droning filled the air alongside bird song and the distant tinkle of the fountain. Nan and Isabella escaped the summer heat by sitting in the shade of the orchard, overlooked by the ancient silver beech. The spreading limbs provided a green canopy to shade mother and child from the harsh sunlight.

Nan spread a woollen blanket under a tree and sat her daughter in the middle. Dimpled arms and legs stuck out from the fine lawn dress. Bright yellow ducks waddled across the front in a line of embroidery that mimicked the toddler's walk. The garment was a gift from one of the villagers. Nan failed at needlecraft, but the loyal women delighted in adding personal touches to the clothing for their beloved lord's daughter.

She watched Bella move with purpose toward a nearby fruit tree. She bypassed the late bloomers, awash with pink blossoms, and headed for the low hanging baubles of an early-fruiting apple tree. Pudgy fingers dug into the bark as she hauled herself up. Dark ringlets shook with the exertion as she peered upward, her eyes locked onto her target.

As a baby she rarely cried, her solemn eyes always open, watching those around her. She only fussed if she was trapped in the nursery, but settled once surrounded by the bustle of daily life. The chubby toddler changed day by day and would soon celebrate her second birthday. The world fascinated little Bella and she longed to explore and dart after whatever caught her fancy. Each day her footsteps grew steadier and already she started to run. *Running to her father.*

The past two years tested them all. It took three months for Nan to fully recover from the difficult labour. Long weeks where Nessy cared for her and Gideon fussed over his new pride and joy. Then one day Nessy slipped and told her there would be no more children.

An ache stabbed deep in her womb as she remembered not the gentle words that spilled from Nessy, but the underlying meaning that cut through her. Empty. Barren. Gideon would never tell his son of his exploits during the war. The estate with no heir except some distant second cousin they had never met. When Gideon no longer walked this earth, his women would be on the street. The spectre preyed on her mind, though he said it made no difference to him. That he would provide for his family, including Nessy, no matter what.

History repeated itself. Nan's father passed his meagre estate to her cousin just a few weeks after her debut. Two months before she turned eighteen her father informed her he was dying and his time on earth ran short. She plotted to find a match in one night to secure her future and succeeded beyond her dreams in Gideon. Her research told her the retired captain was a man of intelligence and purpose, but she never expected to fall in love with him during the course of one dance.

Then she lost that security by failing her one job as a noble broodmare, she delivered a girl. A much loved child who put the sparkle in her father's eye, but a girl nonetheless and unable to inherit the estate.

Nan smiled as she watched Bella. Frustrated grunts came from the child's small frame when she couldn't reach what she wanted. Today she targeted the apples on the low hanging branch. Her entire attention was focused on reaching the deep red fruit and solving the problem of the baubles hanging higher than her hand could grasp.

"You're in a hurry to grow up, little one. You'll be hiding up in the old beech soon enough." She cast a glance at the ancient tree, Gideon said he used to sit up amongst the branches and read as a boy. No doubt Bella would soon be clambering up its gnarled limbs with a book tucked under her arm.

Nessy appeared through the trees, a smile dominated her face. One hand held up her skirts as she raced through the long grass. "Nan, Nan," she called.

Bella turned her head at the approaching woman. "Nesssy!" she replied, her young tongue inserting one too many S's into her name. Then she returned to the task at hand and swiped her arm at the closest fruit.

Nessy picked the apple and held it out for the child. The coo turned into excited chatter as she took the offering in both chubby hands. She plonked herself down on her bottom and began gnawing at the sweet flesh.

Nessy sat on the grass next to her friend. "I have a message from Bill. He has asked me to go away with him." She clutched a scrap of paper to her breast, a faraway look on her face.

Nan caught her breath and stopped her instinct from blurting out the words of denial on her lips. "Go away with him? Surely you won't leave us for too long? Is it for a holiday?" She made light of the proposal.

A frown ruined Nessy's happy demeanour, the edges of her smile turned downward. "He wants me with him for more than a week or two. We need more than stolen moments; he asks that I be by his side, always." Fingers curled around the message and crumpled the words.

"But he cannot offer you what you really want, dear heart. You two cannot be together permanently. For some time his family has insisted he marry, it is why he set aside Dorothea." Cold dread settled in Nan's stomach. She never thought the May to December relationship with the much older man would go this far. Nessy had needed a distraction and gentle Bill proved a steadying influence in the wayward creature's life.

She would be shattered when her beau was forced to forge an alliance arranged by his relatives.

Bill often came to the estate to talk business and politics with Gideon and his gaze always settled on Nessy whenever she entered a room. In 1811 he set aside his mistress of twenty years and mother of ten children to make a noble match. Indeed he pursued many heiresses but had yet to succeed it reaching the altar with one. Nan thought the affair a way to bring two free hearts together for a short time. She watched the romance warm over winter and then bloom in spring. Now summer saw the heat intensify, with no signs the infatuation would fade.

"We love each other, his family cannot keep us apart." Nessy held the letter like a shield, to ward off the intentions of others.

Nan gave a heavy sigh. "We should never have introduced you two. I thought it would be a harmless flirtation, he is so much older than you." How to deflect her friend from her course without tearing her heart apart? The previous year Princess Charlotte died in childbirth and now the royal dukes raced to breed boys and secure the future of the line. "Would you not like an affair with a strapping young man? Have you seen Elijah, the new gardener? There's a man who knows how to trim a hedge."

"How can you think to throw another man at me when I love Bill?" She shoved the note into her apron pocket. The frown hardened on her face. "His age worries me as much as Gideon only having one arm concerns you."

Nan let the retort fly overhead and disappear amongst the clouds. Her friend meant no harm by her words. "I meant you have your whole life in front of you. Bill has never married in his fifty years, why do you think he will do so now?"

"Perhaps he has never found the right woman until now. We love each other and I have given myself to him completely!" Her eyes brightened with unshed tears. "Why can you not see we are meant to be together?"

Nobles rarely had the opportunity to love where their hearts would go. That she and Gideon loved so deeply was unusual amongst their set. "He belongs to his family, ultimately they will decide his course no matter how much he loves you."

Nessy tore up handfuls of grass and tossed them aside. "Am I to have nothing of my own? Am I to spend my life sitting at your feet like a dog, waiting for the tossed scraps?"

Nan reached out for Nessy, to lay a hand on her arm. "You are part of our lives, you know that. You are my soul sister, what is mine is yours. We have never treated you as anything other than a full member of this family."

"Bill wants me with him, to be his as he is mine." Nessy rose and fisted her hands deep in her skirts. "You're just jealous!" Her tone rose higher and higher just as the colour rose up her face.

A fist clenched around Nan's chest. How to stop her friend before she made a decision she would regret? The bright sun lit Nessy from behind, turning her blonde hair into a glowing angel. She looked like a divine figure crying for justice.

Nan stood, unable to stare into the sun or argue from her position on the ground. "No. I'm not jealous. Surely you must see this is doomed? There is no future for you down this path. You must either decline his offer or mayhap go for only a week or two. Make it clear to him this is a summer affair."

Tears streamed down her friend's face. "I love Bill and he loves me, we will be together forever. I am not your servant. You cannot dictate my actions. I will not stay here so you can lord your position over me."

Nan's heart broke for her friend. "Do not do this, Nessy, please," she whispered. "I have your best interests at heart." She reached out a hand, but Nessy stepped backward, beyond her grasp.

"You're jealous. My lover has two arms to hold me and I have a fertile field for his seed." She threw her barb, then turned and ran from the orchard.

Nan bit back her own tears, one hand dropped to her stomach. *She did not mean it*, she reassured herself, no matter how much the insult sliced through her. Behind her, Bella began crying, a high reedy keen.

The apple forgotten and dropped to the ground as the child sensed the distress between her two favourite people. Nan scooped her daughter into her arms and rocked her back and forth. "I'm so sorry, poppet. We cannot stop Nessy now. What will be, will be."

CHAPTER 21

London, Wednesday 5th February, 1862

BRICK donned tweed with a complimentary burnt orange waistcoat matched with a brown bowler. He called it his workingman's outfit. Cara called him high maintenance and wondered what sort of creature she unleashed by encouraging him to use her modiste. His confidence grew in leaps and bounds and he attracted admirers wherever they went despite winter's best efforts to keep everyone inside. His reputation grew and young bucks braved the snow and cold to stop him in the street and ask his opinion on fabrics and styles. He dispensed advice to the fashionably challenged and Cara suspected she would soon be shadowing him and keeping his fans at bay.

With the dapper bodyguard at her side, Cara climbed into the carriage. The mechanical horses pulled her to Belgravia while the cold outside tried to sink into her bones. She pulled the fur-edged throw over her knees and watched condensation form on the window. The felted shoes on the mechanical horses were replaced with spiked snow ones for pushing their way through the streets. They either pulled the carriage over snow or, where it melted due to high traffic, muddy sludge.

When they reached their destination she gave a sigh, pushed aside the blanket, and then stepped out into the frigid temperature. Looking up, she spied another pigeon that had given up on life in a weed-ridden box. The birds above the windows became skeletal eyebrows for the decaying house.

Brick held the door open and she crossed the threshold. The atmosphere in the dark entranceway was no warmer than outside. She hoped Helene was warm wherever she hid today. She made a mental note to talk to Jackson about heating the creaking structure, so they could at least free Helene from the stifling heat of her bedroom and allow her to roam the house in comfort.

Muffled scraping sounds came from under the stairs. Cara brushed aside the tails of her coat and crouched on the balls of her feet. Some creature had gnawed a large jagged hole in the timber. The broken newel post had moved from where she dropped it on a previous visit, the large acorn piece of wood dragged closer to the hole. It lay covered in marks and scratches like a well-loved chew toy.

"Minnow?" she called into the darkened cave, silently hoping it was the little dog. Otherwise it was an enormous rat. *I hate rats. Please don't be a rat.*

A small yip answered her.

"Come on, boy. What have you got?" Knowing the dog's primary food motivation she dipped a hand into her pocket and pulled out the strip of jerky. A trick learned from watching Jackson, who always kept treats about his person for the pug, despite his pretence that he was a stranger in the decrepit house. Cara knew he acted as Helene's canary, keeping her up to date on all the gossip.

She held the piece of dried meat at the entrance to the lair and waved it back and forth, all the while whispering to the dog and promising to remove whatever he was wearing today. Or perhaps Brick could offer the pug fashion advice? A wee waistcoat and cravat would suit him far better than any evening dress.

Sharp nails rapped on the floor boards and the black nose in the squished up face appeared followed by the stout body. Today, somehow, Minnow had managed to escape Helene's bedroom without his usual formal attire or taffeta dress. The dog held something clenched in his jaws.

"I'll do you a trade." Cara held a hand under the animal's head. "Drop whatever that is and you can have the dried beef."

Minnow cocked his head to the side as though considering the proposition. With a cough he dropped the slobbered object into her outstretched palm and took the treat. The curly tail wagged back and forth and he retreated to his hole like a dragon returning to his lair with a piece of gold.

She peered at the pink glob from one eye, the other screwed up. Her gut knew what lay in her hand, she just didn't want to recognise it or think too hard about what she held.

"Where will we find Helene today?" She listened to the old house, waiting for a creak or indication of a direction to follow. A bang came from along the hall.

Leaving Brick to impersonate a Grecian statue in a corner, she followed the noise. Light glinted on one of the metal prongs attached to the object she carried as she passed by a candle in a wall sconce. She shouldered the library door open, still holding Minnow's chew toy at arm's length.

"I found it," she called to Helene as she stepped into the welcoming oasis, the breath of fresh air amidst the foetid stench emanating from the rest of the house. It didn't matter how tight the madness held the countess, she still cared for her books. Helene lavished care and affection on her thousands of children, all tightly stacked in neat rows.

Helene gave a squeal and leapt up from her seat by the fire. She rushed to Cara and brushed her fingers over the extended palm.

Cara dropped her lashes, not wanting to see the open wound in her friend's face. A sigh pulled free from her lungs as the other woman turned, muttering and cooing over the artificial nose. She extracted a handkerchief from within the folds of her skirt and wiped Minnow drool from the hard surface. A click came as she realigned the metal clips with the short prongs embedded in the bone of her face.

Turning back she almost appeared normal, apart from the teeth marks in one side of the nose. And you had to ignore the wild, haunted look in her eyes that constantly drifted off to follow spectres her mind conjured.

"It's good to see you up and about, Helene." Concern for the woman's deteriorating health niggled at her, with only the elderly butler in residence to call for help if needed. Her mind skipped the veil of sanity more frequently and Cara often found herself coaxing the other woman back. How long before her mind chose to stay on the other side? She would not let the doctors throw her friend in Bedlam, wrapped in a strait-jacket and left to dash her head against a brick wall. Perhaps the time had come to talk to Nate about the available options to care for Helene when her mind finally slid away from them.

"I sleep now. Thank you for silencing Henry." She patted Cara's arm. "Screaming in the night tears my soul apart, but silence helps it mend."

A lump formed in Cara's throat. Her own nightmares were greatly reduced with Nate to soothe her screaming. Only rarely did the monsters sneak up on her now, they were too afraid to battle the villainous viscount for control of her slumbering mind. She was glad to give Helene a similar sense of peace.

"I need to talk to you about a book." She took Helene's hands and guided her back to the fireside.

"Books, books, so much knowledge and power contained in words." The milky film descended over her eyes as her mind chased shadows conjured by the disease eating her brain.

"It's about *Suetonius' Secrets*. Do you remember? You gave it to me for my birthday." Cara kept her voice low and gentle. Some days, talking to Helene was like working with a skittish horse and sudden movement or a harsh tone might spook her and send her running. Like a wraith she haunted the house, wandering the dark halls with her torn clothing tangling around her legs. Too many times Cara visited but could not find any trace of her friend. She suspected the old building contained hidden bolt holes. Either that, or more than Helene's *mind* could slip the veil to the other side; could she journey there herself?

The phantom wisp brought her focus back to Cara. "Suetonius. Naughty man, he kept so many secrets to himself and wrote about so few." She raised a finger to her lips as though she held back a secret about the long dead Roman.

Cara tried to lever the crazy train back onto the rails. "Yes, but this secret he did write about, but then someone stole his words."

Helene's eyes widened and she fixed a look on Cara. "Really? I knew it. I suspect Henry is behind this, whispering in somebody's ear. That's what he does you know, starts trouble, never happy with what he has and always wanting more. He is trying to reach our world you know, he would grasp us in his hands." She tapped a finger to her chin.

Cara tried to ignore the comment about Henry. Firstly, she wasn't up to questioning a painting about its involvement. Secondly, she just didn't want to contemplate a painting trying to take over, she had enough problems already. "Suetonius wrote about Nero's Fiddle, but someone took the text from the book. Malachi said the volume was intact when he copied it. So it happened after that. Do you remember who had the book after him? Did anybody else ask you to see it?" Cara held her breath; relying on Helene's memory was a dodgy proposition, rather like standing in the dark at the top of a step stairway and waiting on a bolt of lightning to illuminate the way down.

A smile broke across her face. "Oh yes." She clapped her hands together as memories flooded into her mind and enlivened her eyes. "The prince heard I held *Suetonius' Secrets* and asked to borrow it."

"The prince? As in Albert?"

Helene patted her hand. "Yes, dear, Albert. He is very interested in the occult you know. We often share a brandy and discuss such matters." A frown creased her brows. "He hasn't been to visit for some time, quite remiss of him."

Frustration welled in her chest. A dead end. Literally, unless she cracked out a Ouija board.

"You are on the hunt again."

A hand on her arm brought Cara back from Tower Green and the night she watched Prince Albert's life force drawn skyward by Hatshepsut's Collar.

"Yes, I thought there might be a clue in whoever cut the pages out, but I can't ask Albert, he is—" Cara struggled for the right word, unsure if the consort's death had registered with Helene, "—indisposed."

"Ah, that will be why he hasn't visited for nearly a month."

A month? Cara's mind hurtled down another track. Albert died nearly four months ago. Was Helene losing her sense of time, or was an incorporeal Albert paying visits to Belgravia? Did her gypsy blood really enable her to pierce the shadow of death and converse with the deceased? Could Helene tell the difference anyway between flesh and blood visitors or ghostly ones? Shaking her head, she reeled her brain to focus on the immediate task. "I need to try and track down who might possess Nero's Fiddle."

A deep frown crossed her face and Helene sighed before speaking again. "Ask Nate to take you to visit the Curator."

"The curator? Like at the museum? Was the artifact held on public display somewhere?" Talking to this woman was like getting lost in a maze. Every turn led somewhere unexpected and sometimes you were trapped for hours trying to retrace your steps. She wondered if crazy was contagious because she definitely felt it rubbing off on her.

The smile faded and her eyes focused on a point high up the wall. "A museum of sorts, much like yours. He started your father on his path and later they became rivals. Objects of power will always attract collectors and the Curator always knows who holds them." Her words drifted in and out as she scanned the room, as though her mind had to pull each one from the aether surrounding them.

Cara frowned. *A rival?* She never delved into why her father collected the things; she only knew he valued them more than he valued her. Thinking too much about his engrossing hobby caused her heart to constrict and shatter at the depth of his betrayal.

"Careful though, lest he adds you to his collection. You are special." She tapped a finger on Cara's chest, over the faint scar. Helene's words were another turn in the maze to puzzle over later.

The only thing special about me is how many people seem to want to put holes in me.

"Do you think this Curator will know who has Nero's Fiddle?"

"Fiddle?" The veil descended, the sharp intellect retreated to be replaced by childlike wonder. "Oh I do like music, it has been so long since I danced." She picked up her skirts and started to spin round and around. In a melodious tone she sung a folk song, fast and furious like her turns.

And that's all the information I'm getting today.

With the other woman lost in her own world, Cara slipped through the door.

London, Wednesday 5th February, 1862

CARA stared into the flames dancing in the bedroom fireplace as her mind chased flickers and shadows cast by Nero's Fiddle. *Fire, so beautiful and so deadly. The heat caresses, but the flame consumes.*

Nate picked her feet up, sat on the sofa next to her and pulled her legs over his lap. One hand reached out to caress her nape with lazy strokes. "You look a million miles away. Worried about Helene again?"

She flicked him a smile. "One of many names running through my mind, I am accumulating quite a list."

His touch eased some of the tension from her body as he waited for her to continue.

"What do you know about the Curator?"

His hand stilled and his head shot up. A long moment passed and then the slow caress over her skin continued. "I swear Helene would have made a formidable spy mistress, she hears everything without ever leaving Belgravia."

Thoughts jumbled in her mind, one in particular opened an old wound. "She said the Curator would know who holds Nero's Fiddle and that he started my father on his path." She chewed her lip; the mention of her father sent ghosts skittering into the dark corners of her soul. Her demons raised their heads and sent a warning tremble through her body. Was he her true father? Did it make his betrayal easier to bear if he wasn't?

A shadow passed behind Nate's eyes and he ran a hand over his chin. "If your investigation is heading in his direction then we need to tread carefully."

"Why? Who is he?" She settled on his knee and tucked her head on his shoulder. He wrapped his arms about her. Even though the child in her wanted to run and hide, the woman needed touch to fight the woken fear. The slow beat passed through both their bodies and lulled her nerves, like the *whoosh* of the ocean against rocks. His presence centred her and gave her a place to shelter from the past.

"He's an old noble from Eastern Europe with deep pockets and eclectic tastes. He once asked me to acquire something for him and I declined." He measured his words but didn't withhold information from her, not anymore.

"Did he not offer enough money?" she teased.

"He offered a substantial sum, but my gut told me never to be in his employ. It's difficult to explain, I think you will understand when you meet him."

The name alone sent shivers racing along her skin and pulled at some long dormant memory. "What did Helene mean about my father?"

"I don't know, but we can find out if that is what you want to do." His thumb drew patterns against her neck. "We should be prepared though, you need to have something to offer the Curator."

Cara frowned. "Offer?"

"He won't part with information, he will expect something in return." Carefully chosen words again.

"Something that will appeal to a curator?" *What will he expect? Me?* She remembered Helene's warning to watch he didn't add her to his collection.

"Exactly."

She mulled over the available options and what she could sneak away from their growing collection slumbering deep in the earth. What could they risk being set free? The more she knew about the strange artifacts they gathered, the less she wanted any of them to ever see the light of day. Even the most innocent object could be used against others. Like Boudicca's Cuff, which gave luck in battle to the holder. Its owner was using his charmed luck to financially destroy his opponents. Nate's legitimate attempts to recapture the item he sold had failed. He now plotted to steal the thing back.

"I'll send a message to the Curator and ask for an interview," he said.

She blew out a deep sigh. How did her life come to this point? In the queen's employ searching out otherworldly items of power with the dark viscount at her side? Once she ran to escape, seeking freedom. Now her world was wrapped in bonds she would never break, or ever want to. The more she learned, the more questions she unearthed.

"I need to go see Nan first. There's a chunk of my life missing and it's time to fill in the missing pieces. Is Loki back from France?"

Nate gave a bark of laughter. "We no longer need Loki, plus he muttered something about not being a Hanson cab. We have signed the papers giving him twenty percent of Lyons Cargo and he is busy fussing over his new charge. He is trying to decide on a name for the new long range airship."

"I wonder what the Maori will make of him." She had no doubt the pirate would get up to trouble on the other side of the world, she only hoped he didn't end up as a shrunken head on the end of a spike. She pushed thoughts of Loki aside and concentrated on another pirate as she slid her body over Nate's.

London, Thursday 6th February, 1862

Cara stood on the rear terrace and eyed the object tethered like an enthusiastic dog, bouncing up and down. Four of the men held ropes trying to pacify the tiny ship and make her steady.

She glanced back to her husband. He possessed the skill of a magician, pulling strange contraptions from thin air. Or metal fish from the depths of the Thames. Somehow Nate had acquired a shrunken baby airship. The main compartment was equivalent in size to the body of a carriage with the air bladder rising above.

"What is it?" she asked. "It looks like a landau got amorous with a child's balloon."

The schoolboy grin dominated his face. "Personal airship for short trips. I thought it would be handy for going to see your grandmother and heading to and from Lowestoft."

He took her hand and drew her closer. His crew strained to keep the frisky balloon under control. Brick opened the door in the side and a set of stairs descended with a hiss.

She peered into the darkened interior. Much like a carriage the operator sat up front in his own glass bubble, controls arrayed around two dark leather seats. The engine sat under the body and the burnished propeller attached to the rear. A copper mesh harness attached the air bladder to the main unit. As death traps went it was quite pretty.

Cara raised an eyebrow. "You have got to be jesting. We'll be shot out of the air by a peashooter." Grumbling, she moved closer.

"Where's your sense of adventure?" His smile never budged as she inspected his floating toy.

"I have discovered from living with you that a sense of adventure usually means someone is going to try and kill us." She picked up the corner of her skirt and placed a foot on the bottom step. "This better be peashooter proof." The little dirigible lurched and shifted under her weight.

Brick took a seat next to the operator and gave Cara a thumb's up signal as he pulled their dome down and fastened it.

Men. Always enthusiastic to try new ways to kill themselves.

With a sigh, she climbed the steps. The interior was comparable in size to a luxurious lavatory. A built-in bench seat ran down one side with numerous cushions in a rich green and silver. A tiny table with two chairs attached to the floor occupied one corner. The other corner had drawers and cupboards that drew Cara's eye and hand. Cracking one open she found a well-stocked larder, another held glasses, plates, and cutlery. A drawer revealed folded cashmere blankets, waiting to warm a knee.

Nate climbed in and closed the door. "You might want to sit down before we take off. She gains height rather quickly."

Remembering the sudden jerk from the Hellcat, she plonked herself down and grabbed the handle over the window for good measure. Nate took a seat next to her and hooked his hand through another wall-mounted handle.

The driver started the motor and a vibration rose through the floor of the compartment. Nate gave a signal to the ground crew, who released the lines. Cara's stomach dropped to her ankles as the little ship shot high into the air before equalising. The noise diminished as she got underway and with her nose turned to Leicester, they started their journey northward.

They flew lower than the Hellcat, skimming roads and fields and Cara spent most of the trip with her nose pressed to the window, watching the world pass below. She saw upturned faces, and children raced their shadow as they moved up country. Snow-laden fields gave way to greener pastures as they escaped the wintery angel that had taken up residence over London.

It seemed no time at all before she recognised the village and they flew over her family's fields to the ancestral home of the Earl of Morton. While the small vessel hovered a few feet from the ground, Nate and Brick jumped. They grabbed a guide line each and with help from a couple of gardeners, they anchored the ship to large beams Nan had installed around the lawn.

Cara bounced off the bottom step and ran to her grandmother.

"What a lovely surprise," Nan said wrapping Cara in a hug. "Nessy will be disappointed your pirate captain isn't here."

Cara laughed. Nessy eyed up Loki like he was the last chocolate biscuit on the plate and she was ravenous. For once the pirate met a woman with an appetite larger than his. *What a pair they would have made if Nessy was thirty years younger.*

"Speaking of Nessy, where is she?" The two women were seldom apart.

The smile fled from Nan's face. "Funeral of a dear friend. She will be back tonight."

They entered the parlour and Nan pushed Nate in the direction of the substantial drinks cabinet. "Be a good boy and pour a few rounds to warm us up."

"It's only lunch time," Cara said as she settled on her favourite orange paisley sofa. Her tom cat was camouflaged amongst the swirling pattern of tangerine and brown. With monumental effort he heaved himself over to her lap and raised his head to be scratched.

Nan took the opposite sofa. "I was going to suggest tea, but you have the look, so I think something stronger is in order."

Cara buried her hand in the cat's luxuriant fur. "What do you mean *the look?*"

Nan waved in her general direction. "That one which means you've either escaped out a window again or you have unpleasant news to discuss. Since your husband is with you I assume it's not the former."

She resisted the urge to chew her bottom lip. Nan was right, she did have something unpleasant to discuss. The past. Her past.

Nate handed her a glass of wine. "I'll leave you two to talk before you start lobbing live mortars at your gran." He brushed his knuckles down her cheek and then left.

Cara sniffed the floral aromas circling in her glass before taking a sip. "You never talk about my parents."

The older woman froze, her spine turned to steel. "Of course I do, I talk about them all the time." The words came out clipped. She raised the glass to her face and took a large gulp.

Cara twisted her fingers around the crystal stem. "No, you don't. You talk about my mother as a girl and if you mention my father at all, it is after she died. You never talk about them together, as a couple. Why not?"

Long moments passed, with the tick of the clock a heartbeat pounding out the seconds. Both women sought fortification in the bottom of their glasses.

A shudder ran through Nan's frame and when she turned to face Cara, unshed tears shone in her eyes. "Because it's too hard, to think how they once were."

Cara's mouth dried out, her tongue stranded in a desert. "You always refer to him as *that man*. What did she see in him? If he was so terrible why did you let her marry him? Was it arranged, did he force her?" The words tumbled out, given life by her frantic thoughts. She cast glances at her grandmother's face, waiting for validation of her hidden fear, that Lucas Devon was not her father, that her mother found escape in another's arms.

A tremor shook Nan's hands and the wine sloshed like a rough sea. "Oh child, it wasn't like that at all. Never like that." She took another large drink before placing the delicate goblet on the end table. "God, how he loved Bella. And for her the world revolved around him."

Cara drew a deep breath. Her mother loved Lucas, so he was her father and yet sold her like a broken toy.

"I am so sorry that you never knew the man he was, only the man he became." One deep breath followed another before she began to speak. "The Edington women have always been rather forthright and vocal. I believe the Americans would describe us as smart and sassy. We inspire a passion in our men that steals our breath, but I'm sure I don't need to tell you that."

Cara directed a thought at her internal bond and felt Nate's constant caress deep inside.

"Your mother was always too bright for her own good and your father was the only man who could match wits with her. The summer she turned sixteen, a young man arrived on the doorstep. At twenty-five he was the shining light in the foreign office with a brilliant diplomatic career taking off. He came bearing important dispatches for Gideon. Once he laid eyes on your mother that was that." She took another large swallow of wine. "He loved her so fiercely it was hard to look at them together. He burned for her." Her voice trailed away and her eyes lost focus, reminding Cara of when Helene's mind chased ghosts.

An ache started in Cara's chest and spread through her limbs. *He burned for her.* Her father had loved her mother. "Did she love him?"

Nan chuckled. "Lucas asked Gideon for her hand and agreed to wait until she turned eighteen and had her debut in London. Bella would have none of it. They eloped the summer she turned seventeen, at her insistence. She loved Lucas with single-minded determination and would brook no objection to them being together."

Fierce love ran in their family, the woman each knew what they wanted and set out to seize it. "If he was my father, why didn't he love me?" Cara asked, her voice a bare whisper, an echo of the small child inside who lost so much. The child whose father rejected her and left her to a cruel fate to fuel his own lust for an artifact.

"Oh, darling, it was never your fault." Nan moved sofas, stretched an arm around Cara and then pulled her into a warm embrace. "When your mother died, something inside your father broke. You were such a gorgeous and precocious child, Gideon and I hoped you would fix him."

Moisture welled up in her eyes and threatened to spill down her cheeks.

"We thought you would remind Lucas of her and give him something to live for, but his soul withered without Bella."

Cara shook her head. "He never loved me, he gave me away, Nan. I thought he might not have been my father, which was why he let

Clayton have me." How could a parent give away a child? Had she been so horrid?

Tears rolled down her face as Nan rocked her. "You reminded him too much of her and all he lost. We should have removed you earlier and I can never make that up to you. It destroyed Gideon that he could not save you. He was too sick, we had to hold him down to stop him trying to travel to London and kill Clayton himself. I lost him and you that week."

She never attended her grandfather's funeral, confined to her bed for long weeks while her injuries healed. Another death to add to her tally. The sobs could no longer be contained. "I killed my mother and my grandfather. You must hate me." Tears rolled and blurred her vision.

Nan held her tight. "You give me purpose. You are not to blame for God taking those we love too early."

The parlour door opened and Nate strode in, pulled by Cara's distress. He sat on the sofa and took her from Nan. Drawing her into his arms, he let her grief soak his shirt.

Nan let her cry out the pain for several minutes before she spoke again. Her words were not directed at Cara, but at the ghosts still clinging to their world. "Lucas became obsessed with getting your mother back."

The words filtered through Cara's brain. "Back? But she was dead!"

"He studied languages and ancient cultures at Oxford. When he left the Foreign Service and took up his position as a scholar he sprouted a particular interest in mysterious artifacts. He believed there was a way to return Bella to him. For three years he kept her body in the basement of your house before we managed to remove our poor child and inter her in the family crypt."

Cara curled into Nate, needing the anchor of his touch. "Three years, three years," she muttered, the time period significant but facts slow to trickle to her mind past the newly opened wound. She pulled her thoughts out of the mire. "His diaries, I only have them starting 1844, but he was always scribbling. He must have earlier ones, hidden somewhere."

Nan rose and crossed to her davenport standing by the window. She pressed the centre of a carved flower and released a hidden catch. The side panel popped open and she withdrew a bundle of diaries. "I have them from 1839, the year before you were born, through to 1844. He tucked the completed books in with Bella."

Curiosity fought the pain and won. She wiped her eyes with the back of her hand. "Did Bella keep a diary?" One last strand of hope to know her mother.

Nan shook her head. "That child was too busy living to write about it." She handed over the slender volumes to Nate.

Cara stared at the notebooks. Within, the history of her parents beckoned, and perhaps clues about the Curator that might help in their forthcoming meeting. She reached out a hand to touch the bundle.

"He became involved in something dark, Cara. His obsession with reviving your mother turned into something twisted which consumed what little remained of his soul. Please be careful, I'll not lose you down the same path." Nan stroked her hair away from her forehead, before pressing a kiss to her skin.

"I'll stay with you," Nate said, passing her the diaries.

"No, I need to take this journey alone." She laid her hand over his. "But coffee would be appreciated, it's going to be a long night."

All afternoon and long into the night Cara read her father's diaries. She learned that, tired of the constant overseas travel and separation from his beloved Isabella, Lord Devon resigned his diplomatic post and took up a position with the British Museum in London. His diaries narrated the passion of a new life when her parents moved into the Soho house and every day contained a multitude of blessings.

Next came the hope and joy on learning Bella was expecting after six years of marriage. The fear that consumed him after losing three previous children to miscarriages and the risks to Bella's health. Her father wrote with awe about how he laid his hands on his wife's stomach and felt the child press into his hand for the first time. Their hope soared that this child would live to make their world complete.

His work at the museum diverted his mind and worries. There he came into contact with a wealthy benefactor who sought his assistance in translating old texts. The Curator took Lucas under his wing. That work turned his scholarly interests in the ancient world into a different pursuit.

20 December 1840 and Lucas wrote of Bella's water breaking and their excitement to finally meet their child. Cara knew this part of the story. Her mother never emerged from the birthing room. Nothing but blank pages followed that entry. Ink-smeared blotches where her father's tears fell, words unable to describe his grief. He simply wrote the date. Page after page of damp, distorted dates. Tears streamed down her cheeks and dried. She picked up the next book and flicked through. When the words started again, they showed the man's broken heart had deteriorated into darkness. He transformed into the cold void Cara knew.

Without Bella, he first lost his light, then his world, and ultimately his way.

Leicester, Friday 7th February, 1862

The morning sunlight crept into the room and illuminated the bed. Woken by the increasing light, Nate stirred next to her. Cara watched as he opened his eyes and fixated on the weight holding him immobile. The furry ginger shape reclined on his chest. Passing over the cat, he reached out a hand and brushed a shadow under her eyes. "You've read all night."

She took hold of his hand and gave him a faint smile. "I snuck in, but you were fast asleep so I carried on. Your snoring would have kept me awake anyway."

He gave a sleepy half frown. "I do not snore."

"Do so. Even the cat thinks so." She stroked the tom asleep on Nate's chest.

The cat had his back to Nate and faced his feet. The feline managed to simultaneously deny Nate's existence while sucking up the warmth from his body.

"Damned cat. I thought I was being long-lined off the Aurora with the pressure on my chest." He pushed the animal to one side to sit up. He drew her hand to him and nibbled her fingertips. "Do you want to talk about it?"

"No," the word rasped from her throat. "It's too hard. He spilled his love for her over hundreds of pages and thousands of words, but never had a single one for me." A sob swelled in her chest and she closed her eyes against rising tears. The pain was so raw, like she lost them both all over again.

Nate pulled her into his arms. "You are loved," he whispered against her hair. "Never doubt that for a moment." Between them no more words were necessary. His love enveloped her and became the sword that speared the demons clawing at her mind.

Her world steadied on its axis and she drew a deep breath. She could retell the relevant parts, where it intersected with the Curator. The rest needed to be shut away, the pain needed to mellow and dull before she could face the full story. Nan was right, far too much to bear to see the man Lucas was, not the monster he became.

"During his work at the museum, my father encountered stories and legends about artifacts. After Bella died, one story consumed him. The legend centred on a phoenix feather."

The cat glared at Nate and tried to climb back on his chest, hampered by the fact this particular mountain was now sitting up. Nate kept pushing the cat down but the determined feline kept marching back up the bed. Cara picked him up and deposited him by her side before the two males came to blows.

"Legends said if you placed the phoenix feather in the hands of a deceased person and then cremated the body with dragon's breath they would be reborn from the ashes. He wanted to bring her back, that's why he kept her body. There was a way to give her back her life. He just needed to find the feather and a dragon."

Nate blew out a soft whistle. "He sought two mythical creatures. Only a handful of people know that dragons are real, and even less know where to find a living one. As for a phoenix, I suspect they are rarer still."

The ghost of a smile touched her lips. "Notice neither of us has said there's no such thing as a phoenix."

She annoyed the cat and rolled onto her stomach and propped her hands under her chin. "The Curator used my father to translate old texts and to acquire various artifacts. In return he promised to tell him where to find the feather and a dragon. The diaries ramble after a certain point, but it seems they had a falling out in 1844 and Father left his employ. Lucas was desperate to bring Bella back but came to believe the Curator was toying with him and withholding the information. He suspected the Curator wanted something more from him, something he could not give. I wonder what?"

"We may find out. He has answered my message and said we may call on him this evening."

CHAPTER 23

London, Saturday 8th February, 1862

THE snow piled up on the ground, froze over and still more snow fell. People whispered that God would withhold spring after the unnatural events of October and the queen's heavy mourning for Albert. They spoke that sinners would be picked off by Divine Fire as your name appeared on his list. The churches were packed to capacity with people eager to confess and the Enforcers faced a similar line of petty criminals looking to go straight before they burned. Mutterings on street corners turned to louder voices wondering what England had done to warrant His wrath. Was it connected to their queen and the unholy storm she unleashed last year? Was God sending a message that she was not their true queen?

The newspapers ran headlines about haemophilia and how Leopold's illness was proof something was not right in the House of Hanover. Politicians met in secret and more dispatches appeared in the red box in Nate's study.

The mechanical horses' studded shoes rang out when they hit the cobbles through the dense covering sludge. They pulled the carriage over Blackfriar's Bridge. Cara looked out the window over the Thames, now turned into another highway. The ice grew thicker each day and people could skate on the river. Some braved the cold to dance like winter sprites over the frozen tableau. Lights reflected from overhead airships, lit the scene and charged the air with magic. The other side of the bridge was marred by an open pit, another access site for the underground train line; men and machines laboured to dig under the Thames and connect the ring route.

They hit Southwark, trotted down Upper Ground Street and halted outside what appeared to be a two-storey industrial estate. Shunned by its closest neighbours, the building stood alone. A private jetty brought the Thames into the backyard, although now it gave the owner a private skating rink rather than boat access.

Cara stared up at the brooding visage. With no ground level windows, only the faintest light flickered in arrow slits high in the structure. "It looks like an abandoned factory. Did he employ the same architect your family hired?"

"Wench," Nate breathed hotly in her ear. "You'll understand the exterior when you see the interior." Taking her hand, he tucked her fingers into the crook of his elbow and they walked up the path. Someone had swept the snow to the sides and their way lay clear to the imposing iron door.

A young butler opened the door as they approached. "The master is expecting you," he said in a monotone. A grey flush to his skin combined with his tone gave him all the life and personality of a deactivated automaton.

Cara wondered if he were real or artificial. She veered toward him, thinking a quick poke would tell her man or metal, but Nate kept tight hold of her arm and pulled her back on track.

She stepped into the entranceway; it was stark, beautiful, and cold like the grave. Tones of grey on grey, from the slate on the floor to the washed silk hung on the walls over exposed stone. A cathedral ceiling soared over their heads. Enormous arched timbers formed the doorways to other rooms off the main hall. She wanted to run back down the path, stare at the exterior and then come back inside again.

"It's a castle," she said.

"Yes." Nate took her fur-trimmed cloak and handed it to the butler.

"Disguised as factory." Her brain kicked into action. Why not just build a castle? Why disguise a castle as something mundane and pedestrian? Only one answer leapt at her, the owner wanted a castle but not any attention.

There was no modern electric lighting here. The chandelier above their heads held aloft at least a hundred candles. Even their tiny flames faded from soft yellow to a dull and dirty white as they were consumed by the monochromatic colour scheme. Goosebumps rose over her arms and she rubbed to dispel them. "He could do with the heating ducts you and Jackson devised," she said.

A hum buzzed over her skin and raised the hairs on her arms and neck. More than the cold, it was her body's reaction to an artifact. A big one, something house-sized. She glanced at Nate.

He slipped his arm around her waist. "We're not here to discuss plumbing, remember? Keep your wits about you."

"This way." The butler gestured for them to follow. He strode across the floor and pushed open a double set of high-gloss black doors and then indicated for them to enter. He remained bowed, as though his battery pack ran empty.

Cara desperately wanted to touch him as she passed, but she missed her opportunity with Nate controlling her direction, and she didn't want to make a scene by pulling loose to investigate the domestics.

Within the next room, expensive Persian rugs softened polished marble floors. The same tones of grey dominated, from the palest of white to near black. The interior reeked of simplicity and money and yet a chill took up residence in Cara's bones and refused to budge. It reminded her of when Nate was long-lined off the Aurora. The Atlantic Ocean nearly claimed him and the same iciness nibbled at her limbs.

An enormous fireplace, the height of a man and at least six foot wide, contained a blaze that she swore flickered blue and threw no heat. The flames mesmerised her as they danced from pale yellow to white to sudden flares of blue and green. The spirals of cool colours brought to mind the little male dragon she left in Siberia.

The warmth and life sapped from her body with the onslaught from the pervading damp. She fought an urge to raise a hand to check if the red drained from her hair. She tightened her grip on Nate's hand. Ever since her blood mingled with Nate's in the centre of Nefertiti's Heart, her survival instinct sprang a whole new facet. The entire house stank of a dark object sucking light, heat, and *life* to itself.

A man rose from the high-backed chair by the fire. He wore a smoking jacket of pale grey velvet over black pants. "Ah, Nathaniel, it has been many years since we last met." His voice carried a heavy, unfamiliar accent.

He needs Brick and Amy to inject some colour into this place.

Cara's immediate impression was of vast age. Deep lines marred his face; his hair was aged pure white, and the paper-thin skin with pulsing blue veins lay close to the surface. He looked like he stood on the wrong side of one hundred.

As he neared, her vision danced and blurred. She shook her head. It was as though she saw two versions of the man inhabiting the same space. The other version younger, standing erect and strong with black hair and a firm jawline. He moved with an easy grace and his tone held strength. The young man flickered and dissolved into the features of the ancient resident.

"How old were you when I tried to hire your services?" He stopped a mere step in front of them.

Nate stiffened, his fingers hard at her waist. "I was twenty years old. I trust you found what you sought?"

"Yes, eventually." He moved closer and extended his hand to Cara. The old version dominated and she glimpsed only the odd flash of the younger version underneath. "Lady Lyons."

She gave a sigh of relief that for once she followed convention and wore gloves. The little voice in the back of her head told her not to let him touch her bare skin. Cream satin covered her from fingertip to elbow and as his cool fingers gripped hers, ice water washed over her body and tightened around her heart. The squeeze drifted away when he removed his hand and she breathed free.

"Come, have a seat, so we may talk. I so seldom receive visitors these days." His lips pulled in a smile, but it went no further on his face.

Cara perched on the edge of a sofa covered in grey brocade and bearing a pattern reminiscent of roses several months after a funeral. She took the spot closest to the phantom fire. Nate put himself between Cara and the Curator, his entire body tense and coiled.

The butler appeared with a silver tray holding drinks. He stooped close to his master first, before approaching Cara. She fought the urge to yell 'boo' and see if he reacted. Instead she took the heavy glass of red wine, the swirl of fragrant liquid the only spot of colour in the room.

"I saw you in Goslett Yard, at the bookstore." She remembered the cold presence that drifted over her that day and now she swam in it.

"Yes, I do on occasion venture out to see Malachi." He held his glass but did not drink. "Such treasures to be found in his store."

The Curator's gaze fixed on Cara's frame and she wasn't sure if his comment referred to the books or something else.

"This is no social visit," Nate said, his tone short.

A reptilian hiss came from the older man. "No one wants to converse anymore. Very well, what do you want from me?"

Cara took a sip of wine. Rich cherries and smoky wood rushed over her taste buds. She savoured the burst of flavour in a place so devoid of any character. "I need to know who has Nero's Fiddle."

He gave a short laugh and leaned forward in his chair, the wine glass nursed between both hands. "I thought you came here to talk about Lucas. He was such a willing pupil of mine. Quite an extraordinary mind, until he went rogue and betrayed me."

She drew in a sharp breath. She refused to follow the quarry down that particular rabbit hole no matter how high her curiosity jumped. "My father is dead. I have nothing to gain by discussing him."

"Really?" He quirked a snowy eyebrow. "I thought you might share his curious and enquiring mind. Your life was shaped from the very beginning by his pursuit of certain artifacts. And now you walk such a similar path." His voice washed over her like the tide. Seductive, enticing, and part of her wanted to surrender and learn what destroyed her father.

And then destroyed her.

She didn't walk the same path. She would never abandon those she loved to chase an object. Doubts caressed her mind with a seductive pull; did she want to know the full truth? Did she want to understand his madness?

Could things have been different?

She took another sip of wine and pushed down the questions. "Nero's Fiddle," she repeated. "Who holds it?"

A faint smile touched his lips, but a calculating light shone in his slate eyes. "I will trade you information for information."

The pressure returned in her chest, what would he demand? She cast a glance at Nate, ready and alert, as though he expected to fend off an attack at any moment. Surely there was no physical danger from a man so old? "What do you want to know?"

"The heart," he said, one finger tapped the side of his glass, mimicking a beat. "How does it work?"

She licked her tongue over dry lips. The slow pulse through her body timed with notes beat on the crystal in his hand. "Whatever do you mean?"

"Come, no need to be coy with me. The two of you are bonded by Nefertiti's Heart. A collector of such things knows when they are in the presence of an artifact, the very air has a resonance."

Like a damp cold penetrating every stone, timber, and bone. Something powerful lies within these walls. Does the stone contain or protect?

Revealing their secret could put their lives at risk. If Nate's enemies knew they could kill him by killing her, it would give them an opening to strike against him. The cold shudder sunk further into her body.

"We have all heard the tale of how Nathaniel here was dragged behind an airship for nearly two hours through the frigid Atlantic." He sat back and placed his untouched wine on a side table and the last note subsided. Then he tented his long fingers. A black stare as vacant as a starless sky fixed on Cara. "The crew on the Aurora pulled up a corpse, who then dove back over the side to re-join his airship. It would seem to give credence to the rumours of immortality that surround Nefertiti's Heart. The love of a queen sustaining her pharaoh for all of time."

Nate's fingers squeezed hers. "My lungs were full of water, Cara's were not. The Heart allowed one to breathe for the other." He surrendered a portion of information that the man opposite could discern for himself. The only question was would it be enough to satisfy him?

He hummed deep in his throat. "You're not telling me much. Your lives are shaped by an artifact. I want to know how it works and every single subtle change and nuance it has wrought between you."

Nate gave a short, sharp bark of laughter. "Do you expect me to hand any man knowledge he could use against me?"

The Curator gave a smile that touched his lips but laid ice in his stare. "Perhaps you would allow me to examine your lovely wife instead? A moment to caress the skin kissed by Nefertiti, the most beautiful of queens."

The barest suggestion of a threat to Cara and the cold temperature in the room dropped to glacial. She expected to see an icicle hang from her nose. The beat between their hearts slowed and time suspended itself, waiting for the next move.

Is this what he really seeks? Not knowledge of the Heart but to lay his hands on me? Helene's warning shot through her brain. Careful he doesn't add you to his collection.

"Come, Cara." Nate took the wine from her hand and placed it on a table. He rose and tugged on her hand, pulling her to reluctant feet.

The undercurrents in the room mesmerized her. So much converged here; her past, Helene's warnings, her father's actions, and some ancient power. A storm brewed and she wanted to study the gathering clouds, to learn how they could defeat it before it overwhelmed them all.

Another tug from Nate and disappointment trickled through her limbs. If they left now where else could they find much needed information about the Fiddle?

The Curator rose from his chair to mirror their movement. "Some years ago the item came up for auction. Only one other man recognised the old lyre for what it was—Nero's Fiddle. I am somewhat embarrassed to say the other noble outbid me." He spread his hands wide at his loss. "I do not usually lose what I have set my mind to obtain. It has only happened twice."

"Noble?" Cara seized on the word and tried to crane around the bulk of Nate's body. "Who?"

The corner of his lips curled in a smile more reminiscent of a grimace than anything filled with warmth or humour. "Albert."

The curse flew from Cara's lips before she could call the words back.

The Curator gave a harsh bark. "Quite extraordinary, isn't she?" he said.

Nate gave a half bow. "Thank you." He took Cara's arm to lead her from the strangely disguised castle.

Except she couldn't force her feet to move. The questions flooded into her mind and she wanted to bombard the elderly gentleman as though he were a tutor keen to quench her thirst for knowledge. A prickle over her skin told her so much rested on this interview, she just couldn't comprehend what, exactly.

The Curator approached with one hand extended. The candles in the overhead chandelier threw a long shadow, his spectral fingers danced over her cheek long before his physical touch would reach her. His visage flickered and the young man appeared, hunger in his gaze as he sought to touch her.

She stood still but inwardly recoiled, gut instinct screamed not to let him lay a hand on her body, even as the strong face behind the old one drew her curiosity to the surface.

Who was he?

She never saw Nate move. One moment he stood beside her, the next instant in front.

"She is not yours to touch." His tone stayed low and conversational but along their bond he growled. Chest to chest, he stopped the other man from reaching Cara.

"No need for such an overreaction," the Curator said.

A snarl curled Nate's upper lip. "We both know words alone would not stop you from taking what you desired."

"A touch, that was all. A moment to bask in the sun of youth and beauty." His image wavered as the handsome young man threw the challenge to Nate. As though the anger of the confrontation centred him and enabled him to suppress the elderly visage.

A huff of moist air left the man and he took a step backward, young fading to ancient as he retreated. Only then did Cara see the blade Nate pressed into his abdomen. Four inches of bright steel pulled free of his clothing; a slick of clear moisture ran along the length. Nate pressed a button under his jacket sleeve and the blade slid back up into the sheath strapped to his forearm.

The Curator bowed to Cara as though nothing had happened, with no sign of injury or distress. "Perhaps you will visit with me another time, Lady Lyons. We have much to discuss and I have so much knowledge to offer you."

She nodded, unable to form words, her brain about to explode with all the strands it tried to unravel.

Keeping Cara close to his side and beyond the reach of the Curator, Nate led her from the mansion.

Safe in their carriage, she leaned back against the blue velvet interior and let the fabric caress her cheek while her mind rampaged and examined every detail of the evening. It took several minutes before she uttered another oath.

"I'm glad Jackson is no longer at your back, he seems to have influenced your vocabulary." Nate rapped on the roof and the carriage moved forward.

She flashed her husband a smile. "Actually I learned cussing in Texas, from the experts."

Her brain picked one thread to being the conversation. Nate slid a blade four inches into the other man's gut. "Explain to me why he wasn't picking his entrails up off his expensive carpet."

A smile touched Nate's lips. "Yes. A rather handy trick to have in your repertoire, is it not?"

She replayed the moment he withdraw the knife and the way the light played over the edge. "There wasn't any blood."

He rubbed a hand over the back of his neck. "But the blade was wet."

"Whatever runs through his veins was clear, like water." A chill lapped at her body like the lick of the tide. "Whatever he hides in there is dark and damp with sinister depths." The house pulsed with a menace far worse than her family home in Soho, where the house would often send a stray charge of electricity to Cara's fingertips when she flipped a light switch.

"Rather like the Thames at this point." Nate drew her closer.

"Perhaps that is why he lives here, his castle perched on the edge with its feet in the water. Do you think he holds some artifact that needs water close by?"

"Possibly. You will need to consult your books. After you brush up on your Latin," he teased, injecting much needed lightness into the brooding tension.

"So much is happening in that house," she muttered to herself. "Another thing, did you see the dual images? He's ancient but young at the same time. It made me cross-eyed to look directly at him, like two versions of him kept shifting over each other."

The carriage gave a gentle sway as they headed home over the bridge. "I suggest we worry about the Curator another day. Right now we need to figure out what Prince Albert was up to with Nero's Fiddle."

"He said we have much to discuss. That my father betrayed him. What do you think he meant?" Already she wanted to return and ask a myriad of questions. But if she did, would she ever leave?

Nate curled a large hand around the nape of her neck. "I don't know. Do you really want to cross paths with him again?"

She chewed her bottom lip. "But we will have to, eventually. One day we will have to find out what dwells in his house. Not that I want whatever he possesses under our home in Lowestoft, I'm much too fond of the warmth."

Nan & Nessy

Christmas 1818

SUNLIGHT streamed in through the high windows in the morning room and belied the frigid temperature outside. Although it had yet to snow, the ground froze over. Hardwood burned on the fire and provided a slow heat that warmed the entire parlour. Bella wore festive red with a white fur edging and looked like a cherry covered in whipped cream. The family decorated the room for Christmas and only one thing remained to be lavished with good cheer: the tree.

The child approached the fir tree with a miniature silver armillary sphere in her outstretched hand. With monumental effort the youngster lined up the metallic string with a bough and shoved the ornament over the green needles, where it nestled up against four other arrow pierced globes on the same branch. The tree took on a distinct lean to one side with the unbalanced weight distribution.

Nan watched the child's labour. Laughter skated through her body and she didn't know how much longer she could hold it inside. The tree soared to nine feet tall with a spread of over four feet at the base and yet Bella insisted on placing every single ornament in the exact same spot.

The rest of the tree remained barren and green while one bough became the sole recipient of the child's decorating skill.

"Obstinate child," she murmured.

"She gets that from you, once locked onto your target you are both hard to deter." Gideon smiled at his wife.

Her parents had tried to direct her attention elsewhere and her father picked her up to reach higher, but she steadfastly refused to release a bauble in any other spot. If anyone dared moved a bauble when she turned away she threw herself to the ground in a tantrum. Bella's determination to hang every ornament in the same spot butted up against Gideon's need for military precision. Nan suspected the man would soon develop an eye twitch at the uneven distribution of the brightly coloured troops on the expanse of green territory.

The earl paced and tried to rein in his natural instinct for order and control even while he tried to contain his growing mirth at his beloved daughter's antics. "She's going to make the tree topple over at this rate."

Bella returned to the open crate. She leaned in and gave the remaining ornaments close inspection before emerging with a sixth armillary sphere. Her attention wandered over the tree and zoomed in on her favourite spot. She gave a cry of triumph and wandered to her selected branch.

Nan burst into laughter. "Do you want to remove the ornaments and rehang the tree in an appropriate and military-approved pattern?" Every year of their married life her husband decorated the tree like he was on manoeuvres. Each object had to be placed an exact and equal distance apart. He ranged the knick knacks like troops and armaments, larger items at the bottom rising to the more delicate glass blown trinkets at the pinnacle.

He paused before answering and Nan wondered who would win his internal debate, the cavalry captain or the doting father?

"And disappoint my daughter? Certainly not. I'll get some wood, we just need to prop up this side. And perhaps tie the top to the dado rail. And maybe build a low supporting structure." He gestured around the tree, imagining ropes and pulleys to enable it to survive Christmas without toppling over.

A cough from behind caught Nan's attention. She turned to find Nessy in the doorway. Six months had passed since she fled from the orchard but to Nan it seemed more like six years. Never before had the two friends been parted for such a long time, and they parted on such angry words.

Her chest constricted. Relief to have her friend back was overlaid with pain at what her presence meant.

"I had nowhere else to go." Nessy stood immobile, her hands fisted deep in her floral skirts. Eyes bright with tears met Nan's gaze. "Bill has married as his family directed and I am cast off."

Nan's heart broke for her lifelong friend. To love but to be turned aside. She opened her arms and Nessy flew to safety.

Sobs racked her frame. "Oh, Nan, the last few months have been horrible. His family was so cruel. They made me sleep in the servant's quarters. I was such a fool to think they would accept me."

Nan stroked her friend's hair. "Any man would be lucky to have you, the loss is entirely his."

"He tried, he really did." Nessy spoke up for the man who broke her heart, loyal to the very end. "At first it was wonderful, to have so much time together and he treated me like a princess. I would cook his dinner some nights and laid his clothes out in the morning."

Gideon reached into his pocket and passed over a linen handkerchief and Nan shoved it into Nessy's hand. She paused in her tale as she gave a noisy blow.

"Three months ago his family began interfering; they said it was not appropriate for Bill and me to sit at the same table. They said I was not good enough. Every week there was a parade of noble women before him. They discussed them like broodmares. Talked of bloodlines and which would be most likely to breed an heir." Tears choked her words. "I wouldn't have been surprised if they shoved their hands into the women's mouths to check their teeth."

A familiar lump rose in Nan's throat. Gideon had every right to cast around for another wife, another mare to service in the hope of fathering a boy. She could well imagine how the sight of prospective breeding partners would shred her friend's soul.

"He stood up for me, but the arguments flew more often, weekly sometimes and they raged long into the night. I used to sit on the stairs and listen." A wail burst forth from her chest and her words became lost amongst the tears.

Nan caught Gideon's raised eyebrow over the bowed blonde head. They knew the relationship was doomed and Nan tried to dissuade Nessy from her course of action. When they parted ways Nessy was convinced jealously fuelled Nan's words. Noble families rarely let sons marry where their hearts lay. Bill sacrificed his love to try and save his family, the match arranged for him by brokers. The bride with suitable bloodlines imported from Europe like an expensive horse.

"Last month Bill had to move, to be closer to the family. I went with him. I would follow him anywhere." She gripped Nan's hand.

"I know, dear heart. You love him, of course you wanted to be with him."

Nessy nodded. "They were horrid. His family forced me into the servant's quarters. I wasn't allowed to use the front stairs. Every day they treated me worse, trying to make me leave." The tears stopped all conversation as she cried out her heartache.

Bella did her best to offer comfort. She rummaged in the wooden chest and walked over to the sofa. "Nessy?" she said, and with the last astrolabe ornament in her grasp, she placed it in the crying woman's lap.

The selfless action made Nessy raise her head. She wiped away the tears on her cheeks and with a deep inhale she took the bauble. She held the string, the little arrow piercing the rotating globe. "Thank you, Bella. Isn't it wonderful? Would you help me find somewhere to hang it?"

The child nodded her head and with a serious look, regarded the one-sided tree. After long moments contemplating her options she took

Nessy by the hand and then led her directly to the bough struggling to hold up the weight of five other identical ornaments. She pointed.

"There," she said with a solemn expression on her face.

"The perfect place for it, precious." Nessy kissed the child on the top of her head and added one more trinket to the overburdened branch.

They all gave a laugh as the tree lurched to one side, pulled by the relentless weight. Gideon arrested the sideways motion and the footman rushed over with an end table. The two men managed to prop the table under the tree so the ornaments could stay exactly where Bella placed them.

Nessy straightened and turned to face her friend. The worried look settled between her brows. "Can you ever forgive me? The things I said—"

Nan hushed her and reached up and removed the broken comb from her hair. "There is nothing to forgive. I know the words were thrown in pain. We are two halves, you and I."

Nessy extracted the other half of tortoiseshell from her pocket. They held the two pieces together to make a whole. "Friends forever, no matter what," she whispered and then hugged her friend.

"There is more to my tale." She smoothed her skirts over her stomach. Her gaze darted from Nan to Gideon. "I am with child."

Nan's eyes widened and focused on Nessy's midriff. Only the tiniest bump visible under the cotton of her dress. A hand drifted down her own body. She remembered the first time she felt Bella stir and flutter under her skin. A sensation she would never again cherish.

"Bella will adore having company in the nursery," Gideon said. He placed his hand on Nessy's shoulder. "Congratulations, Nessy. We are blessed to add to our family. You are, of course, back for good?"

Nan looked at her husband, her daughter and then her best friend. Tears shimmered in her eyes. Gideon could divorce her and marry another woman to bear his heir. She had tried to urge him to think of the future. He refused. It was the one topic that provoked a violent argument between them. She could not have children, but they would welcome Nessy's offspring. "Yes, of course Nessy is back with us. And Bella will adore a little brother or sister."

Nessy kissed Gideon's cheek. "I hope it's a boy. I want my son to grow up to be the sort of man you are. I want you to teach him how to ride and shoot and torture worms with a fishing hook."

A son. A tiny sliver of hope entered Nan's soul. The child could save the estate. Everyone knew how close the three of them were, it would take no effort to let people think Gideon had fathered Nessy's child. He could adopt a boy and make him his heir.

They would be safe.

CHAPTER 25

London, Monday 10th February, 1862

EXHAUSTION settled over Fraser's frame and pushed his head toward the desk. Warm hands dropped to his shoulders and massaged his tired muscles.

"You work too hard, Hamish," the woman behind him murmured as she worked.

"I cannot stop," he said. "There are always monsters to hunt and slay." One particular monster took more of his energy and focus than any other. He laid his traps and herded his prey. Close, so close now.

"Exactly, they will always be there, waiting in the shadows. The monsters will win if you work yourself into an early grave or sink so low you become what you hunt." She lifted her hands, depriving him of her touch.

He imagined her hands on full hips, ready to berate him for spending too long at work again. A smile on dark red lips would entice him further into the dark with her promise of pleasure. His body ached and he raised a hand to pull her to him. "Faith," he whispered as he turned and reached for her.

Only to find himself alone.

He inhaled and frowned. The faintest trace of lilacs lingered in the air. He only saw Faith when he took the laudanum, his imagination must have supplied her scent. He shook his head to clear the fuddle.

Did I slip and take it with my tea, or fall asleep at the desk?

He sat in his chair for so long, staring at his blackboard, he couldn't remember if he was working late or starting early. He ran a hand over his chin and scratched the emerging stubble. He needed to go home and shave, if only he could bear the thought of the cold and empty house.

The dull grey clouds blanketing the city parted company and allowed a shaft of sun to break through. Morning light bounced off the metallic turbines on the roofs opposite and shot bright slivers over his walls, highlighting the names on his board. Rising from his chair, he stretched tired muscles held too long in one position. Scrawled names and dates covered the board dominating one wall and his mind followed one line lit up by a sunbeam.

Three deaths in a most violent manner and the prospect of a phantom killer on the loose spooked the population. Winter clung to London, every day they sunk deeper in the cold dank grip. The underclass was convinced God had turned his eye to England's capital and that he hovered above, seeking out his next victim to smite. Paperwork grew, cells were overcrowded and tempers flared. He wished the super would disperse the sinners to the churches, the priests had far fewer forms to fill out.

Three names and three occupations; a physician, a lady's maid, and a country midwife. Some thread bound these particular lives and drew them all together. An idea niggled in his brain, a constant scratch like a dog at the door wanting inside. He patted his jacket pocket but found it empty. The purple glass bottle absent, left behind in his small parlour. He felt a glimmer of relief; he did not suck the poppy at work. Not yet. Then a huff of air escaped his tired lungs. His mind needed to fly, to dip, and soar to find the path they needed to follow. And he needed to shave.

The neat pile of typed notes drew his attention; the secretary finished the last hand-scrawled page the night before. They spent hours talking to those who knew the three victims, covering decades of history trying to find the commonality. The lives of the first two intersected all the time, the physician attended the duchess at least once a month over a forty-year period. He and Penelope knew one another and the acquaintance grew as the woman rose through the ranks of attendants from housemaid to the most trusted position of lady's maid. Mundane illnesses and intimate social events threw the two together on a routine basis. Fraser knew they followed the wrong path concentrating on Nigel and Penelope. The answer lay in the extraordinary, not in the everyday.

Claudette Foreman was the fly in his ointment. A country midwife with no known association to the other two, at least none visible on the surface. The itch told him it was there, he just needed to keep digging the find the truth.

The silver ring rested on top of the file. Watery sunlight filtered through the window and played over the crest. A bird with outstretched wings and something covering its feet. Water? Grass? The pattern was so worn by years of long use he couldn't make out the etched detail.

Dropping back to his chair, he dragged over the large and dusty peerage tome. A burgundy strip of ribbon marked his place and he flicked the book open. Crests, titles, and estates stretching back to the Doomsday Book swam in his vision. His gut told him the ring was his linkage. Why would a country midwife have a signet ring? Years of experience taught him anything out of place, however small, usually bore a larger significance. Or did his mental dog have him barking up the wrong tree?

Connor pushed his way into the office and dropped the morning paper on his desk. "Damned fish wives at it again, they should find some other piece of gristle to chew." He gestured to the headline, where the reporter announced a growing movement for an investigation into the allegations surrounding Victoria's parentage. Medical experts weighed in on the fate of the little prince and commented there was no sign of haemophilia in the House of Hanover, proving the Duke of Kent could not have fathered the queen. Some priests even weighed in, saying God's disapproval of the current reign was the cause of the coldest winter in hundreds of years.

"At least they are taking a break from declaring God is seeking vengeance on random English citizens. Although the French are delighting in spreading that tale," Fraser said as he flicked a sideways glance to the paper and then returned to stare at another prancing animal on a field of fleur de lys. The hand outstretched to the mug of tea never made contact due to the gunpowder that exploded in his brain as a vague thought coalesced and ricocheted around his head.

"Good God." He leapt on the paper and he devoured the lead news story.

"Not you too." Connor crossed his arms and leaned on the window frame. "Didn't think you'd believe such drivel about the queen."

"Victoria's legitimacy is the key!" He smacked the paper and gestured to his blackboard; the lines untangled themselves and began to make sense. "What if there was a very old secret, one that has been unearthed and brought into the light of day? What would somebody do to protect that secret from being revealed or confirmed? Perhaps tidy away a few loose strands before they talked?"

A deep crease formed in Connor's forehead. "You'll have to catch me up. You think Queen Victoria is having the old servants snuffed out to keep the reporters quiet?"

Fraser's hands took on a life of their own and drew patterns in the air before picking up the newspaper. "Rumours have circulated for decades that the Duke of Kent was not Victoria's true father and that her mother dallied with John Conroy. Nobody ever gave such stories any credence, until little Leopold was born and diagnosed with haemophilia."

The newspaper danced across Connor's field of vision as Fraser held it aloft. The frown still sat on the sergeant's face. "But that's all it is. Gossip."

Fraser's eyes lit up as his brain ploughed a new field. "People gossip, but a hereditary disease that follows a predetermined medical pathway is much harder to refute than vague rumours. Haemophilia plagues the prince, but it is a disease not known to afflict the Duke of Kent or anyone of the Hanover line. Rumour is, the evidence is so compelling that parliament will soon order an enquiry."

Connor let out a soft whistle. "If the queen is offing people who know something about her parentage, do you really want to piss her off?"

Fraser punched his sergeant in the arm, a rare smile on his face. "I'm well used to annoying the aristocracy. Send a message to Lady Lyons, see if she can trace the artifact to anyone connected with the royal family."

The frown still occupied space between Connor's brows. "What about the midwife though, Foreman? How would she be involved?"

"How indeed." Fraser picked up the signet ring. "This is the final clue, I have only to find out who it came from and why. Thank you for the tea, Connor, it will recharge my brain."

Taking a large slurp of hot, sweet tea he dropped into his chair.

"You need to go home and shave. You look awful," Connor said. "Before your mind disappears chasing rabbits I have another little piece of news for you."

Fraser's head shot up. "Oh?"

"Your man in the rookeries is getting close." Connor picked up the overcoat on the floor and hung it on the rack behind the door.

"How close?" Fraser dared not breathe; this could be the break he pinned his hopes on.

"Saul Brandt's daughter is not happy about her dad being offed." Next Connor tidied a pile of reports on the chair and placed them on an empty shelf. "When she's in her cups she does an awful lot of angry talking."

Fraser let out a whistle. "He is close. Tell him to stay quiet and keep his ears open and let me know when she is angry enough to come forward."

Connor gave a salute. "He knows. You don't ask questions in that place unless you really like fish and want to end up in the Thames." Impromptu housekeeping done, he headed out the door.

Pushing aside the Rookery murders, Fraser turned to the book before him.

It took another two hours and the assistance of a magnifying glass to find the matching crest.

"It's a phoenix," he muttered. His finger rested on the small text as he identified the relevant house and then he let out a whistle. "The Earl of Morton." He stared at the little ring, the legendary bird rising from the flames licking at its feet. "I don't like co-incidences, especially not those that touch the Lady Lyons and her family."

Ideas and theories spun in his brain as he moved from his office down the stairs to where the street-level Enforcers worked. He sought out Connor in the crowded and noisy floor. Pick pockets and bobtails sat on wooden benches along the walls, waiting to be released after a night in the cells. He danced out of the way of two large Enforcers who manhandled a struggling ruffian to the underground prison.

Connor sat at a large desk, staring at the keys on a typewriter as he tapped out a prostitute's name, one painfully slow letter after another.

"Another trip to the country, my friend. This time to Leicester." He held up the little ring.

"You found where it came from?"

Fraser couldn't keep the grin from his face. "Oh yes. And I think Lady Lyons will want to be present for this particular conversation. I shall ask her to join us there tomorrow."

London, Tuesday 11th February, 1862

THE knock on the bedroom door came just before dawn. Cara pulled herself awake as Nate rose and spoke to the man outside the door. He returned to bed with a strip of paper and flicked on the small bedside light.

"For you, from Fraser. Also, apparently there is an issue we need to deal with at Cleopatra's Needle."

Cara sat up and took the slip. "Urgent issue at Cleopatra's Needle, bring blanket," she read out. They exchanged looks and Nate shrugged. She read the second part of the message. "Interview at Leicester Wednesday, require your presence."

"Why is he going to Leicester?" Nate asked as he pulled on trousers and looked around for a shirt.

Cara's sleep fuddled brain tried to connect the two sentences but gave up without caffeine. "Something to do with Nero's Fiddle, I assume. Let's go sort out the first issue."

Dawn struggled to illuminate the cloudy sky as Cara and Nate stood on the Victoria Embankment and stared up at the imposing monument. The obelisk was a gift to England from the ruler of Egypt in thanks for

Nelson's victory at the Battle of the Nile. It took decades for engineers to figure out how to move it to London. Eventually two airships undertook the perilous journey with the stone in a specially constructed and reinforced cargo net strung between the two vessels.

An Enforcer stood with his back to the monument. He nodded as they approached. "There's a party of visiting dignitaries due to view the Needle this morning, please have him gone within the next hour," he said.

Cara's gaze dropped to the base, and the very naked, very drunk, pirate chained at the bottom. To be fair he wasn't completely naked, someone had covered him in pine sap and a dusting of feathers. Shivers ran over his body and shook his plumes, and his lips had turned blue. The semi-circle of scars on his side, from his shark encounter, were picked out in bright white against his chilled skin.

"Why are you chained to Cleopatra's Needle?" Cara asked. She dropped the blanket over his shoulders, while she wondered if his piercings had frozen and tried to keep herself from looking. "And why are you covered in feathers and sap?"

"Because I lost a bet and that pencil dick bastard Jackson has no sense of humour."

"I think it's pretty damn funny," Nate said, as he walked around the stone to see what held Loki in place.

He had his arms stretched out behind him and held together with a large chain and padlock. Rattling came from behind the stone as Nate set to work picking the lock holding Loki prisoner.

Cara shook her head. "You're going to freeze out here. What bet did you lose?" She was grateful for the blanket or she would have stared openly.

"One involving a fair English rose and God knows how, but he plucked her first. I can only assume the woman was overwhelmed with pity for him. He was supposed to just feather me. But no doubt driven by jealousy of my mighty shaft, he chained me out here thinking the snow would knock a few spare inches off. Lucky I am so well-endowed it takes more than a little snow to affect me." He gave her a wink.

A clunk came from behind the monolith and the chain holding Loki's wrists fell slack. Nate walked around the base holding one end and a padlock. "Let's get you into the carriage and I'll unlock the handcuffs where it's warmer."

They helped him up and ensured the blanket stayed in place as they made their way back to the carriage. Only a few hardy souls were out this early and the escapade went unnoticed by all except the late watch Enforcer, who reported the incident. He still stood guard to one side and gave a nod as they moved away, to continue his rounds.

"What do you think, my peach, now you have seen all of me?" Loki said as Cara stepped up into the carriage. "I do believe the great erection behind us suffers by comparison."

She kept her expression sober, unlike the pirate. "I think it's been a rather cold night."

Loki clutched the blanket to his breast. "Ouch. Keep in mind this is me in the cold, imagine what I'm like when you take me inside and I warm up." He gave a roughish grin.

They settled in, Brick jumped up top and the carriage moved off.

"Don't try to deflect the conversation. What woman are you talking about?" She tried to remember the barmaids at the local pub, the most likely objects of attention, unless they were sporting with one of the housemaids.

He rested his head back against the blue velvet and fixed a dark stare on her. "You don't know, do you?"

Her fingers tightened on Nate's leg. "It's too early and too cold for games. Don't know what?"

Loki's eyelids dropped and a smile pulled on his full lips. "It's your friend Amy."

"What?" Loki's words about plucking roses slammed back into her brain. "What exactly has Jackson been up to in Lowestoft?" She turned to Nate, a frown on her face.

He shrugged. "Domestic relationships are not my forte." He pointed a finger at Loki. "But you can get your feathered arse on that airship, it's time you headed out."

"All good to go, just as soon as she is christened." Loki opened his eyes and rearranged the blanket around his body before looking across to Cara. "The lovely Amy is an untouched flower no more. Jackson has her holed up in the cottage shagging her senseless."

Cara choked on the air trying to fill her lungs. Nate rubbed her back and she thanked god he could breathe for her, because her mouth opened and shut but wouldn't admit anything to her airways. Finally she managed to suck air in and expel words. "Oh no. Amy is still fragile after events with Burke." She turned to Nate, her hand clenching. "I need to return to Lowestoft." What on earth was happening at the estate?

He unhooked her death grip on his trousers and took her hand in his. "We don't have time. We have an interview with the queen this afternoon, a function tonight and Leicester tomorrow."

"Blast. The day after then. I swear if he has hurt her, I will castrate him and feed tiny pieces to the fish." Her mind whirled, trying to digest what events unfolded on the Lyons estate while she worked in London. The mere suggestion of Jackson *shagging* Amy spun her world on its axis. In what universe was that even possible? She planned to send an aethergraph message to Amy as soon as they returned to the Mayfair house.

Loki laughed. "Just my sort of entertainment. I want a front row seat before I'm exiled to the Pacific."

Cara fidgeted with her skirts while they waited in the outer office.

"Nervous?" Nate asked with a twitch to his upper lip. He leaned against the wall and looked relaxed, despite the fact that the queen had summoned them and they had an indelicate topic to discuss.

"Yes, I keep expecting her to yell *off with her head.*" She walked back and forth, her gaze flitting over the paintings lining the walls.

Behind the solid wooden doors a voice rose and fell. The wood sprung apart to reveal the derriere of the queen's secretary as the man backed from the room.

A cry of 'damned reporters' hit their ears before he pulled the doors to and then turned.

"Give her a moment," he said, straightening his cravat and then the points of his waistcoat as though the diminutive queen had held him by the throat up against a wall.

Great, the queen's in a temper and we're bearing bad news.

Cara paced for another minute, then Nate pushed off the wall and reached for her, stilling her movement. He took her hand in his and gave a squeeze. "Shall we get this over with?"

She nodded. Nate signalled to the secretary, and he ushered them into the queen's presence.

Cara expected to find the queen in an agitated state, but the monarch sat at her desk, her head bowed. Crisp piles of papers aligned with military precision awaited the royal signature. A black lace mop covered her hair and bobbed up and down as she read a dispatch. She was clad in black taffeta, still in full mourning for her husband. Some said she would never surface from her grief.

Cara dropped a curtsey and beside her Nate bowed.

"Lord and Lady Lyons."

With their presence acknowledged, they could stand; no messing around today. The queen remained seated, a quill in her hand which she dipped in a cut crystal bottle. "We believe you have a report to make?" Her focus drifted back to the dispatch and the pen nib hovered, waiting to drop in the right spot.

"Yes, Your Majesty," Nate said.

Cara bit her tongue, not wanting to articulate what ran through her mind. Although, she had so many different thoughts whirling around sometimes it was hard to know which one to grab. She was just as likely to blurt out Loki had a piercing just like the late prince consort. The rational part of her brain that maintained a semblance of control pointed out that *that* wouldn't be a very good conversation opener. Although it could explain why she grieved him so hard.

"There have been some unusual recent deaths which we believe are caused by a particularly dangerous artifact," Nate said.

The scratching of pen on paper ceased. The cold blue stare pierced through Cara, not Nate. One eyebrow rose. "Do elaborate."

"Three people have died by what appears to be spontaneous human combustion. Such deaths are incredibly rare, so rare as to stretch credulity when there are three in a matter of just two months. Inspector Fraser is investigating for the Enforcers," Nate said.

"God's fire," Victoria muttered, then waved her hand to continue.

Cara took a breath to still her mind. "There is an artifact called Nero's Fiddle which replicates that effect."

The eyes narrowed. "We hope you will seize and dispose of this lethal object."

"There is a matter of some delicacy involved, ma'am," Nate said.

The piercing gaze flicked from Nate to Cara, assessing them. "Then please speak plainly."

Cars stayed silent, letting her husband drop their news. She found in situations like this, it was better to remain silent and let Nate try and keep them out of trouble. Or he could keep the queen talking while she slipped out the door and ran for it.

"We have learned that the artifact was sold to Prince Albert several years ago and was last known to be in his possession."

The queen's lips pursed as though she sucked a lemon and the pen clattered into its silver holder. With knuckles clenched on the green leather blotter, she rose. "Your mongoose is chasing the wrong snake if he thinks to sniff at our door."

Cara bit her lip and reached out for Nate's hand. *Try telling Hamish to lay off the aristocracy.*

"We understand the prince had an interest in matters beyond the physical realm," Cara said, trying to weigh how much to tell the queen. She doubted mentioning he often dropped in to visit a syphilitic countess in Belgravia would go over well. Especially not if the queen found out her husband's spirit still found the time to gossip with Helene on a regular basis while his wife mourned his loss.

Victoria turned her head, her attention lost out the window for a moment, before she spoke. "There were books and objects of an other-worldly nature among Albert's possessions. They remain undisturbed in his apartments. Have our secretary procure someone to escort you there. Once you find this fiddle undisturbed, we trust you will speak to the inspector."

Somehow Cara doubted Nate would speak to Fraser unless he did the talking with his fists or a blade. "Let us secure the item first, ma'am, so we can be sure it is not behind the deaths and will not cause any in the future."

She gave a curt nod. "One other thing, Viscount Lyons. We are still waiting for your answer to our question."

Nate froze, his attention on the queen. His fingers tightened on Cara's hand.

"Have you thought any more on our proposal or will you be gracing the House with your presence since you are now responsible for two seats?"

"I'm not of a political mind, ma'am. I believe my new position in the crown's service will require a large deal of travelling, so I regret my seat may remain vacant for some time."

Cara kept down her snort. Nate wanted to spend all day with the politicians about as much as she wanted to be stuck doing tea and biscuits with their wives. Neither of them was suited to the superficial games of social niceties.

"Very well. We would be most pleased if you dropped other, more nefarious pursuits to dedicate yourself to our employ." The queen took up her pen, her change of focus their cue they were dismissed.

"Ma'am," Nate murmured.

It didn't quite sound like an agreement to Cara's ears, more like a play for time.

In the outer office, Nate relayed the queen's order that someone escort them to Albert's suite. The secretary called for a guard, who led them through the maze of corridors to the private apartments on the next floor.

With the passage of time, her beloved's rooms became a mausoleum. Despite the fact he had died four months earlier nothing had been touched or moved, except to perpetuate the idea that he would return. That day's newspaper lay on the bedside cabinet; no doubt each morning the old one was removed and a new paper put down. Fresh flowers stood in a vase at the end of the mantle. A red velvet smoking jacket was tossed over a chair, waiting for its owner to return.

The guard closed the door and left them alone with each other and the spectre of the dead consort.

"What did she mean by being responsible for two seats?" Cara had a list of questions in her head and limited time to rattle them all off.

"The queen is holding me responsible for not just my seat but that of the Earl of Morton. I am supposed to sit for both titles until such time as—" He waved his hand at her midriff. Their relationship defied the rules of convention, Nate married her before she ever met him, then he proposed and they had yet to have a ceremony. Children had never entered the conversation. Not once.

"Until I breed the requisite heir and a spare?" *Children.* A shudder ran down her spine. She enjoyed her freedom, a child seemed such an adult responsibility. Assuming a woman survived childbirth. The act nearly stole her grandmother and took her mother; her line was not well suited to the activity of breeding. The odds were stacked against her should she become pregnant, or would the heart allow her to draw on Nate's strength should the time ever come?

His arm slipped around her waist and his lips nuzzled her neck. "Stop thinking about it."

"How can I not think about it now you have raised the topic? It's not as if we sleep in separate rooms like most married nobles." A child.

Her stomach gave a lurch at the very idea. "We could always have you neutered and remove the possibility?"

The look on his face would kill pigeons in flight and pluck them stone dead from the heavens.

Men. So touchy about their testicles.

"Why don't we discuss this later? I think right now we need to find Nero's Fiddle." He pulled the shoulder of her gown sideways to kiss along her collarbone.

She danced away from his arms. "Then stop touching me," she said. The man was incorrigible. Given the amount of time he devoted to divesting her of her clothing, surely it was only a matter of time until she quickened. While Nate had a supply of the new rubber French letters, they were thick with a hard seam. The most charitable description was to call them *unwieldy*. Plus they smelt funny and were prone to sliding off. She looked after her body by taking an infusion of the plant Queen Anne's Lace early in the morning. Although no method was truly fool proof. She could carry even now, unless she was barren. A hand fell to her stomach, wondering. They had been intimate for eight months now. How long did conception take?

She took a deep breath, willing her gut to stop cavorting around and making her nauseous. The more she thought about the possibility of being pregnant the more her stomach revolted and threatened to revisit breakfast.

"Stop worrying about it," Nate said. "Take a deep breath."

She hadn't realised she was only breathing out; in would help. She took a breath and then another. The shake in her hands subsided. Pushing down thoughts of what might be happening unseen in her body, she returned to their current mission. Where would a prince hide an ancient artifact of power?

She started with the bookcase while Nate went through the drawers in the dresser. A perusal of the prince's collection revealed a number of old tomes that her fingers itched to add to her pile. She would have to ask the queen if she could borrow or acquire the texts to aid their job as the royal artifact hunters.

"How big is it?" Nate asked, having looked under the bed and found nothing but a gaily painted porcelain bed pan.

"It's a lyre, hard to tell from the text but perhaps a foot square."

Nate stood at the end of the bed and surveyed the room. "If it were me, I would have a hidden compartment for my valuables. Look behind paintings and furniture. And check panels for signs of wear from fingers."

They searched all afternoon and found nothing.

"So close, where could it be?" Cara kicked the bureau. "I should get Helene to ask Albert next time he pops in on her for a chat."

Nate raised an eyebrow. "It will turn up. We know it came this far, we just need to find who Albert may have handed it on to." He stuck his head out the door and signalled for the guard, who led them back through the maze.

The man chatted as they walked the long corridors. "We all miss him, lovely chap," he said.

Cara nodded, lost in her own thoughts. "I'm not surprised the queen is trying to keep his room intact." The whole nation knew the depth of the queen's grief, but not her culpability in his end. He died tearing Hatshepsut's Collar from around her neck. "It must comfort her to see his things."

"And others feel the same way," their guide said. "You're not the first people to go looking for something in there."

The chill returned and slithered down Cara's spine. "What do you mean?"

"The Prince of Wales took a few mementos of his father, including his man." They came to the main staircase and foyer and the man bowed to leave them.

"He took his father's valet?" Nate asked, halting the man before he disappeared back in the palace.

"Yes, he moved service from father to son, Edward inherited him. Must be handy to have a valet trained in serving a king, no need to train one up." He gave a wink, and having answered the question, he left, scuttling down another corridor.

Nate and Cara exchanged looks as they crossed the courtyard to their waiting carriage. If anyone knew what happened to the prince's possessions it would be the valet, constantly in the prince's room and presence.

"What do you think Edward took, apart from the valet?" she asked.

Nate shook his head. "No idea; best we ask, I believe he will be in attendance at Skittles' soiree tonight."

CHAPTER 27

London, Tuesday 11th February, 1862

CARA'S message to Amy was to the point: *What the hell is going on with you and Jackson?* The reply made her want to bash some heads together until the truth fell out. *With Jack. Will explain all when I see you.*

Her friend couldn't drop a bomb like that without a full and detailed explanation. She left her mourning a broken engagement and now she was doing unspeakable things with Nate's former bodyguard. She screamed and tossed the paper but instead of exploding it fluttered to the ground. Events left her no time to fret; they returned from their audience with the queen and searching Prince Albert's rooms and had to begin dressing for the oncoming evening.

"What do I wear to a soiree at a courtesan's house?" she asked as she prowled through the bathroom to the spare bedroom she used as a dressing room. Her mind needed to concentrate on how to approach Prince Edward, not about unseen events unfolding at Lowestoft.

"Something scandalous," Nate answered.

"That's most of my wardrobe according to the *ton*," she muttered. Emily, her maid, threw open the doors to the robe, so they could pick a gown.

In the end she felt nostalgic and picked the grey silk chiffon with silver stars and no back. The dress Nate had commissioned for her to wear the night she first appeared on his arm. The gown clung to her frame and moved with her. Perfect for an evening amongst the demi-monde.

"It's probably too modest," she said to Emily as the maid pushed the diamond pins in to her hair. She rose from her seat and picked up her fur-trimmed coat.

"I think you look gorgeous, milady," the maid replied, dropping a curtsey as she took her leave.

"So do I," Nate said from the doorway. "You will outshine them all."

"You're not bad yourself." He didn't just wear formal clothes, he commanded them. The tight cravat and stiff lines moulded to him and his will. He appeared a master of everything, including fabric. A smile spread over her face. "The only possible improvement would be if it were pirate day."

"I'll schedule one just for you."

The way he said the words, with his tone low, licked over her skin and a hot shiver slid down her spine. "I think we should leave now, or not at all, because what you are conjuring up in your mind won't get us any closer to Nero's Fiddle."

Skittles held court in Mayfair, a mere stroll away for Nate and Cara. He indulged her by walking through the frigid evening, Brick trailing behind. Cara looped the train of her skirt over her arm so the hem didn't drag through the slush, although the street sweepers kept the footpath clear of snow in the wealthier suburbs.

Even before they approached her doorway, it was evident where the courtesan lived. Light, warmth, and laughter spilled out onto the street. The neighbouring houses appeared dour and subdued.

The butler showed them through to an elegant and warm parlour. Amongst twenty-five men there were only four other women present, courtesans not keen on sharing the spotlight, even with their sisters. Their coats were taken and Nate kissed Cara's hand before singling out one man for his attention.

Always business before pleasure. She wondered what he discussed tonight that could not wait. *Although I guess this is business before business, since we need to corner Bertie.*

Conversation flew and buzzed around the room. Each woman held court with her own group of men. Skittles detached herself from the throng and approached.

"Lady Lyons." She kissed both cheeks and drew her into the warmth. "Always lovely to have your company."

"Please call me Cara, I hate formality." A glass found its way into her hand.

"Cara it is then." Skittles tucked her hand into the crook of Cara's arm. "Do you think you and Nate will start a new trend of husbands and wives entertaining together? You are quite a scandalous pair, appearing in public together all the time. Perhaps you should strike off on your own?"

Given Nate's over-protective urges she doubted he would willingly let her out alone at night; he much preferred to keep her in his line of sight. "I doubt there is any danger of the *ton* following our lead. Most men can't stand to be in the same city as their wives, let alone the same room."

Laughter tinkled from her throat. "True, most men come here to forget their bonds of matrimony for a few hours."

Cara cast around the crowded parlour. "I hear the Prince of Wales is here this evening."

Skittles gave a light chuckle. "Young Bertie is indeed trying to find his feet amongst us."

She gestured to the tall, thin lad on the edge of the group. Cara had quite overlooked him. His open expression drifted from one décolleté to the other. He drained his champagne in one gulp, set the glass on the tray and took up another.

"He looks overwhelmed." She found it hard to believe they were a similar age, but then her life had a more brutal beginning and dealt her harsh lessons in looking out for herself.

Skittles sipped her champagne and leaned closer to whisper. "Although we all mourn the prince regent, his death has let Bertie slip the parental leash and he is relishing the freedom. I think he will be quite the patron for some lucky demimondaine."

Although only a year younger than her twenty two, he appeared childlike. Life had not yet marked him physically, and everything around him was new and open for exploration. As the heir apparent he could have whatever he wanted, he had only to reach out his hand and take it.

The call came to go through for dinner and Cara sat opposite Nate. The prince sat to Skittle's right, in a place of honour. He was being favoured.

Must have cracked open his pocket book.

The women were evenly dotted around the table, so each reigned supreme with their direct neighbours. The grin never left Cara's face. Not only was she welcomed here, but the people surrounding her at the table talked. Really talked, about issues that mattered in the world, not the best doily pattern to crochet or the right shade of silk for a needlework aquilegia. They discussed politics and argued long and hard about the civil war in America. Some agreed with the abolition of slavery. Others, like those with plantations paying for their place at table, saw the merits of owning their workforce. The women were outspoken and passionate in their opinions and the men listened.

Acceptance by the *ton* came at the cost of becoming a decoration. To be seen and admired at the appropriate occasions and never, ever, having a voice. Deep within her, Cara set free the last tiny sliver of desire to ever be accepted by the matrons. She watched the childhood indoctrination disappear out the window and into the winter night. Then she turned and embraced her new place. *This* was her society.

After dinner they adjourned to the parlour, the wide double doors to the billiards room flung open, so the party could continue. The women did not hide away from the men, they joined them in brandy, cigars, and raucous laughter.

A young buck stumbled toward them. Fortified by the courage he found in the bottom of his glass, he gave Nate a nudge. "I say, Lyons, it's not the done thing to bring your wife to these shindigs. As lovely as she is."

Nate narrowed his eyes at the man.

Cara tightened her grip on his arm. "Play nice," she murmured.

His gaze shot to her. "What is your definition of nice?"

"Don't stab anyone, I'm pretty sure this lot will bleed like stuffed pigs."

He dropped a kiss on her neck. "I will try, just for you. His father holds Boudicca's Cuff. The artifact pays for his place here and I need to find where it is, so I can steal it back to line our pockets instead." He turned to join the men. "Don't blame me because you chose badly, Simmons. You should have left your horse in the stable instead of marrying her." He plucked a glass of brandy off a silver server and moved to join a small group of men.

The courtesans moved like dancers among them, clothed in rainbow colours. Laughter swirled toward the ceiling. Tiny flashes of red, orange, blue, and green danced over them all as light fractured from the myriad crystals hanging off the heavy chandeliers.

Cara touched Skittles on the arm. "Would you introduce me to Edward?"

"Of course," she said. They approached the gangly prince. "Bertie, this is a friend of mine, Lady Cara Lyons."

"Your Royal Highness." She dropped a curtsey.

"Lady Lyons." He took her hand and raised her up, his touch damp and clammy on her skin. "It is so lovely to meet you at long last."

"I am flattered you know who I am." She reclaimed her hand by using it to take an offered crystal flute.

"Of course." Once the words were out, colour rushed from under his collar, making her wonder what exactly he had heard about her. "You were present when my father died."

"Ah. Yes. A terrible event." The prince's sacrifice removed Victoria from under the artifact's thrall. "I only wished Nate and I could have stopped the tragedy from occurring."

"Your presence gave my mother comfort."

"What little we could do, sir." She remembered how the queen clung to her dead husband in the pouring rain; there was no solace to offer. She cast a glance at her husband across the room. Tall, broad, and darkly handsome, she saw beneath his cold façade to the river of heat that ran below. A shiver ran through her body. No level of comfort could ever console her should he die. Although she wouldn't have long to grieve; she would follow him to the grave in such an event.

"Speaking of your father, I'm trying to locate an antique he had in his possession. The queen gave us permission to look in his room, but we could not locate it." She drew him to the side of the room, not wanting the gossiping ears to swallow up every syllable. "It's an old fiddle, or more accurately a lyre, dating back to Roman times. Do you recollect seeing it amongst his things?" She held her breath, waiting to hear that he knew of the deadly weapon.

He gave a casual shake, his fingers stroking her wrist. "No, I have no interest in musical instruments or dusty antiquities, I enjoy much earthier pleasures."

If you don't stop touching me you'll be in the earth. She cast a glance at Nate. He looked up and his brows drew together at the sight of the prince's attentions. She sent a promise along their bond and he gave a nod, leaving her to deal with the young man.

Frustration bubbled under her skin at the false lead. The guard was sure that items were removed from the consort's rooms. "Such a shame, I know you were close to your father and had hoped it would jog some memory."

Emboldened by all the alcohol he had consumed over the evening his hand crept higher, to stroke the inside of her elbow. "My father's man might know something. He was always pottering around in his suite and would know of his knick knacks and such."

A ping of hope flared in her mind. "Oh?" She resisted the urge to pull her arm back and let him continue his caress, hoping it was enough of a trade for more information. She gritted her teeth; her demons became agitated by the unwanted contact, but she needed to make it through the next few minutes. "Who is that, his man?"

"Dalkeith, he moved to my household after my father's death. Very capable chap, knows what it means to serve royalty." He gave a wink and leaned in closer. "Now that you have me all stirred up, I am reminded, Dalkeith did ask if he could select a memento from father's rooms."

Bingo! She contained herself from letting out a whoop of excitement. They were back on the scent in their hunt. "Would you mind terribly if I could ask him what he selected? It would mean ever so much to me to have the lyre for my collection." She dropped her lashes and licked her lips.

"For you, dear lady, of course." His whole demeanour brightened and he leaned so close his breath feathered her skin with an alcoholic burp. "Lyons is a dashed lucky bugger, although there is a certain convenience to a married woman." His suggestion hung heavy between them. "I have yet to decide where to lay my royal favour." He raised his hand to stroke the side of her face. "I will be king one day, a woman can climb no higher than me."

Nate will squash him like a bug if he ever hears that suggestion. It's time to derail his train of thought. "These rumours about the queen's legitimacy are horrid, it must be a terrible strain for you. I do hope they die down."

He drew back his hand and curled his fingers into a fist. Blue fire burned in his eyes and his nostrils flared. "The peddlers of those rumours should be put down like the curs they are. How dare they defame my mother and attempt to usurp my position as Prince of Wales." He tried to keep his tone low, but spittle marked his lower lip as he spat out the words. "Dalkeith is right, those behind this slander deserve to burn."

Burn. Her brain sprung to attention. "Burn? A harsh sentence for unfounded gossip, surely?" She tapped his arm with her fan, trying to make light of his growing rage.

Red anger flowed into his cheeks. "They deserve God's fury for daring to suggest I am not the legitimate heir to the crown. Let the Lord strike them down for their vicious slurs against their anointed ruler. I am the first in line, the crown *will* be mine one day and no gossip will take it from me!"

The other guests cast glances in their direction, the prince unable to keep his voice low.

"Of course, little minds with nothing else to occupy them, sir," she murmured. She took one fist and unfurled his fingers, trying to calm his ire. "You will be a mighty king when your time comes."

"They will not strip this from me, not now I am off my father's leash and free to enjoy my position. I have not waited this long in the shadows to be labelled a bastard and cast into penury."

She remembered Nolton's cold promise of evidence against Victoria's mother and wondered how much Bertie knew. The comment about the rumourmongers deserving God's fury was too much of a coincidence and the prince had the most to lose should the rumours be proven.

"Society is the brighter for your star joining us, sir." Cara caught Skittles' eye and gave a subtle eye roll, hoping the courtesan would intervene before Nate threw the prince out a window. "Do tell me you will be a regular patron at Skittles' wonderful soirees? I have so enjoyed our tête-à-tête."

She danced her fingers up his arm, gave him a wink and just like that the runaway train slammed into a wall. The prince's eyes widened and he took a deep breath. He clasped her hand.

"How kind of you, Cara. I can call you that, can't I?" The harsh light vanished to be replaced by the puppy dog looking for validation. "And do call me Bertie, all my close friends do."

"Bertie." She smiled and then flicked open her fan and used the small object as a shield. Made of enamelled metal, each segment was finished with a razor tip she could thrust into a man's gut should he become too forward. Nate shot her a look that said he expected the accessory to be intimately acquainted with part of Bertie's anatomy by now. Ignoring her husband, Cara fixed her attention on the prince. "Do let me know when it's convenient for me to chat with your man about the lyre, I would be ever so grateful."

"Bertie," Skittles called and wrapped her hands around the prince's forearm. "Cara has monopolised you enough, do come and talk to me about your adventures at university in Edinburgh and Cambridge. I hear you are quite the rogue." She bit her lower lip, leaving the skin glistening and wet.

The prince swallowed, his tongue darting out to lick his lips, his mind fixated on the beautiful courtesan. He drifted from Cara without a backward glance.

She gave a soft huff at his retreating back. "So much for my appeal."

An arm encircled her waist and pulled her to a warm chest. "If he hadn't left you I was going to be forced to call him out." Hot breath washed over her skin. "When he started pawing at you, I thought you might have opened him up with your fan. Are you all right?"

She leaned against him and remained silent for a moment, waiting for her demons to slink back to their dark corner. "Yes. Old fears are back, but I know I can conquer them again." Her brain searched for a light-hearted topic. "It's really not fair you know. You commission these wonderful toys for me, and I can't find an opportunity to use them. I still haven't skewered anyone with the stiletto in my parasol and now I'm not allowed to use my fan."

"I like knowing you're armed." He nuzzled under her ear. "Although I could have saved some money and just bought you a champagne bucket."

She laughed. "Even unarmed I am never defenceless."

"Remember that. You are never defenceless nor unprotected," he whispered his words low so only she would hear. "The prince looked quite agitated, whatever were you talking about?"

"He is rather disturbed about the allegations about his mother's illegitimacy. His new man has suggested those behind the tale deserve to burn with God's fury."

Nate swore against her skin. "Rather co-incidental choice of words."

The prince's words chased each other around her brain. "Too much so. Dalkeith used to be Albert's man and Bertie said he removed a couple of objects from the prince's rooms."

"Bertie?" He stiffened behind her.

Cara turned to see a frown settle over Nate's face. She stifled her laugh. It wasn't the coincidences that had him worried but her use of the nickname for the prince. "You know I do believe I could wrangle an invite to the prince's private chambers, to discuss this further."

Nate growled low in his throat. "I don't think that will be necessary. We just need to have a conversation with Dalkeith. Once we figure out what Fraser wants in Leicester."

CHAPTER 28

London, Wednesday 12th February, 1862

C A R A christened the baby airship *Bobby*, because it bobbed up and down like a balloon. The men shook their heads, raised eyebrows, and muttered about having to call the diminutive dirigible *Bobby* which just encouraged her to find nicknames for everything and everybody. Her attempt to match man and endearing epitaph shut them up lest any of them end up called Snookums.

They ate a quiet breakfast, each lost in their own thoughts. Cara was conflicted between rushing to Lowestoft to interrogate Jackson about his intentions toward her friend and her need to protect Nan and Nessy from whatever imaginary conspiracy Inspector Fraser thought they were involved in. She took out her growing frustration on her boiled egg. With a sharp knife she slashed it in half and toppled off its head. Wielding a slice of toast like a sword, she rummaged around in the egg's cavity.

Nate watched over the top of the newspaper and kept quiet.

More surprising he maintained his silence when she gave a cry and lobbed another piece of buttered toast against the wall. It stuck and then dribbled down the dark blue paper leaving a sticky trial.

"I'll kill him if he has taken advantage of her," she said, as the butler picked up the toast and placed it on an empty tray. Watching the man clean the mess of the wall made her stay her hand from any further childish outbursts. "Sorry," she said as he took the offending toast away.

"Let's put out one fire at a time," Nate said. "Shall we leave? I'm sure we all want to hear what Fraser has to say that involves your family."

Rugged up in warm clothes, they climbed into *Bobby* and headed for Leicester. Cara pressed her face to the window and watched the snowscape below. The dirty grey of London gave way to the crisper view of the country. She watched farmers fork bright yellow hay off the back of wagons to feed hungry sheep and cattle. Children in brilliant blue and red woollen coats built snowmen and pelted each other with snowballs while their parents worked. The farther north they flew the more the ground greened. Grass poked through its winter blanket, ready to shake off the cold and embrace spring in a few more weeks.

Inactivity chaffed; her body needed to do something, anything, to burn off the building edge of anxiety. She couldn't even prowl around the tiny swinging carriage. At least the Hellcat allowed her to circumnavigate the outside deck. She shuffled back and forth along the bench seat, took one stride to the bolted-down table and back again.

Nate sat immobile in the corner. Arms crossed over his chest, he watched her from under half lidded eyes. "Now I understand why you dove out a window if your father confined you to your room. You seem incapable of being restricted to a small space."

"I can last a whole hour sitting with Malachi, he is helping me with my Latin." She gave a mischievous grin.

One black eyebrow arched. "He might be ancient, but I will call him out if he gets any ideas about you."

Close to the estate they saw plumes of smoke as the Enforcers' slow and ponderous steam carriage chuffed up the curving driveway. Cara guessed they had an early start to make such good time. They passed over the top and split the cloud in two before they set down in the garden. Little *Bobby* only needed the help of two workmen to be made secure to the bollards. Cara and Nate ascended the stairs in time to meet Fraser and Connor at the front door.

"What have you been up to?" Cara managed to whisper to her Nan as they showed the men into the front parlour. "Why does Inspector Fraser want to see you?"

"I'm sure I don't know what you mean, dearest." She kept the smile on her face but the worry etched itself between her brows. "Tea, Duffie," she yelled down the hallway to the cook. "And bring some plates of those divine smelling savouries you are concocting down there, the scamp is far too skinny."

Nessy gave Cara a hug. "You need curves, girl. Men love curves to explore, don't you, Nate?" She gave the viscount a wink.

"Don't worry about what he likes," Cara whispered to Nessy as they took their seats. "I'm more worried about what you two have been up to."

Nate hung back in the hallway until Fraser and Connor crossed the threshold. Only then did he trail behind and enter the room; his focus never moved from the object of his disdain. He took up position at the window with one hip resting on the sill and arms crossed over his chest. Cara saw the slight bulge in his sleeve, hiding the knife strapped to his forearm. Despite her urging, he never carried a gun. He preferred a blade; he said it made any encounter more personal.

Connor stood in a corner and tried not to bump an Aspidistra off its delicate stand. Each move elicited a clank or whirr from the gadgets dangling from his bandolier. He leapt back when a leaf touched him and the sudden movement set off a glow stick. "Sorry," he muttered as he tried to cover up the bright green light. He thrust the stick into his pocket and glared at the plant.

Fraser took an indicated arm chair, across from the women. The orange tom cat claimed Cara's lap and fixed Fraser with his golden gaze; a sneer curled his lip and exposed his fang. Finally he and Nate had a foe in common.

Everyone stared and waited as the inspector extracted his notebook and pencil.

"Thank you for coming, Lady Lyons," Fraser said. He rubbed the back of his neck, where Nate threw visual daggers, as though he felt the cold stare behind him.

"How goes the investigation?" Cara asked. "I assume that is why you called us all here?"

He leaned forward in his chair, his attention fixed on the tray brought in by the rotund cook. He waited as she set out tea, biscuits, and savouries. "I believe the deaths are centred on the rumours of Victoria's illegitimacy and the pivotal question: who has the most to gain by proving her unfit to rule."

Cara cast a glance to Nate. Her pursuit of Nero's Fiddle led her first to Prince Albert and then his son, Edward. If he discredited his mother, he removed himself from the line of succession as well, which made no sense given his eagerness to exploit his royal position and newfound love of shopping. His motive could not be to support the accusation, but to silence it. "Our enquiries would lead us to believe you need to look at the problem from the opposite direction."

Nan played mother and poured tea and then handed out cups. Fraser raised an eyebrow as he took the offered drink.

"Who has the most to lose?" He mulled the words over as he sipped, his eyes closed in a moment of enjoyment before they snapped open again. "You think the murderer is close to the queen?"

Nessy circulated the nibbles and Connor pounced on a cream and jam scone like a man who had forgotten his breakfast. "Oh I do love a man with a strong appetite," she said and the colour raced up from under the sergeant's collar. With a laugh she continued around the room and left the plate on the table in front of the inspector.

"What have you learned to draw such a supposition?" he asked once he swallowed an enormous mouthful of fresh baked scone.

Under dropped eyelashes, Cara regarded her husband. He appeared to be staring out the window, uninterested in events inside the house, but she knew he would be listening to every word and movement his enemy made. She just hoped the knife stayed in its sheath, they didn't need the added complication to their lives of him gutting one of Her Majesty's Enforcers.

She turned her attention back to Fraser. "Nero's Fiddle was purchased some years ago by Prince Albert. Nate and I have searched his rooms but could not find any trace of the artifact. Last night I talked to Prince Edward, who mentioned that his new man removed some mementos of Albert from his suite, after his death."

Fraser leaned forward in his seat, hanging on her every word.

Cara picked up a silver spoon with the family crest on the end. "A man who believes those behind the rumours of illegitimacy deserve to burn with God's wrath," she said, stirring her tea.

"Burn? An interesting choice of fate to use." The scone dangled in his fingers, cream perilously close to dropping on the carpet. "A name, Lady Lyons, what is his name?"

"Thomas Dalkeith. He served the queen's consort and moved to the Prince of Wales' employ." The orange cat dug his claws into Cara's skirts, reminding her of his presence and that he had been too long without affection. She balanced her cup in one hand and stroked his coat with the other. "I believe Prince Albert also removed certain pages from one of my books, which detailed how the lyre worked."

Fraser shovelled the remnant of scone into his mouth and then dropped back in his chair and closed his eyes. Cara could almost smell the smoke as his mind processed the information. "Dalkeith, Dalkeith," he muttered under his breath.

The eyes flung open and he grabbed his small leather bound notebook. Pages flicked over as he scanned the contents as he sought a particular entry.

"Ah." He slapped a page and peered closer at the neat print. "Dalkeith was the most loyal and trusted companion of the old duchess. Mrs Dalkeith died just over a year ago. So our web pulls tighter and tighter around the fly."

"You think the younger Dalkeith is related to the older?" Nan asked.

"I don't believe in coincidences, Lady Morton. Given the age discrepancy I would place my money on Edward's new man being a son or nephew of the older Dalkeith."

Nessy gave a sharp intake of breath and covered it up by munching on a crisp savoury.

"You think this Dalkeith is killing people who know something about Victoria's legitimacy?" Porcelain gave a rattle before Nan's fingers tightened on the cup in her hands. "Why is he not torching those reporters who are peddling the scandal?"

"Parliament has initiated a secret inquiry into the rumours," Nate said while still staring out the window. He turned back to the room. "They gather the names of those closest to the duchess to see who is still alive. They are to be questioned about the year preceding Victoria's birth. The belongings of the deceased are searched for diaries, letters, anything that might hint at an affair with John Conroy."

"The killer must have caught wind of the enquiry," Fraser said. "Gossip will always spread, Lady Morton, but silence those who remain and could speak the truth and all it will ever be is unsubstantiated gossip."

This time Nan nearly dropped the cup and she placed it on the table before it crashed to the floor. The shake was visible in her hands.

"Which brings me to why I am here in particular." His hand dove back into his trouser pocket and emerged with the signet ring, which he rolled between his thumb and forefinger. Flashes of light danced over the tiny phoenix. "Claudette Foreman wore this." He dropped the item on to the end table and everyone watched it spin on its side before laying still. "A woman involved in this conspiracy. A woman who died a horrible death because of something she knew."

Cara picked up the ring and stared at the faded image. She looked up at the panel carved into the centre of the marble fireplace. The phoenix with spread wings, flames licked at his feet and the family motto: *I will arise.*

"Your murder victim wore a ring with our family crest?" She directed her question at Nan, wondering how her family could possibly be involved in the conspiracy about Victoria and one man's murderous attempt at vengeance. Or clean up.

"Claude was a gentle and kind soul. She saved my life, you know," Nan spoke, her hands folded in her lap. "Your mother wouldn't turn, three days I laboured to no avail. The midwife asked Gideon to choose, me or the child, she was so certain only one of us would survive. Claudette was just an apprentice, only fifteen years old at the time. Such slender hands." She stared down at her own, lost in that horrible moment when two lives hung in the balance. "She saved us both. Gideon gave her the ring to say thank you and said we would always be in her debt."

Cara frowned. "This doesn't make any sense. What has this to do with Queen Victoria and her legitimacy? Where is the connection? Why would someone go to the trouble to kill a country midwife because she delivered my mother?"

Nan and Nessy exchanged long glances. Nessy twisted her hands in her apron and gave a sob. She chewed down on her knuckle and tried to settle next to Nan on the settee.

"We called on her services again, nearly three years after Bella was born," Nan said.

Understanding crept over Cara. The traumatic birth of her mother left her grandmother unable to bear another child and meant there was only one other woman in the room who would have needed the services of a midwife.

"Oh, Nessy," she whispered.

Nan patted her friend's shoulder.

"Lives are at risk, Lady Morton. The lives of you and your friend if you are involved in this old mystery." Fraser extracted the pencil from the spine of the notebook.

Nan shook her head. "Some secrets are best left undisturbed, there is nothing to be gained by dredging up events from over forty years ago."

"But this secret has been agitated by the ill health of Leopold. Even old tongues can still wag and this is about to be dragged into the daylight by Parliament. There is someone, probably Dalkeith, ensuring the conspirators are permanently silenced." He took another sip of his tea, his tone quiet and soothing, waiting to draw forth the require information. "Greed is a powerful motivator. Some men will go to any lengths to protect their wealth and positions."

If Dalkeith wielded Nero's Fiddle he would never let the issue rest. Cara's research told of how the artifact burrowed into the user's brain and fuelled their desire for revenge, blinding them to reason.

"We would never tell." Nessy jumped to her feet. She paced back and forth, her hands fisting in her skirts. "I will take her secret to my grave."

"You need to tell us, Nessy, or that might be all too soon." Cara's mind whirred. What on earth had Nan and Nessy done, how were they involved in the rumours swirling around Queen Victoria? Did Nessy have intimate knowledge of the duchess' Welsh secretary, John Conroy?

"In 1817 Nessy fell in love," Nan started narrating the story from long ago. "Then for a time my dear friend left us, trying to forge a new life with her beloved. But their relationship was not to be. Nessy returned to us Christmas 1818 with news. She was with child."

Nessy's hands moved to her stomach, remembering the swell of her child within, the life that struggled to make itself known in May 1819.

CHAPTER 29

Nan & Nessy

May 1819

THE sideboard held an array of breakfast options, from black pudding and Haggis sausage to toast and four minute eggs. Silver warming trays were held aloft on their stands, everything secure and bolted to the table top so Gideon could help himself with one hand, without needing to steady a bowl or plate.

Nessy let out a large burp. "Pardon me, but that sausage is repeating." She placed a hand over the large swell of her stomach. "It's given me terrible indigestion."

Nan smiled at her old friend. "Are you sure that's all it is?" The baby dropped the previous week and her time neared.

The hand drew circles over her apron. "What do you think, wee blighter? Is it time?" She laughed as she stood, then one hand gripped the back of her chair and she doubled over. "Oh," she cried.

Nan rushed to her side. "What is it? Is it the baby?"

She straightened her body. "Just a twinge is all, my back has been killing me all night." She moved to pat Nan's arm, but her hand stopped mid-air. "Oh dear," she whispered and looked down at the growing pool of water between her feet. "I've done a puddle like a naughty puppy."

"I'd say baby is keen to put in an appearance," Nan said. "Time to fetch the midwife, Gideon."

"I'll send one of the boys to ride for Claudette and tell one of the girls to fetch a bucket and a mop." Gideon left the women alone in the breakfast room. He would direct people and events to the best of his ability, but childbirth was in God's hands, not his.

"Let's get you upstairs and comfortable," Nan said, leading Nessy away while silently she prayed her friend fared better with the oncoming ordeal than she had.

A stable boy rode hard to the village and returned with young Claudette. The midwife declared it would be a hard and fast labour, Nessy dilated quickly and her screams accompanied every inch her body yielded for the baby. By lunch time Gideon left the house, unable to listen to Nessy cry, swear, and growl. Nan sat with her friend throughout, determined to offer the same support she once gave her and prayed she wouldn't have to choose between friend and babe.

For once, God listened and everyone's prayers were answered. Nessy was blessed with a swift delivery, Claudette had the easy job of catching the infant and delivering the afterbirth. By dinner time a dark-haired girl lay against Nessy's breast. Gideon sent a message to Bill, to let him know Nessy had delivered his child safely.

Bella clambered on to the big bed and gawked at the small bundle in wonder. Nan breathed a sigh of relief that her friend survived and that there would be more laughter in their nursery. She worried the absence of playmates made Bella a serious child. "You must think of a name for her, she is quite lovely and must have a pretty name to match," Nan said.

"I don't know." Nessy wiped a tear from her eye. "I wanted a boy, for Gideon."

Laughter came from the foot of the bed. "God has blessed me with another woman. I shall teach the new mite alongside Bella to ride, shoot, and do military manoeuvres. They will be the equal of any boy, you wait and see."

Nan smiled at her friend then turned her face to worry her bottom lip. A girl could be more accomplished than a boy but what did it matter? She could never inherit a title or hold together an estate.

Dusk ticked into night when the noise came from above. The airship blocked out the emerging moon as it hovered over the topiary lawn. Gideon and three of the male staff stood on the dewy grass. A cry of, "Look out below," was heard before a rope dropped to the ground. The rope was attached to the bottom of a swing, to hold the platform steady as those above lowered a man over the side. Once his feet touched the grass he undid the harness around his waist and strode toward Gideon.

"Bill," Gideon said as the two men shook hands. "We did not expect you, but Nessy will be gladdened by your presence."

"Are they both well?" the older man asked as they entered the house.

"Yes, an easy delivery and a healthy girl. Come, I will take you to her."

They discussed small matters as they walked to the house and climbed the stairs. The earl pushed open the bedroom door.

"Bill!" Nessy's tired demeanour perked at the sight of her former lover.

"I'll leave you be," Gideon said as he closed the door and allowed them privacy, knowing these few moments would be all the time Bill could steal to see his daughter.

An hour later the older man descended the stairs and met Nan and Gideon in the hall.

He stopped in front of them, his hands thrust deep in his pockets. He cleared his throat twice before he could cough out the words troubling him. "I have asked something momentous of Nessy. Something not for myself, but for another who is bereft at this time."

A frown passed between husband and wife. Before Nan could speak, Bill continued.

"I will leave her to make her decision, but it is most vital she makes it quickly. If things are to be done, we must act before morning and the upmost secrecy must be kept. Send me an aethergraph with her decision."

Gideon nodded and showed Bill to the waiting airship. He left in full dark, a shadow raising up into the belly of the enormous troop ship. The propellers drowned out the noise of settling birds as the airship turned toward London.

Nan raced up the stairs and found Nessy cradling her daughter and crooning a lullaby, a hand stroked her dark locks.

"What is going on? Bill said he asked something important of you, what was it?" Dread clutched at her heart. She prayed Bill did not want Nessy to leave them, to set her up as his secret paramour under the nose of his new wife.

Tears shone in the other woman's eyes. "He has given me the chance to save our family."

Nan perched on the edge of the bed. "Our family does not need saving, dear heart. I don't understand. What does he want you to do?"

Nessy traced the child's face with a fingertip, as though memorising every pore and contour. "A family member delivered a child today. It was a long and difficult labour, like your own. The surgeon tried, but failed to save both and the baby did not draw breath. The midwife has advised the mother that she will never bear another, her arms will be as empty as her womb."

Nan watched Nessy's constant stroking of the child, face, limbs, hair. Alarm grew in her stomach as she watched the new mother soak up her child. As though she did not expect to see her tomorrow.

"Bill has asked if I would consider giving our daughter to be raised in the dead child's stead." A tear slid down her cheek and dropped on to the baby's swaddling clothes, leaving a dark spot.

Nan grasped her friend's arm. "No. No. He cannot take your child."

Nessy patted her hand and turned her attention back to her sleeping child. "She would be loved and raised as the legitimate daughter of a noble couple."

"She will be loved here, Nessy. No one can care for your child more than us."

A shake of her head. "The world will only ever see my darling daughter as the bastard child of your companion. What future is there for a common-born girl of unknown parentage?"

Nan kept shaking her head, trying to stop her ears from absorbing Nessy's words. "She will be raised in the nursery with Bella. You know we would never treat her any differently. You are the sister of my heart and your child is one of our family."

"Here, yes, but beyond this estate?" Tears fell down Nessy's face. "And what if anything happens to Gideon? With no heir you know we will all be out on the street with only our wits to support us. Four women and not a single man to protect us."

"We are not lacking in wits, my dear, we would survive quite well I'm sure." Moisture threatened Nan's vision. "Please don't do this, Nessy. Not your child. Don't give up your child."

Tears coursed down Nessy's face but an odd calm settled over her. "A woman with no child, ever, can you imagine the depth of her grief and emptiness? Can you imagine your life without the joy Bella brings?"

Nan's heart broke; Bella was the jewel of her life. Could she have lived without her little girl and a barren body? Nan's tears fell silently, dropping to her hands where she clutched at Nessy. "You cannot seriously consider this."

"Bill has made me a promise. There is some benefit to him being a noble after all. He has connections, he has promised to make things right. I have made my mind up, Nan. This is for the best, for my darling girl and for us."

"No." Nan sobbed at her friend's sacrifice and they joined hands over the child, feeling the rise and fall of her tiny chest as she slumbered. Her face at peace, with no inkling of the catastrophic decision about to be made for her future.

"She will live a privileged life and Bella's future will be safe." Nessy squeezed Nan's hand. "Send word to Bill, I will not be swayed."

Plans were swiftly put into motion. Claudette wrapped the child in a warm blanket. Nessy removed the bracelet from her wrist and tucked it around the child's neck, the small pendant against her skin. One kiss on her forehead and she passed the sleeping newborn to the midwife.

"You know what to do?" Gideon asked as she cradled the precious bundle to her chest.

"Yes, there is a carriage waiting below for us, with the physician inside. I will deliver her direct into her new mother's hands."

"Thank you." Nessy turned her face to the pillow where tears spilled down her cheeks as the sobs shook her body.

Leicester, Wednesday 12th February, 1862

CARA let rip an oath that was a unique blend of cussing she acquired in Texas and a touch of something she learned from Jackson.

"Quite," Nate commented from by the window. His lips twitched at his wife's creative invective.

Fun-loving, man-eating Nessy was the queen mum.

"Your child went to the Duchess of Kent." Cara stared at Nessy, trying to comprehend that her grandmother's lifelong companion was in fact the queen's mother. Or more accurately, Queen Victoria was the love child of her grandmother's common-born friend. If this juicy tidbit of gossip hit the newspapers it would push the American civil war from the front pages as furore erupted across England and Europe. Victoria would be forced to abdicate. If the crown went to Prince George, her cousin, England would become a vassal state of Germany. The British people would rebel before they bowed to another country, which would leave a scramble to find an heir not already occupied ruling another country. The power vacuum could lead to civil war on both sides of the Atlantic.

She blew out a whistle. Perhaps Nolton had been on to something when he tried to wrest the crown for himself. At least he was English and legitimate. Although probably too dead to be of any use now.

Fresh tears shimmered in Nessy's eyes at the memory of the heart wrenching decision. "Her child did not live and she had no hope of any other. My babe was born at the same time. Bill asked if I would surrender our child, to live in her daughter's place."

"And so the conspiracy is revealed," Fraser threw in from his couch. His pencil scratched over the notebook as he copied down every damning word.

"We never imagined the succession would fall to her. The duke had two older brothers, everyone expected them to father multiple children. We only sought to offer some comfort to a distraught mother." Nessy sat by Nan, who embraced her friend and wiped away the fresh tears.

Cara let out a long breath; her mind spun and tried to grasp all the random threads and implications. "Nolton said the duke was not Victoria's father and he was right. But he missed out the tiny fact that the duchess wasn't her mother, either."

Fraser sorted through the confusion to bring the discussion back on track. "The duchess's companion must have known and passed knowledge of events to Thomas Dalkeith, somehow. Perhaps a deathbed confession to cleanse her soul before she met her maker?"

"Who else knew, Nan?" Cara asked, wondering how many people had carried the secret and calculating how many corpses they could expect.

"On our side, me, Nessy, Gideon, Bill, and Claudette. On the duchess's side of the deal, her physician, her companion, and a maid who was present at the child's stillbirth."

"Out of those only you two are left alive." Nate pushed off from the window. "We need to find Dalkeith. If he is trying to silence the conspirators then his attention will turn here, next."

Connor stiffened in his corner, his fingers curled around the arm, his body tensed to intervene if the viscount came too close to the inspector.

Fraser turned in his chair. "We need to do so without alerting him that we know. Otherwise he may scarper with the artifact."

Cara knew what she had to do and Nate was not going to be happy with the arrangement. "After my discussion with Bertie last night, I am sure I can elicit an invitation to his private rooms, which will give us an opportunity to locate Dalkeith. We should be able to nab him before he ties up the last few strands of this web."

Nate's growl rumbled through Cara's body, but he never made a sound. He wouldn't voice his dissent with her plan in front of others. "We'll find out where he is, quietly."

A sneer touched Fraser's face for a second before he turned it into a smile, however cold. "It would appear that we must work together once again, Lord Lyons, but please don't try to throttle me this time."

"What?" Cara glanced from Nate to Fraser and back again.

"You deserved it," he said and moved to stand behind Cara.

"We are missing something here," Fraser muttered. As he thought, he tapped the end of his pencil on the arm of the sofa. The soft rhythm filled the room until the noise stopped and he pointed the pencil at Nessy. "Has anyone pulled your hair recently?"

Nessy frowned and raised a hand to her head where the grey intertwined seamlessly with the blonde. "Pulled my hair? No, why do you ask?"

"Of course!" Cara said. "The killer needs a hair from you head to make the artifact work. He needs it to string the lyre." They could yet save Nessy from bursting into flames, as long as the killer didn't have a hair she was safe. "As he plays the lyre, the hair will smoulder and burn and so does the body of the victim. He cannot touch you without a hair from your head, it is the connection between artifact and prey."

A gasp came from Nan, who held a hand to the side of her head. "A man, in the village yesterday. I was jostled and the basket fell from my hands. I felt a tug on my head under my bonnet. He apologised and said that his gauntlet became caught as I bent over. I thought nothing of it, market day is so busy and people are always bumping into one another." Her voice trailed off as they all realised the implications.

"Oh, Nan. Because of grandfather's ring the killer thinks you are Victoria's mother, not Nessy." Cara would not let anyone harm her grandmother. She certainly was not going to be Dalkeith's final victim. She would see to that. She punched John Burke for hitting Amy, there was no limit to what she would do if anyone physically harmed her family.

"We must take Nan and Nessy back to London with us." Cara turned to Nate.

"No," Fraser said. "They are better here, exposed."

Cara hissed. "You will not use my grandmother as bait for one of your traps."

Nate's hand curled around her shoulder. "Think, Cara. The killer needs proximity. Nero invited his enemies to a feast. What is the maximum distance to make the lyre work?"

She narrowed her eyes at Fraser. "Thirty yards, perhaps up to a maximum of fifty, but the closer the better. What is your point?"

His thumb stroked along her shoulder. "How many places are there to hide within fifty yards of the house in Mayfair? Or that distance from a carriage in the streets?"

She didn't like it, not one bit but could see his rationale. The Leicester house sat alone in a five-acre field. The only cover was the trees and gardens, and familiar faces surrounded her grandmother. A stranger would be far more visible here than on the busy London streets.

"We leave Brick here and we finish this tonight," she said, holding Nan's hand.

Nate nodded in agreement. "I don't like sending you in alone." His hands still rested on her shoulders.

She looked up at her husband, wearing his best game face and scowl combination. "I doubt Bertie will agree to an intimate tête-à-tête if you are there and we need to confirm it is Dalkeith silencing those involved. There is still the very slim chance it is Bertie, and I know how to extract the answers we need." She planned to test Helen of Troy's fan and find just how willing and compliant it made men. It could be a very handy little item to keep nearby.

Fraser rose to take his leave. "We will return to Headquarters and look into the history of the Dalkeiths and do some quiet digging. I believe our man stood at the top of poor Claudette's stairs so he could question her."

Cara rose and bent her head closer to Fraser. "You think he will want to make sure Nan is the last person to know?"

He nodded and flicked a quick glance to Lady Morton. "Yes, why else would he be inside her home, why did she try to reach him? I believe some conversation passed between the two."

Fraser and Connor climbed back into the steam carriage and headed for London at top speed. Cara used the house's aethergraph and sent a message to Skittles, asking her if she could arrange an assignation with the prince.

They paced, waiting for the reply. The second hand on the clock overloud. Each tick fell into a void and seeming to take several seconds to move.

The day moved into early afternoon before the answer came. *Seven o'clock.*

"If he touches you he bleeds," was Nate's only comment.

CHAPTER 31

London, Wednesday 12th February, 1862

THEY stood in the shadows cast by a brick wall as they waited in a small cobbled courtyard. Night fell early in the harsh winter. Black velvet reached down and embraced them from a starless sky. Nate's breath skated over the nape of Cara's neck as he stood close. The heat from his chest soaked through her back and she swayed against him, needing a physical touch in the dark. A reminder he was flesh and bone, not some spectre sent to tease her senses. Despite the growing threat to her grandmother's life, calm lulled through her body coming from Nate.

"You relish this. The hunt, the danger," she whispered, as she waited for the door to open that would lead her through to the prince's private suite.

"Hmmm. I believe spymaster is a better use of my skills than politician." The Prime Minister still tried to pull him to Parliament, but Nate dug his toes in like a stubborn mule.

She gave a sigh. She couldn't figure why he still hadn't taken Victoria's offer even though he implied he would. Before she could ask, Big Ben struck the hour. "Time," she said.

For a moment his arms tightened around her waist. "I will be near. Make sure Bertie is not involved and you have only to ascertain Dalkeith is there, no more and leave. Fraser is not far away; he wants to take the man alive, to see him brought to justice."

She turned and stood on tiptoes to kiss him. "Don't kill anyone in front of Fraser, he's a stickler for law and order and you might find yourself in a tower I can't spring you from."

A segment of wall broke away and a faint light revealed a man holding the hidden door open, a glow lamp in one hand. Pulling her fur hood over her head, she walked toward the figure, Prince Edward, and the man who planned to kill her grandmother.

The door closed behind her and the only light came from the phosphorous lantern held by the servant. Stones loomed over Cara in the narrow stairway as they spiralled up inside the thick wall. She wondered how many women had been ushered up and down these stairs over the centuries to secret assignations with members of the royal family. Quite a few she figured, judging by the worn tread in the centre of each stair.

He pushed through a door that revealed a parlour more opulent than anything the courtesans would favour. Now off the leash of parental restraint, the prince found bottomless lines of credit open to him. Anything bright and garish found its way to his rooms, from gilded candlesticks to gold-worked carpets. The door closed and blended into the velveteen wallpaper and moulding, the passageway concealed from the casual glance.

Cara stumbled through an Eastern bazaar with strange and beautiful objects clustered around every surface and expensive embroidered silks from India draped from the ceiling.

Bertie stood at the fireside, his posture rigid in his deep blue Turkish gown and fez. A golden tassel slumped over his forehead. Cara bit her tongue to stop the laughter. The prince arranged his tableau for impact, to impress her. He failed and it only highlighted the stark difference between Nate's calm command and Bertie's puppy dog eagerness to please.

"Your Royal Highness." She dropped a curtsey as the servant took her cloak. She hoped it would be Dalkeith, but this retainer looked closer to sixty than thirty.

"Bertie, please," he said, moving from his spot to grasp her hand and draw it to his wet lips.

"Why don't we have a nice chat and get to know one another?" she said, smiling while willing him to release her hand.

"Chat? Yes, let's chat." He indicated the chaise and sat, patting the seat next to him. The glazed look in his eyes as he lingered over her décolleté suggested chat was the last thing on his mind.

Bother. Cara had limited time and didn't want to waste it handling the prince with kid gloves. She tugged on the cord around her wrist and flicked open Helen of Troy's fan. The faint scent of sandalwood drifted on the air with each stroke of the artifact. The delicate object was painted with a scene of naked Greek gods and goddesses in various poses of enjoying one another's company. The risqué art work grabbed the viewer's attention while the fan worked its magic.

"You want to chat," she said, hiding all but her eyes behind the fan.

Bertie's eyes widened and fixed on the scene dancing before his face. "Yes, I want to chat," he intoned.

"You were telling me all about your man, Dalkeith."

"Dalkeith, yes, good man. Knows what it is to serve royalty." He didn't blink, his attention focused on the vignette before his eyes.

With his full attention and no wandering hands, Cara got straight to the point. "Did you ask him what he took from Albert's room?"

"Yes, some old Latin scribblings Poppa used as a bookmark. He liked the penmanship."

The missing pages. If he has them I bet he has Nero's Fiddle as well.

"Anything else?"

"Some toy instrument." His voice was monotone, as though he was hypnotised by the movement of the ancient fan.

"Have you used the instrument, Bertie? Did you play the fiddle?"

A frown settled between his brows. "No, I'm sorry, do you want me to play for you?"

Cara gave the fan an appreciative look. *This really does make them eager to please.* "Where is Dalkeith now?"

A slow shake of his head. "Gone. Some old relative is about to die, he has gone to see her off. Took a horse from the stables at lunch time."

Cara gave a huff and snapped the fan shut. *Gone. We have to get back to Leicester.*

Bertie blinked and rubbed the bridge of his nose. He let out a big sigh and raised puzzled eyes to Cara. "Where were we?"

He gave a shake, and then leaned in close. He reached out one hand and grasped the fabric of her skirt and pulled it up to reveal her ankle. His tongue left a slick trail over his lips as he took a handful more and watched the silk slide up her calf to her knee.

She wasn't having any of this, so waved the fan at him. "We're having a lovely evening, but I'm afraid we drank far too much champagne, which accounts for your terrible headache." *I'm so sorry Bertie, but I have to do this.* Cara reached out with one hand while Bertie remained fixated on her exposed flesh as he pulled her skirt higher to reveal more leg.

She struck him hard with the object and he fell forward, into her lap. She stood and rolled him onto his back on the chaise just as the secret door pushed open to reveal Nate.

His gaze flicked from the dented champagne bucket at her feet to the unconscious prince. "Déjà vu," he said as one black eye browed arched.

She retrieved the bucket and dropped it back into the cradle. "It's becoming my favourite weapon. Far less mess than pistols or blades." She turned the bucket so the dent was behind on the holder's upright arms and dropped the bottle back in place.

He gave a deep throated chuckle. "Perhaps you would like to try fry pans next?"

"Only if I can try one on Jackson first." She grabbed her cloak. "I gave Bertie the suggestion we had a lovely evening, but he got drunk. He knows nothing about the fiddle, so we don't have to worry about wrangling with royalty this time round. His valet took it and the missing pages from Albert's room, but we have to go, Dalkeith is not here."

"I know, Fraser sent a messenger to say they have headed back to Leicester. Dalkeith left earlier today. The dirigible is waiting for us on the roof."

She tossed the cloak around her shoulders and headed out the door into the passage built into the wall. "I like the fan, by the way. I'm going to use it on you, to make you do as I wish."

He took her hand and kissed her exposed wrist. "I already do, you know I am yours to command."

"Only so long as it falls in line with what you want to do," she said as they took the same secret stairwell higher up, to the roof.

He followed close behind. "You wouldn't be happy with a man you could push around, and we both know it."

They climbed into *Bobby* and Nate waved to the driver to set off. Cara changed in the small airship, stripping off the silken gown to don buckskin trousers and corset. For once Nate kept his hands mostly to himself and handed her the shoulder and hip holsters. She draped her body in the familiar weight of the pistols. A wool frock coat kept out the worst of the winter chill and she pulled a cashmere scarf around her neck.

The dirigible flew back to her family estate in pursuit of the killer. Inside its distended belly, they sat on the padded seat, the English countryside passing close underneath.

"I want you to go on ahead and be with your Nan and Nessy. Organise Brick and the household men into patrols."

She frowned. "What do you mean go on ahead? We're in a teeny airship, there aren't any other options."

He picked up her hand and stroked his thumb over the pulse in her wrist. "When we spot Fraser I'm going to drop down on him. We need to plan our approach with Dalkeith."

The small touch elicited a big response in her body, arcs of electricity raced up her arm and through her torso. "You can't even stand to be in the same room as him, and you'll voluntarily sit in that horrid steam carriage with him?"

He gave her a smile. "I want to make sure he won't take it the wrong way if I inadvertently kill the man while *assisting* the Enforcers." Having ruined her equilibrium, he released her and rose to stare out the window.

Nate's version of assisting would be his sense of justice in action. Dalkeith threatened their family and Nate would make sure he paid. Cara watched her husband, one of his hands braced on the roof of the dirigible. The other clenched and relaxed into a fist by his side. The only outward sign he prepared himself for the fight ahead.

"Tell me something," she said, waiting until he turned to face her face, before continuing. "If your family had maintained their wealth, would you still have gone off pirating and causing trouble?"

A mere second passed as her words registered and then the smile spread over his face and revealed even white teeth. Always the predator.

"Yes, you would have," she murmured. "Put us both out of our misery and take Victoria's offer."

"What do you mean?" He turned and leaned against the side, she held his full attention.

She gave a small laugh. "You're more grumpy than usual because, for whatever reason, you haven't made a final decision. Become her spymaster, it's the only obvious path."

"Do you know what you are asking?" His fist opened and clenched again. "I have played the spy game for some years, but only as a free agent. It is not a normal life, I will tear you from the normality of London and throw you into the path of danger. There will be travel, intrigue, and people trying to kill us."

She smiled. Men thought they were so intelligent and yet they could be so dense. "Given the life I have led, it all sounds perfectly normal to me." She glanced out the window and saw the Enforcers' carriage puffing along the road below, the plume of smoke bright against the night-time sky.

The driver manoeuvred the baby airship to keep apace just above but out of the drift of the noxious smoke. The flap in the roof opened and Connor's head appeared and peered upward.

"You might think you are protecting me, but do you think I would ever be happy hosting boring dinner parties for fatuous politicians and their dour wives?" She rose as he prepared to leave the moving vessel. "How long do you think I would last before I shot someone over the jellied eels?"

He looked out the window, judging their height above the carriage before turning back, his piercing gaze locked on her face. "I couldn't make that choice for you. I need you to be safe."

She snorted. "If you lock me away to keep me safe I will never be happy. I need to be free and protected. Take the job or I will start shooting politicians in the foot."

Relief crossed his face. "I needed to hear it from your lips." Nate slid the door open and the wind rushed in to the small space. He placed a large hand on either side of her face. "God, how I love you." He gave her a brief fierce kiss and then turned and leapt from the airship onto the roof of the conveyance below.

He dropped to his knees, one hand held the roof tie for balance. The dirigible pulled ahead. He cast a glance through the small flap into the carriage to find Inspector Fraser and Sergeant Connor staring back. Mask in place, Nate slid his body into their territory and pulled the flap shut behind him.

Inside was cramped, smelly, and damp. Small porthole windows on either side were the only connection with the outside world and the main source of illumination, assuming the sun were up in the sky. Connor held a small glow lamp that cast a faint green glow around the interior. It reminded Nate of close quarters on the first pirate airship he crewed. At least this didn't smell of feet.

"Nice of you to drop in," Fraser said, his tone colder than the ice clinging to the metal of the window frame. "My instincts were correct about Dalkeith, he is indeed the son of the duchess's companion who died last year. Quite the fervent royalist according to his few friends."

He shifted trying to find a comfortable spot on the hard wooden seat. "Let's cut the civilities. Do you have any reinforcements meeting you in Leicester?"

"No. There is only one local constable and I did not see the point in troubling him for one rogue valet clutching a musical instrument." Amazing how his façade changed when no women were present. This Inspector Fraser was harder and sharper. He gave a piercing stare from narrowed eyes as he assessed the unwanted intruder.

Nate nodded. Dalkeith hardly represented a threat to safety unless he was carrying a Gatling gun. "He will be caught tonight, the only question is will he still be breathing."

Fraser spread his hands. "Naturally I would prefer he lives to stand trial for his crimes."

He curled his lip. "Victoria will have us cover up the use of the artifact. There is enough hysteria in London already and the people can never know of its existence. What exactly will you charge him with?"

"Murder by means of an unknown incendiary device," the inspector said.

This time he couldn't hold in the snort of air. "The whole of London believes the deaths to be the result of Divine Fire. With no evidence to the contrary, he'll walk."

Fraser's smile dropped and his mask slipped. "That's not my decision."

Tension grew between the two men. Connor's head swung left and right, following the conversation.

Nate stared at his blunt fingernails, considering his next words, the real reason for his drop into this hideous conveyance. Cara was wrong, this cheap vehicle far more of a death trap than the miniature airship. "You build your career on pursing the wrong cases."

A cold laugh vied for space in the small compartment. "I have no interest in a career, only in justice. Wrong-doing must be brought to light, no matter who committed it, or how highly placed."

"You waste your time." A prod, testing if he would reveal the existence of any real evidence.

Fraser inclined a fraction, enough to bump up against Nate's personal space. "All it takes is one single person to talk. I'm sure Dalkeith is well aware of that principle."

They understood each other, tested one another and the storm brewed. Soon it would not be contained. "Twice now you have tried to sway Cara's opinion of me. There won't be a third opportunity."

Connor leaned forward on his bench seat but Fraser put his hand on the sergeant's arm, stopping his motion. "Are you threatening me?"

Nate leaned back and smiled. No matter how smart Fraser thought he was, he would not win. "I'm sure you have a file on me, Fraser, you should know I don't threaten people. I make promises."

The carriage came to a shuddering halt. Nate flung open the rear doors and jumped down into the brisk night.

Leicester, Wednesday 12th February 1862

CARA jumped from a foot in the air, hit the ground running and kept going. She ran up the stairs and burst into the darkened house. She stopped the maid in the hallway. "Where is Nan?"

"Library, ma'am," the girl said, dropping a quick curtsey.

Cara headed farther into the house to the double height library. She pushed open the door to her grandfather's inner sanctum, now sheltering her grandmother and Nessy.

"He's here, somewhere," she said, her gaze checking he wasn't hiding behind an ornamental palm.

The walls were lined with soaring bookcases. A brass catwalk ran around the room at the first floor height. A spiral staircase in one corner was the only access way up and down to the upper level of books. An enormous desk sat before the only window, its legs carved like griffon bodies, standing guard in each corner and holding aloft the top with its green leather inlay.

Nan and Nessy sat before the fire, the shutters pulled over the tall window, the mythical creature desk guarding their backs. A stack of woollen blankets and buckets full of water and sand were arranged around the sofa.

"Oh good, you're back." Nan removed the glasses perched on the end of her nose. "There's something I have to tell you, dear."

"It will have to wait, Nan, where is Brick?" Cara itched to move, to do something to protect her family. Shooting was too good for Dalkeith, he needed a slow end. Maybe they could stake him out over fast-growing bamboo in the green house.

Nan waved a hand in the direction of the window. "Stalking around the house. Now it really is important. I remembered something about when this horrid man pulled my hair in the market."

She gave a sigh and willed her feet to stay put for a few moments longer before she ran in search of Brick and nodded for her grandmother to speak.

Five minutes later, she headed out through the kitchens. "Seen anyone we don't know around, Duffie?"she asked on her way past.

"No," the cook replied, stacking the dishes away under the shelf. "Only that gent who fell off his horse."

Cara halted, her feet nearly to the door. "What?" Her comment was a throw away, she never expected a positive response.

"There was a gentleman out for a ride. He fell off, hurt his leg. The lads put him and the horse in the stable to rest. I took him out some supper." Duffie folded the tea towel into a neat small square.

The warning itch crawled up Cara's spine and pounded on her brain. "When, Duffie?"

She looked up at the enormous kitchen clock, used to track every meal and snack prepared under its watchful face. "About an hour ago? He felt much better and said he would be gone by dark."

Cara jogged outside and found Brick crossing the lawn. "Nate is not far behind with Fraser. What happened to the man in the stable?"

"Just been there. Gone. Up and scarpered." The line of Brick's suit was completely ruined with strange bulges and lumps.

Cara wondered just how many different weapons he had strapped around his body. "Damn."

"We'll find him, you said he has to be close to the house." He fell into step next to her.

"Thirty yards, fifty max," she said, peering into the dark. She hoped her affinity to artifacts worked and alerted her to the presence of Nero's Fiddle.

"Let's keep circling," Brick said; his breath frosted on the air and curled up to the sky. "Most of the house is clear lawn in that distance. He'll turn up, he has to expose his position to get close enough to his quarry."

They moved around the side of the mansion, ears and eyes straining to notice something amongst the moving shadows of the trees and shrubs. The pulse through her body stuttered and then synchronised as a familiar shadow cloaked in darkness strode toward her.

"Where's Fraser?" she asked. This monster in the dark would never harm her.

"Going around the other side with his sergeant," Nate replied.

As they rounded the old wing of the house, the shiver skated over her skin despite the thick coat. She turned her head even as the musical note carried across the crisp air. "There." She turned and ran.

He stood on the back lawn. A single shaft of moonlight struck him from above, a celestial spotlight for the man about to call forth God's fire. He held the small lyre in his hands. Two sinuous curves made of ebony and walnut that danced and swayed to the music as though made of serpents, not wood. A beautiful and deadly item. It only had six strings and one glowed compared to the others. The single strand held the note like a tuning fork. The hair shimmered as it vibrated.

"No!" Cara cried as she hurtled toward him.

His head shot up. The corner of his lip tilted in a sneer and then his other hand came up holding a pistol. She slid to a stop, Nate grabbed her from behind and rolled her to one side as a shot fired across the lawn.

A cloud drifted over the moon and darkness dropped over them. Under the enveloping blanket, their target vanished.

"I thought we had this conversation about you throwing yourself in front of bullets?" Nate breathed against her ear.

"Sometimes my brain forgets to tell my hand to draw." She swung her head around and her hand remembered the pistol at her hip. She tried to figure out where Dalkeith might have run under the covering darkness. The estate lacked London's street lights, something to remedy in the future.

"Well, at least he has fired at us. Now I can kill him without Fraser tut-tutting at me." Nate's hand moved down her arm and he clasped her fingers. "Where did he go, Cara? Close your eyes and reach out to the lyre, you are more in tune with the artifacts than I."

She took a deep breath, shut her eyes and surrendered to the black abyss waiting for her. The pulse of their joined hearts was the music of her body. Like an ocean kissing the shore it washed through her. She lowered the volume and listened for a clue. A faint ping shot down her spine and she turned to face the direction of the noise.

"The tree," Nate whispered, his senses following the lead. "He's up the old copper beech."

A frown crossed her face. "Oh no, I love that tree," she muttered as they crept past the clipped buxus hedging to the ancient guardian of the back lawn.

Fraser and Connor approached from the other side. Nate held a finger to his lips and pointed up at the spreading canopy. The Enforcers nodded their understanding.

Winter stripped the tree of all greenery but its twisted outstretched limbs could still easily hide a man. Or a man and a woman, as it proved one summer's day. With a trunk as wide as a carriage the bracts created platforms and hidey holes where the young Cara hid, played and read. Now it concealed a man with vengeance on his mind.

Another tinkle of notes drifted down followed by a high-pitched scream from the house.

Cara froze. "Nan," she cried.

"Come down, Dalkeith," Fraser yelled to their treed prey. "You have nowhere to go."

"Not until this is over," a voice answered.

"It is over. There are more tongues than you can silence and you are stuck up a tree," Fraser said.

The scream tailed off and was replaced by pale yellow that bounced out to the lawn as people moved through the mansion. Electric lights were turned on as staff rushed toward the source of the ungodly wailing.

Cara's attention split between the man in the tree and events unfolding in the house. She held her breath, waiting for the call to return to her grandmother's side.

Fraser paced around the trunk, his service pistol drawn as he tried to find a target amongst the branches. "You don't have to do this, Thomas. Those people didn't have to die."

They spread out; each of them two yards apart as the circled the beech.

Laughter filtered from above. "Old tongues can wag, they all need to be silenced before Parliament can ask its questions."

"You cannot hide the truth by killing innocent people. It will be brought into the light. Too many of us know now." Fraser holstered his weapon looked for handholds.

Nate touched Cara's shoulder. "I'll go up and end this, unless you want at him?"

She shook her head. "There's no maniac in an exo-skeleton and no military airship. It's just a valet with a musical instrument, he's all yours."

He caressed the side of her face. "You should go, be with your nan, see what you can do."

Cara stood her ground. "I know what I'm doing, I'm not hiding inside."

Another strum, a clear note hanging on the air and screaming rolled from the house.

"End this," she whispered. "Now the lyre has hold of him, he cannot stop."

Nate knew this tree, having climbed amongst its canopy before in pursuit of a far more pleasurable target. He could visualise in his mind where Dalketih would stand. There was one spot where the ancient trunk formed a hand and provided a level palm to cup a person, or two if they were very close. The person hidden by the tree had a clear view of the house, but no one below could see you.

He grabbed a gnarled piece of trunk and began to haul himself up the side of the tree. Fraser did the same from the other side. Years of experience in climbing the netting on an airship bladder made scaling a tree an easy task. He reached the desired spot ahead of Fraser, who huffed, scratched and scrapped as his boots slipped.

He leaned against the trunk in the shadows and watched his prey, waiting for his attention to be fixed on the inspector. Perhaps they would tussle and both fall from the tree solving two problems in one hit.

Clouds drifted past and a shaft of moonlight revealed Fraser's bowler hat as a knot on a branch. "You cannot escape, Dalkeith. We have the tree surrounded."

"I will end the slander and keep Edward secure as the heir. He will reward me." The valet kept talking as he played Nero's Fiddle. "Victoria is our queen. If Parliament forces her to step down it will throw England into chaos. I am preventing civil war." His laughter tinged with madness as the artifact wrapped its tendrils tighter around his brain.

Nate's fingers caressed the hilt of his dagger as he waited for his moment.

"No, it won't. We're British." Fraser hauled himself up and balanced on an outstretched limb, three feet from their target. "We'd have the succession sorted by tea time."

"I will not lose my position." The notes stopped as he slammed his hand against the strings. "I am a king's man, not the valet for a poor nobody!"

"Ah, so you seek to line your own pockets, not just to protect the royal family." Holding on to an overhanging limb with one hand, Fraser fumbled at his waist for his revolver.

"Edward will rule and reward me for my loyalty. I will have whatever I want." Dalkeith plucked another note. The hair strung in the lyre burned bright, soon it would catch fire and crumble away to dust. Cries and shrieks came from the house. "You cannot stop me," Dalkeith yelled as he took a step backward on the branch.

Fraser edged along his branch, one hand grasped his revolver and pointed it at Dalkeith.

Nate coughed into his hand, alerting the valet to his presence behind him.

The man turned his body and snatched at the pistol tucked into his trousers' waistband while trying to maintain his balance on the limb and his hold on the artifact.

As Dalkeith moved, Fraser fired and the shot echoed through the night.

Nate jumped for the branch above his head and swung his feet, connecting both boots with the man's chest.

A branch snapped. Dalkeith yelled as his body was propelled one way by a bullet and another by the force of Nate's kick. His arms flailed for something to grasp and in doing so he dropped the instrument of his revenge.

Twigs cracked and he dropped from the sky like Gabriel flung to earth.

A thud and silence.

❧⦿❧

Cara and the two men rushed to the fallen man, his leg twisted under his body at an unnatural angle. Light glistened on his shoulder as a growing stain spread over his jacket. Relief flashed through her that it wasn't Nate. A soft moan came as they rolled him flat on his back. The moan turned into a sharp cry as Brick took hold of his ankle and realigned the leg.

Connor removed handcuffs from his utility belt and secured the prone valet.

Two more shadows detached from the tree and touched the earth. They stood over the downed bird.

Fraser peered close and gave the injured valet a quick inspection. "Looks like his leg is broken and a shoulder wound where I winged him. We'll bind the wounds for now and Doc can deal with him at Headquarters."

Connor searched in his multiple pockets for a roll of bandage while Brick cut two sticks to length as splints.

Nate held out the small wooden lyre to Cara. "You should take this, don't let anyone else touch it."

The frown left her face as soon as her hand slid over the smooth wood and she understood why Nate handed it over so fast. The artifact *called* to her. Tendrils crept into her mind and plucked forth her darkest desires and deepest fears. It played a haunting tune in her brain, begging to be of service to her, to end her pain by eliminating those who hurt her. The instrument promised to deliver anything she wanted, so long as she plucked the human hair strings. She gasped as it tried to seduce her, preying on her secrets. Like a siren's song the music flowed through her body and drew her closer so it could burrow deeper into her psyche.

She took off her scarf and wrapped it around the side of the lyre, so her flesh no longer touched the warm wood. She breathed out a huff. *I don't need you for revenge; the bastards who hurt me have already been dealt to.* She glanced at Nate. *What would Nero's Fiddle find deep inside him? What would it promise him?*

She shivered and tucked the small instrument under her arm. "Let's go check if my grandmother is singed."

Fraser and Connor lifted Dalkeith and carried him off, over the lawn and back to their smoke-filled vehicle. Cara headed back to the house with Nate and Brick, leading the way to where her Nan and Nessy hid. They walked through to the doors and into the plush oasis. The smell of burnt hair hit their nostrils first. A woollen blanket in the middle of the floor smouldered and seemed to be the source of the noxious odour. A small lump underneath of indeterminate origin.

"Oh good, is it over?" Nessy asked, jumping up from her seat.

"Yes," Cara said. "Let's crack a window open, it reeks in here." She placed the lyre on her grandfather's desk as she passed and then threw open the casements to let in the fresh breeze.

Nate glanced at whatever lay under the blanket and frowned on seeing Nan sitting before the fire, a crystal tumbler in her hand. "Why aren't you burning up?"

"You're lucky I like my men forthright, other women would take that as an insult." Nan raised her glass to Nate in a silent salute.

Cara smiled, for a rare moment Nate looked lost. "Nan has a wee confession to make about her encounter with Dalkeith in the market."

"Oh that." She raised a hand to her head. "An old woman's moment of vanity."

"What?" The frown deepened.

Cara swallowed her laughter. "Nan was wearing a wig. Dalkeith and Nero's Fiddle dealt a fiery death to a hair piece."

Nessy pressed a drink into Nate's open hand. "Drink up, lad, it's been a long night."

A footman entered with a brush and shovel. The maid bundled up the blanket and the man swept away the remains. The floor sustained a scorch mark and no more. In short time the crime was cleared away.

Cara nestled next to Nate on a sofa. He looped an arm around her shoulders and drew her close. "I thought you were rather cavalier about the fate of your nan."

"It was a risk, but we assumed since the hair he took came from the wig, Nan was never in any danger. I asked them to play it up if anything happened, to buy us some time. If we were wrong, they were to send someone outside immediately to fetch me. So long as no one came running from the house, I knew it was horse hair being torched."

"Well played." He sipped his drink and stared into the fire. "Probably not so well for a horse somewhere, that has spontaneously combusted in a farmer's field."

"No worries there, the hair came from a broodmare we lost last spring," Nan said. "I'll let God worry about the semantics of burning a creature already grazing in his dominion." They clinked glasses and watched the fire dance in the grate. This one safely confined and not posing any threat.

Cara warmed the drink in her hands. "And so the queen's secret is safe, that she really is illegitimate."

"No, she's not," Nessy said from her corner.

"But she's your child," Cara said, trying to figure out how to broach the subject that Nessy wasn't part of the legitimate succession.

"Bill and I were handfasted in front of a priest. Even though his family refused to recognise the ceremony and demanded he married someone else, we were bound to one another before God." She smiled at the memory of her lover.

"But even if you were married in a recognised ceremony to Victoria's father that doesn't mean she has any claim on the throne." Cara frowned and hoped her grandmother would explain the technicalities to Nessy.

Nan smiled at her granddaughter. "You're not asking the right questions, dear." She turned her attention to her lifelong companion. "Tell them Bill's full name."

A wide grin split Nessy's face. "Oh, why he was William Henry of the House of Hanover."

"Or King William IV," Nan said.

Cara choked on her whisky. "You married King William?"

Laughter rumbled through Nate's chest as the implications all fell into place.

"Well, he wasn't king then, he was just Bill and we were in love. I ran away from here and to show the depth of his love we were handfasted. That means you are married for a year and a day. Victoria was born under that bond, so she is legitimate."

Nan took up the old story. "The Regency was plagued by a series of tragedies and after the Napoleonic war there was a rush to secure the succession. Bill's family exerted pressure on him to marry a noble girl, to produce an heir to the throne."

Nessy continued the story. "I was pregnant the same time as the Duchess of Kent, we both delivered on the same day, except her child died at birth. Bill saw how distraught she was and he formed the plan that gave comfort to her and saved the estate for Nan and Gideon."

"But you gave up your daughter." Cara wondered how a woman could give up her only child. "That can't have been an easy decision."

Nessy's constant smile fled and in her solemn expression Cara saw the echo of Queen Victoria. "No, but I saved my family by doing so. I know what I sacrificed, but never forget Victoria was greatly loved. She grew up a princess. If she stayed with me she would only ever have been the by-blow of your grandmother's companion. By handing her over that night I allowed my daughter to come into her true inheritance, for she is queen."

Nan folded her friend in her arms. "Do not think we will ever forget what you did for us."

Cara let out a low whistle. "So the gossip sheets are right, Victoria is not the child of the Duke of Kent. But she is the only legitimate heir of King William. No wonder the old king had a soft spot for her, she wasn't his niece but his daughter."

"Funny how life figures these things out, she truly was his heir." Nate stroked Cara's hair.

Only one little thing plagued her mind now, their next interview with their employer. "What do we tell the queen?"

Nessy held up her hands and gave a sad little smile. "Nothing. There is no need to make this public, the matter is finished. Let her live her life."

CHAPTER 33

Buckingham Palace, 1830

THE equerry coughed into his hand to attract the attention of the king. The man before the window turned and the servant held out the slim envelope. William tore open the edge of the packet and extracted a pencil drawing. It showed a young girl at her lessons. Dark curls fell around her face as she copied the text laid out before her.

"How does she fare?" he asked, while he memorised the image in his hands.

"She is exceptionally bright, Your Majesty. The tutors delight in teaching her."

He nodded. "Good. You are dismissed."

The servant clicked his boot heels and left the monarch alone with the drawing. He returned to the window so a shaft of sun illuminated the girl as he traced a finger over the ringlets. A hand tightened around his chest at the solemn expression rendered in the drawing. The duchess kept an iron control on the child and she had little contact with the world beyond Kensington Palace. Servant gossip said the girl was not even allowed to run up and down the stairs, that someone must hold her hand, least she stumble or fall while walking.

Or as though her mother feared someone would steal Victoria away from her.

It took the use of his contacts to have a household member sketch the picture. He grabbed any scrap of her life he could extract from behind the walled palace. He thought his position would afford him greater access to Victoria.

His daughter.

But the canny duchess kept him at bay, least he influence the child or worse. He doubted she knew the identity of the child's natural mother or father. The midwife said only the mother resided at the estate of the Earl of Morton. There was nothing to connect him to Victoria. The world believed him to be her uncle, only four souls knew the truth. They gave him an unrivalled gift, his true heir and his daughter would rule after him. He would not forget his promise or the enormous sacrifice he asked of the woman he loved. Now he was in a position to keep his word.

It was time to repay his debt.

The secret order went out to the most influential lords in the House. He spent time picking the exact composition of his quorum. All men with secrets. Dirty little secrets that left evidence.

They gathered under darkness, in the private chamber at the palace. William waited until they all assembled before addressing the group. "My lords, I have called you here to pass a bill, in private."

Outrage flared amongst them. "Sire, this is not the forum. Any bill must be argued in the House."

He waved them down, silencing their protests of democracy as he continued. "You have before you a simple bill of no effect to anyone except to the one noble concerned."

Frowns and mutters were exchanged, but they allowed the king to say his piece, curiosity outweighed outrage as they waited to hear what was proposed.

"Henceforth the estate of the Earl of Morton is exempt from the rules of primogeniture. His estate and fortune is to pass to his eldest child, male or female. In the event of his direct heir being a girl, the title and seat in parliament will remain in stasis until such time as a direct male heir is born."

The assembled lords glanced at one another. Questions rolled from their lips pointing out the extreme precedent such a move would set. Chaos would ensue if women were allowed to inherit. William silenced them once more.

"You do not need the intricate details, my lords. One estate, one man, one exception to primogeniture that will not spread to your fortunes. Sign or I may be forced to ask indelicate questions about your own affairs."

He met the gaze of each man in turn. In a hidden safe he held letters and signed confessions, all he needed to exert gentle pressure on those assembled. He would go to any lengths to deliver on his promise. Any lengths to protect his daughter.

They muttered about the unorthodox proceedings, but they all signed the decree.

William IV affixed his official seal and Nessy's family had their security.

Lowestoft, Thursday 13th February, 1862

NATE
could not contain Cara and as soon as the baby airship hovered above the ground she jumped and took off. She fled past startled retainers and ran into the transformed house. She paid no attention to Amy's subtle decorating her mind focused on only one task.

"Amy?" she called, hoping to catch a sound before she dashed in the wrong direction.

"Parlour," a muffled voice replied.

She pushed through the doors to find a scene of domestic contentment. Amy curled up in front of the fire, needlework in her lap. Jackson sat in a wingchair with an open book.

"What the hell has been going on?" she demanded, levelling a finger at Nate's second.

"Whatever are you talking about, doll?" Jackson said as he closed the book and set it down.

Amy parked the needle and dropped the fabric into a basket at her feet.

Cara brushed her jacket aside as Nate entered the room. He slipped a hand around her waist and removed her pistol from the hip holster. She shot him a scowl but turned back to her immediate target. "Loki said you were shagging my friend." She nearly choked on the words; there was no way sweet, innocent Amy would do anything like that.

"Big mouth that one," he said the corner of his mouth pulled up in a sneer.

Amy rose from her spot and moved to sit on the edge of Jackson's chair. Putting herself in the line of fire should Cara remember the gun nestled by her armpit.

Jackson wrapped his arm around Amy's waist and pulled her close to his side. The smile on her face was wide enough to light the Tower of London.

"Oh, Amy. What have you done?" Cara shook her head, trying to fend off what she would hear next despite the obvious visual clues.

"All sorts of deliciously wanton things, actually." She gave Cara a wink.

"How could you? You detest him." How could she cosy up to the man she referred to as Nate's dog? And how could she look so damned content about it, the woman positively glowed with happiness.

"I know he's a gruff bugger." Amy patted the protective arm around her body.

"Sitting right here, princess," the cur in question growled.

"And Lachlan made such grand gestures. He painted the sheep pink and wrote my name on them. What Jack did by comparison was so small and inconsequential." Another pat for the hound and her smile was bright enough to chase away the winter gloom and light the room.

"Still here and can still hear you," Jackson said.

Cara hid a smile, she rather liked the way Amy breezed over Jackson's objections, completely oblivious to how her comments sounded.

The words spilled from Amy in a gush, as though she could no longer contain them. "Then you all went away and left me alone with Jack and oh, the things that happened. Davie got injured and I rummaged in his gut and stitched him up, I saw a unicorn at the lake, Jack kissed me when I lost at chess and then after Hunter kidnapped me—"

"He what?" Cara lunged at Jackson, but Nate held her back. "Did you know about this?" she demanded of Nate as she struggled to break free.

"No, but it would appear Jackson dealt with it and Amy is unharmed," he said as he pinned the hand reaching for her remaining pistol. He lifted it from the shoulder holster and put it on the side board with its matching companion.

She locked her sights on the henchman and his arm tightened around Amy as though he were prepared to throw her behind him and take the hit. "Do you think I would ever let anyone hurt her?" he said.

The air left her lungs in a rush. One look at the couple and she knew Amy was loved and protected. She certainly didn't look any the worse for falling into the clutches of the local thug.

"Are you all right?" she asked.

"Oh, yes. Being kidnapped was frightfully boring, but it gave me lots of time to think about my future. Then Jack rescued me and Lachlan blew the top off the pub."

Cara kept looking from one to the other trying to absorb everything.

"My princess," Jackson murmured and stroked a hand up Amy's arm.

The woman looked like if she got any happier she would explode in a mess of pink paint and glitter all over the room. One segment of Amy's recent history jumped at Cara's curiosity more than the other events. "What do you mean you saw a unicorn?"

Amy held up her arm to show a horsehair bracelet. "When I came to Lowestoft Jack gave me this bracelet made of unicorn tail. He's looked out for me and made my wish come true."

None of this made any sense, except that the gruff ex-boxer really was a crème brûlée. She tried to stay impartial and weigh his pros and cons. She knew he was only a few years older than Nate. Not really old at all, but the loss of his family weighed him down. He had proven his loyalty over and over and she could not fault him there. Nate paid him well, but he spent little, so he had a nest egg hidden away. Plus he came with the house by the lake. His was a man of worth and life taught her they came in all sorts of guises.

Helene asked her to find him a creature of light and joy. Who better to redecorate his life than Amy? They could have kept her abreast of developments though. She needed every little detail, starting from the beginning. She couldn't change events so she would just have to make the best of the situation. Plus she had never seen Amy so ecstatic.

"As long as you are happy," she said at last.

Amy gave a squeal and leapt up to hug Cara. "Thank you for understanding."

Jackson held up his hands in surrender. "Just don't shoot me again. It happened, how could I resist when my angel sent me a princess to open the windows in my soul?"

Amy frowned and looked from her lover to her best friend. "Yes, don't shoot him. I don't give my permission for that sort of nonsense. Jack has quite the gooey centre under that tough exterior. He would leak all over the new carpets."

"Huh!" Cara pointed a finger. "Told you." She felt vindicated about her assessment of her former minder. She plonked herself down on the sofa. "So what are your intentions to my friend, now that you've debauched her?"

"I'd make an honest woman of her, if she would let me." His attention never strayed from Amy as she returned to him.

Amy swatted him on the arm. "One day. I shall revel in being scandalous first."

"If you have children eventually and it's a boy, would you call him Jackson Jackson Junior?" Nate asked, his voice impassive; but laughter ricocheted along their bond.

Cara smirked, poor child if they lumbered him with such a moniker. One hand dropped to her stomach at the talk of children and family. Perhaps offspring wouldn't be so bad after all? Then the tiny voice in the back of her head warned that soon they would have to face the Curator.

She would have to confront her past and peel back her father's association with the rival artifact collector. Ice slithered down her spine and sucked the humour from her bones. When she thought of her future she saw only a void, cold and empty.

Nate placed a hand on her shoulder and the moment passed.

"Time to celebrate, I think," Nate said as he picked up the bottle of champagne from the cradle. "New beginnings, for all of us. I have a new assignment from Victoria to add to our other duties."

"Yes." Cara took a deep breath. The unnatural cold of London could wait a few more days. "You need to tell me what exactly has been going on out here. Every tiny sordid detail."

She fixed on the metal bucket. She moved to hand Nate glasses and when he finished pouring, she slid a finger along the rim of the cooler before curling her grip around the edge. "Although we must watch the champagne doesn't go to Jackson's head."

MOSEH'S STAFF
ARTIFACT HUNTERS BOOK 4

All things must come to an end...

LONDON is in the frozen grip of an unnatural winter and Queen Victoria wants answers. Cara and Nate know who – the Curator. The queen's artifact hunters just don't know *what* is responsible. Cara is on the trail of an ancient and powerful artifact capable of freezing a city and stirring demons but first she must confront her past and her father's history. Only in learning why her father became a disciple of the Curator can she hope to learn what the old noble holds and why he is so fascinated by her.

Then tragedy strikes and the bond forged by Nefertiti's Heart is severed. Nate without Cara succumbs to his darkness and he lashes out at those he holds responsible for her loss. Meanwhile, in the shadows, Inspector Fraser waits for his opportunity to pull down the man known as the villainous viscount.

With London entombed in ice and all hope lost, this could be the end...

MOSEH'S STAFF:
CHAPTER ONE

WOODEN planks covered the windows; nails stuck out at crazy angles, as though someone unused to wielding a hammer put the boards up in a hurry. They could have blocked out the light, but the haphazard construction left gaps between each slice of timber. Cara glimpsed enough to tell night from day, morning from afternoon. Moments of quiet from full on terror.

It only took three days for her to fear dusk. As the shards of light retreated with the approach of night, the men returned. She pressed her ear to the door, listening. Waiting. A light tread headed down the hall, and she raced to the far corner of the room. She tried to make herself small and insignificant, burrowing into the wainscoting as close as her frame would allow. She curled into a ball, her arms around her knees, spine flush with the wall. A sob broke off in her throat as the footsteps neared her prison.

Day three, and no one had come for her.

Three days, and no one stopped the horror.

Her muscles protested every movement, and her body ached, not just the welts from the beating or the dark ring of bruises around her wrists, but in other places. Would he tear her in two, rend her body like her mind and leave splintered pieces scattered on the floor? Another cry welled up as she forced the memory away, tried to forget what they did to her each night. Every footfall made her heart leap into her throat. The lock clicked as the key turned, and then the door handle rattled.

Her pulse faltered.

She screwed her eyes tightly shut and buried her head between her knees. She couldn't breathe, her heart jammed in her throat trying to escape even if she couldn't.

The boot tread continued into the room, then stopped.

Don't see me. Don't see me.

A hand gripped her ankle and dragged her from the corner.

"No!" she screamed, her hands scrabbled for purchase on the smooth floor. She tore her nails trying to find a knothole to stop her slide.

No one heard her cries. No one would save her. As seconds stretched into hours, she experienced an epiphany; she either laid down and gave up, or fought to escape. In the space between one heartbeat and the next, she made a choice. She might be outnumbered, outsized, and overpowered, but she would never give up. She kicked and clawed, striking out blindly with her eyes shut. She didn't want to see his face. Couldn't bear to see him grinning at her as he did those things to her body.

Large hands captured her wrists and held her tight, stopping her torn nails from digging into flesh. The panic in her chest erupted at being confined. She tried to scream, but the terror constricted her throat, and only a high-pitched keen escaped.

"I have you, cara mia," he said.

The fear short-circuited her brain and constricted her vocal cords, only a whimper managed to pass her lips. Her body shook as she lashed out at anyone, anything, and adrenaline pumped through her veins, giving her the strength to fight on.

"No. No, no, no, no!"

"You're safe, cara mia. You escaped and they were punished. They will never touch you again."

Something about the low tone soothed the raging fear. Her mind stilled for an instant. Something was different this time. Arms wrapped around her and held her close, but not to hurt—to protect. A steady beat next to her cheek pulsed through her with the lull of a soft wave.

The cry of terror turned to a sob of relief.

"Safe?" She stuttered over the word, not daring to say it out loud. Still unwilling to open her eyes, lest this prove a cruel trick.

"Safe," the familiar voice whispered.

Safe. Dear God, she was safe. It was over.

The child in her cried with relief while Nate stroked her hair.

"I will always protect you."

Some foul creature tortured her brain with a brand of pure sunlight. She cracked open one eye as she sat upright and dragged the blanket with her. A shadow opened the curtains, outlined by the ring of fire that burned across the floor. The figure turned. The fog slowly lifted, and Nate walked toward her. He picked up a mug of coffee from the end table, placed it in her hands, then sat on the bed. For once, he didn't hide his worry; he wore it openly on his face and in the piercing blue gaze.

"The nightmares are back and each time they grow worse." He reached out and tucked a short strand of auburn hair behind her ear.

She didn't want to think about it. She thought the nightly struggles were confined to a dark corner of her mind months ago. Until recently. She inhaled the sharp aromas wafting off the mug and curled her fingers around it tighter. "I thought I had defeated them, but they have arisen and claw themselves free in my mind."

"You had a couple the first few months we were together. Then none until early this year." He cupped her face, and his thumb stroked her cheek. "Now they are almost weekly and stronger. You struggle so hard to be free, Cara."

She closed her eyes and turned her face into his palm. "They nearly broke me, part of me wanted to just lie down and die. It would have been so easy. I realised it could take weeks for Nan and Grandpa to find me, but I didn't want to be the sort of person who just gives up. They wouldn't. So I chose to fight."

"How do we make you free?" he whispered.

She took a sip from the mug and let coffee vapour drift up to her brain. "It's linked to what's happening out there." She waved at the window with its thick white frosting. Even though they approached the middle of March, London lay frozen—but far worse affected the city than just the temperature. The cold pervaded the atmosphere. The people were morose and laughter diminished, the life and vitality sucked from their bodies from some unseen force.

She shook her head. "Something bad is coming, and the demons are rising up with it."

Cara stood in the secretary's office and plucked invisible dust motes from her clothes. Unable to rest, her hands kept fussing with the lush fabric of her skirt.

"We're not in trouble," Nate whispered from behind her. He reached around to take her hand and still the nervous movement.

She snorted. "Name one trip here that hasn't resulted in trouble."

His lips twitched. "Fair point. But no one will try and kill us here. Not today."

The secretary pushed apart the doors and announced them. They stepped into the queen's personal domain. Victoria, dressed in full mourning garb, stood in front of the world map that covered one wall. Her hand rested on the Pacific Ocean between Australia and Aotearoa.

"We hear your endeavours in the colonies are successful, Viscount Lyons." The queen launched straight into business, not letting them teeter in their uncomfortable positions.

They rose from their brief bow and curtsey. "Yes, Your Majesty. The new long-range airships take immigrants and supplies out and will return laden with cargo," Nate replied.

The monarch's hand swept upward and over China. "We look forward to the taxes from your new trade to supplement our treasury."

Cara swallowed her sudden laughter so hard that tears sprung to her eyes. She coughed, trying to put the air back into her lungs. Nate didn't pay taxes, McToon, the canny Scottish lawyer, saw to that.

Ignoring his choking wife, Nate spread his hands. "I labour to benefit Queen and country, ma'am."

Victoria made a noise deep in her throat that mimicked Cara's scoff of disbelief, then flowed to the window. With her steps made invisible by the enormous crinoline, she appeared to run on wheels. She raised a hand to the glass and traced a passing flake. "Why does the snow keep falling?"

Cara chewed her lip. Was it a rhetorical question? Better to steer a neutral course. "It is an unseasonably late winter, ma'am, but it has happened before."

The queen turned and fixed her with a piercing gaze, so similar to Nate's in many ways. It tore through your protective layers and left you exposed. She needed to add only the most delicate arch of her eyebrow to express her complete disdain for Cara's words. So hard to reconcile her with the fun-loving Nessy, her natural mother.

"We approach April, Lady Lyons. Not only does the Thames remain frozen, but our scientists tell us that each day the ice thickens when it should melt. We are well aware this phenomenon is wrapped around London, but elsewhere in our dominion, spring approaches." Her hand curled into a fist, the steady gaze faltered. She looked away for a moment and when she met Cara's gaze again, her face softened, the lines visible on her brow. "Is this our doing?"

Hatshepsut's Collar discharged its energy into the sky and unleashed a storm upon London. Many speculated that the unnatural winter was triggered by the lightning that shot upward to the sky that October night. The more poetic said the very heavens grieved for Prince Albert, and winter would last as long as the queen wore full mourning.

"No, ma'am." Cara had thought exactly the same as the more pragmatic citizens and read every book Malachi could provide that alluded to the Collar. She could find no reference to it altering the weather beyond the short-term effect of the lightning. The storm should have cleared within one or two weeks. As days turned into months, it became obvious the cold grip was localised and worsening. The rest of England warmed, daffodils popped up their heads, and lambs cavorted in fields. It was more than the snow, for a dread settled over London as though the damp crept into the populace and chilled their spirits. Long-buried demons clawed to return and haunt the people. Tempers flared as the citizenry turned fractious and the Enforcers were overrun with petty crime and disputes.

Cara reached out for Nate. They both believed they knew who was behind the abnormal winter. When the Thames froze, it radiated out from Southwark, confirming their fears. They just didn't know what had such an effect. What could be so powerful as to distort the weather over an entire city? Cara believed the timing was deliberate, if only she could discern the reason.

"We shall investigate, ma'am." Nate squeezed Cara's hand, silencing the protest on her lips.

"Good." Victoria nodded and returned to her desk.

"If I may make one request, ma'am?" Cara halted the queen's return glide.

"Yes?"

Cara took one step forward. "Amongst Prince Albert's things are a number of books he collected on matters of unusual phenomena; they may assist our enquiry if I could have access to them."

"Very well, I shall have them delivered to you." She took her seat and pulled a dispatch from the pile in front of her. The audience over, she no longer saw Nate and Cara, and it was their prompt to leave just as invisibly.

Cara chewed her lip all the way home while her stomach roiled and rolled. Everything converged, her nightmares returned and when she turned her mind to their new task, it recoiled and cowered as she once did. At the mansion, she stripped off her outer layers and handed them over like an automaton. Nate guided her to his study with one hand at the small of her back.

"It all centres on the Curator. We need to learn more about him," Nate said as the door snicked closed behind them. He peeled off his jacket and tossed it over the back of the sofa. "We need to dig into his history and try to figure out if there is an artifact that could do this."

Cold gripped her and slowed her heart. "I can't do this." She shook her head and paced the study.

"Why?" Nate asked, watching her constant movement.

How to put it into words? The dread stirred in her gut, a sixth sense told her this investigation would not end well. The little voice told her to turn back, that she was being led up the garden path of a very elaborate trap. "We cannot go up against the Curator and whatever he wields."

"Don't you want answers?"

"Perhaps I would rather not know." The Curator. She shivered at the remembrance of his cold touch sucking all the warmth from her body. Did he have something that allowed him to do that on a grander scale, to take the heat and hope from an entire city? The old nobleman set her father on his path to destruction. The man who fed his obsession with resurrecting her mother. The man whose face appeared in her nightmares and obscured Clayton's features. What was the connection? Her mind drew back. Better to not know, it whispered.

She stopped in front of Nate. "You have your new position as the queen's spymaster. Let's leave the cold and go to Russia, I long to catch up with Natalie."

The set of his jaw said he wouldn't be swayed, but he took her hands in his. "Don't you want peace, Cara?"

She raised her gaze to meet his. The nightmare grew in intensity, thrusting her back into her fourteen-year-old body and making her re-live the terror over and over. She grew tired of fighting, perhaps it was time to run.

"I want peace for you," he said. "I would do anything to tear that memory from your mind so it never disturbed your sleep again."

She took a deep breath and willed her rampaging stomach back under control. "I know. But part of me thinks I can outrun this."

He smiled as he drew her into his arms. "You tried running, but I still caught you." He stroked her back. "Let us lay the past to rest, once and for all, so we can move forward with our lives. Plus, the queen commands it, and we are the only ones with some idea of what is at play. We cannot let the people of London freeze. What of your friends in the Rookery?"

Her mind battled her heart. She spent many afternoons in the St Giles Rookery; she found the children there smart and eager to soak up the knowledge from the teachers Nate employed. She would not see her little friends freeze. Yet still the fear bubbled up, the nameless worry that preyed on her mind in her weakest moments.

"What if I lose you?" A solitary tear slid down her cheek. "What if this is the fight we cannot win?"

"Impossible." He breathed against her hair. "It's just the idea of digging up the past that has wakened your demons. We will fight this, and him. Together."

She nodded, the demons laughed, and the dread remained.

ABOUT A. W. EXLEY

BOOKS and writing have always been an enormous part of my life. I survived school by hiding out in the library, with several thousand fictional characters for company. At university, I overcame the boredom of studying accountancy by squeezing in Egyptology papers and learning to read hieroglyphics.

Today, I write twisted historical novels with heart. I live in rural New Zealand surrounded by a weird and wonderful menagerie consisting of horses, cats, a mad boxer, and chickens who think they are mini Velociraptors.

Web..www.awexley.com/
Facebook...www.facebook.com/AWExley
Twitter...@AWExley
Pinterest...www.pinterest.com/AWExley/

Be the first to hear about new releases, occasional specials and giveaways. My newsletter comes out approximately four times a year. Follow the link to sign up http://eepurl.com/N5z5z

Made in the USA
Middletown, DE
10 December 2019